BIG FLAME AND LITTLE BUCK

JJ HOLBERT

Dedicated to those that have been diagnosed with a mental illness, and to the people who love them.

Also dedicated to Plainfield, Vermont — my muse.

1

1983: A CONCERT, A WRECK, AND A
PHONE CALL

The first time Candice Bates asked Dante if something was wrong with Pat was in the winter of their junior year. While Pat Bates and Dante Zuckerman didn't exactly have senioritis yet, they had already been making travel plans for the summer of 1984, when they would be free: Florida, where it would be warm; Montreal, where they could drink legally.

By this time, they all had licenses and most of them had cars. Lyle Laguerre had been working at his family's body shop, Dante at The Apothecary, Jeremy Ibey at the general store. Pat farmed some for Jimmy Kleets, Jr, but his dad said he could start working at Rock of Ages quarry with him when he was a senior. As for girls, well, Lyle stayed true to Donna, Jeremy hadn't quite gotten lucky yet, Pat played the field and never seemed to settle, and Dante was still waiting to get it on with Shannon.

It was the beginning of junior year when Lyle, who everyone called Lincoln due to his height, and Pat started hanging out together on double-dates. Dante usually ended up at Jeremy's on weekend nights to play video games. Dante kept wanting to ask Shannon out, but knew she liked Pat, though Pat knew that Dante liked her, so he kept away from her. Dante wondered how long that truce would last — Shannon was getting prettier every day. If only he could stop turning beet red anytime he got near her. His chronic blushing had long ago earned him the name Strawberry, which he grudgingly accepted so he didn't get called something worse.

Since middle school, the boys managed to gather at the crumbling cabin near the railroad bed as often as they could. The tracks had been removed years ago, so once cars were in the picture, Pat or Lyle snuck off there with their girls sometimes, until it got too cold. After that, Lyle and Pat went their separate ways on dates, usually romancing in their vehicles, white puffs of exhaust from running engines, heat blasting against the winter nights, steamed-up windows.

Then changes happened, especially with Pat. He started talking less about his conquests and just talked less in general as winter deepened. He became moody and avoided hanging out with anyone. It got chalked up to the painfully long winter, the first snow flying before Halloween and the last covering up flowers in early April. Their remarks about "fucking winter" eventually led the group to rename it "Winterfuck". They each took turns feeling low at some point every winter. In turn, they would grow listless and refuse to hang out saying, "I don't know, I just don't want to", but they would always snap out of it, when the boredom of being at home got to be too much.

But when Pat stopped taking his phone calls, Dante felt something more was up than a week of Vermont winter blues. By the middle of winter of their junior year,

Dante noticed that girls hadn't really been hanging around Pat's locker like they used to do. He had asked Shannon about it, and she just shrugged and said, "Well, look at him. He doesn't even seem to care anymore. Even Andrea called him up and he wouldn't hardly say anything, much less ask her out."

Dante looked at Pat, his best friend since third grade, more closely and saw what was different- his hair hung down straight, greasy. His eyes lost their "Paul Newman sparkle", as his mother had always called it.

At first, Dante kept asking him what was wrong. "Is it a girl? Is it Lincoln? Jer-Bear? What'd they do? It's not me, is it? Is your dad being a hardass again?"

"No. I don't know. Nothing. It's nothing."

Then Candice, Pat's mother, stopped Dante on his way out the door one night. Dante had been over just to hang out, but Pat was being lame, so he was leaving early to catch dinner at home.

"Dante, should I be worried about Pat? All you kids go through phases like this, especially in the winter, but this is Pat we're talking about. He's stopped showering. He stopped fixing his hair 24-7. He just comes home and sits in his dark room."

"I don't know, really. He won't say much."

"His grades… well, they've never been off the charts, but I am beginning to think he's not going to school at all anymore."

"We have some classes together — he's there. You know, sitting there."

"Keep me posted, you know, if you see anything, like he's not going to school or something. Come by a bit more, alright? Do homework together?"

"No sweat. I'll come when I can." And he did, often

bringing a paper sack of mood-lifting vitamins, herbs and supplements from his mom, which she put together special at the store after Dante confided that Pat seemed down. The baggies and bottles piled up on Pat's dresser, unopened. Dante never mentioned that to his mom.

More often than not when he came over, Dante would sit on the floor and read through all the comics he'd read a million times before in the dim light and Pat would lay on his bed staring out the window. It was weird and annoying. Shannon kept asking about Pat and if he was okay. Dante wasn't sure if he was more worried that Shannon asked so much about him, or that Pat really was feeling bad.

When spring came, Pat improved considerably. For a while, things got back to normal, signaled by Pat coming to school with his trademark feathered hair, taught to him by his kid sister Kitty courtesy of *Teen Beat* magazine years before. He also started fooling around with girls again, including the wrong girl, which nearly cost him his friendship with Dante.

~

It was after the accident that Pat's mom became nearly desperate with worry.

Months had passed since Candice called Dante for the first time to come over, to stay over, and keep an eye on Pat. Now it was the middle of summer before senior year and the boys — Pat, Lyle, Jeremy, and Dante — were all home after the crash in Boston three nights before. No one had seen each other since the hospital, where they'd repeatedly gotten in trouble with the nurses for sneaking into each other's rooms with their rolling IV's. Since then, parents were keeping them all in lockdown while they healed, phone calls only.

It was his mom who picked up the phone. Dante was finishing a bowl of breakfast Kashi in the kitchen and could clearly hear her "hmms" and "oh mys". He figured it had nothing to do with him, but she stopped him as he started to make his way up to his room. School hadn't started yet and his folks were giving him time off from work at The Apothecary and he was bored, broken and sore after being in a car that rolled over twice.

"Dante." His mom's voice was low and somber. He turned to her, one foot on the stair, his arm held by a sling across his midsection.

Her hand was covering the mouthpiece. "It's Candy. She, uh, I mean Pat is um..." Dante took his foot off the stair and took two steps closer to her.

"What? Is he okay?"

"Yes, I'm sorry. It's just that he's really, really... well, depressed, I guess. He won't get out of bed, or even change his clothes. Three days now, since the accident. She's asking for help."

Dante reached for the phone. "Mrs. Bates?"

Candice's voice was shaky and wet. "Hi Dante. Could you... um, come over? Pat isn't doing good and I was just hoping..."

Dante looked at his mom and mouthed, "Can I go?"

"Of course."

WHEN DANTE GOT THERE, Kitty was in her bathing suit on the rocking chair on the porch. She had a sour look on her face. As Dante went up the steps, she grumbled, "I can't go to Number Ten Pond because mom won't take me because of Pat. No one can come get me, either."

Dante had always wondered why that pond had just a number for a name. And it seemed to him more of a lake than a pond. Maybe he'd always be a city boy at heart.

He shrugged. "You can ride a bike, can't you?"

Kitty huffed. "I guess." She hopped off the rocker. "Mom. I'm riding my bike to Number Ten." She slung her towel around her neck and flip-flopped past Dante down the steps.

Pat was lying in bed with ice on his knee and wearing his concert tee, the one he got at the Foreigner show. It was white with three-quarter length black sleeves and looked like the cover of the band's featured album; a large black number four, like you'd see during the flickering of a movie when the film first starts rolling. There was blood on the right shoulder. If Dante was remembering right, Pat was wearing all the same clothes from that night. Pat didn't even glance at Dante as he came through the doorway.

JEREMY WAS the first of them to get his driver's license, which created a domino effect and soon after they all had them. Jeremy had to drive the night of the concert because Pat's truck couldn't hold them all. Lyle's Brat could have, but two of the seats were outside, bolted into the bed of the truck. No one was even sure if that was legal on a highway, much less in Massachusetts, where the concert was. Dante's Tercel had so much rust that they joked he would have to run it like a Flintstone soon. Jeremy hadn't gotten his car yet, so he begged his older sister Lisa to borrow her

Chevette and in exchange, he had to do her chores for two weeks. Jeremy had learned about the Foreigner concert by overhearing a Greyson College kid while he was working at the general store. It was Lyle who got his parents' credit card and called to order tickets.

After the three-hour drive to Boston, they were in awe at seeing so many cars and people in one place. They had to park what seemed a football field's length away from the arena entrance. It was still light out and they could see the mass of fans gathering in the upper section of the sports stadium. They had walked about halfway across the packed parking lot when they got herded into a rowdy keg party. Looking at each other with shocked and happy expressions, they downed three beers each. Jeremy outdid them all by accepting a beer bong after two beers and puking twenty minutes later as they waited in the line to get in. They all fell to the ground laughing, even Jeremy, despite the dirty looks from the other fans in line.

"Holy Shit! Jer-Bear tossed his cookies!" laughed Dante.

"You'll probably be next, Strawberry. Oh, right. Well, I can't call you that anymore, so Schnante it is!" Lyle teased. "You already pissed yourself laughing!" Lyle cracked up some more as he staggered to standing.

Dante stood up quickly. "Fuck you, Lincoln. It's just beer."

Lyle belched. "Is not."

"Is, too!"

"Dude," Pat said, pulling Jeremy up with him, "Why do you always have to fucking do this? Lincoln pushes your buttons and you fall for it. He's just an asshole. Don't let him get to you."

"Oh, great, I'm the asshole now." Lyle rolled his eyes.

Jeremy swayed in place. He punched his finger in the air at Lyle. "Lincoln's an asshole." His finger swung to Dante, "Straw... No, *Schnante* is an asshole." He swung again. "Pat Bates is a superior asshole, but he gets away with it 'cause the girls think he's hot. And me?" He pointed at himself and inadvertently leaned back on his heels from the effort. "I'm the biggest asshole of all. Plus —"

"That's right, sweetie, you're all assholes," said the woman behind them with shaggy bleached hair, black at the roots. "The line's moved ten feet. Now get going so we don't have to smell your puke anymore."

Once they got inside the stadium, they were star-struck by the hordes of girls in tight jeans and hundreds of guys with styled hair, short in the front like Pat and Lyle's, but sometimes reaching all the way to waist-level in the back. Tipsy and unused to crowds, they had some trouble finding their seats, as well as staying together while cutting through the beer and bathroom lines. Jeremy got separated for a good ten minutes and told them later in the car ride home that he had stuck to the rule his dad taught him about the woods- as soon as you realize you're lost, just stay put and you'll get found in no time. It worked.

They all shopped for concert tees together. Jeremy got the same one as Pat. Pat bought a size too small to show off his muscles. Dante and Lyle got black ones that had the band's name in fancy writing. All shirts had a list of tour dates on the back. Still sloppy from the quick beers, they all pulled off the shirts they were wearing and put on the concert T's. They tucked the old shirts into the waist-band at the back of their jeans giving them T-shirt tails.

Once they figured out where their seats were, the four

of them bumped and staggered their way up the steep concrete steps to their section. When the lights went down and the band came on, the crowd exploded and Jeremy went hoarse within the first ten minutes from yelling. Dante and Pat's fingers were a blur of air guitar. Lyle burned a black mark on his thumb from tribute after tribute with his lighter. When at last the finale of "Juke Box Hero" reached its crescendo and the concert was over, they were drenched in sweat and stone cold sober. They stood in a subdued cluster long after the house lights came on. No one wanted to be the first to move, to end that perfect moment, to start the long exodus back to their concertless lives in the wooded hills. After the crowd had noticeably thinned, Jeremy, who was driving and wouldn't have the luxury of sleeping on the way home, took the first step toward the exit. The rest of them fell in line behind him.

"Uh, hey, Pat Bates." Dante glanced at Candice who stood behind him, large black circles under her eyes. All parents had been visibly shaken since the accident. She gave him a soft squeeze on the shoulder and left.

No response from Pat, who stared at the ceiling.

It felt too motherly to go sit on the bed, so Dante sat on the floor, legs crossed. "Dude. The shirt. It's like... you know."

Pat mumbled.

"What?"

"I know."

Dante leaned back on one hand, his other arm still tucked in a sling. He was glad it wasn't winter — he wasn't sure he could drive one-handed through ice and snow. "Can you believe Jer-Bear got to go home the very next day? The lucky bastard. I mean, how does a person end up getting thrown clear and only have a dislocated shoulder and a chipped tooth?"

Pat shrugged.

"I mean, it wasn't his fault, right? That guy clipped us trying to get to the off ramp. But how fast was Jer-Bear going? I never really got a good answer from him."

Dante didn't realize how much he had pent up inside him. He really hadn't talked with anyone about it since they got home, not even his parents. They were not the kind to press, always took the approach that things happen when the time was right. "You know what the fucking problem was for us? It was that ghetto blaster Lincoln insisted on bringing because the tape deck in the car wasn't working. Banged all over the place when we flipped over. Hand to God, it musta pinged each one of us like a fucking pinball. Even Lincoln in the front seat. All except for Jer-Bear, that douchebag."

Dante saw a twitch of a smile on Pat's face. "He is a douchebag, isn't he." Pat shoved himself up onto his elbows. "How's Lincoln?"

Dante shrugged. "Well, you know he had busted ribs and a cut on his head from the boom box, so I guess he's just resting at home. You haven't talked to anyone?"

Pat shook his head.

"Me either. Check out my fat-ass lip. Hurts to talk. Guess you're a real lucky bastard. Guess what?"

Pat sat all the way up and grimaced. He had a bruised abdomen, a sprained knee, and a black eye. "Ow. What?"

"Shannon called me and asked me to go to Burlington with her to see a show. I guess she had fun on our first date. Ow, fuck." Dante's cut on his lip hurt the most when he smiled. He'd been waiting for her for a long time, no thanks to Pat. "You know, when we're not hobbling around in pain anymore."

Over the years, Pat had tried to resist her flirting and some days he was a really good friend. But there was the first kiss at Number Ten, plus three more; two that Dante knew about and the other he didn't. The first was at Tony McGuires Spin-the-Bottle party in ninth grade. Pat won two-minutes-in-the-closet with Shannon. Shannon giggled for most of it, but they did kiss, with tongue, for at least five seconds. Dante didn't talk to him for two weeks. Pat told her that he didn't want to go out with her, but that maybe wasn't the whole truth. He just hadn't known why Dante wouldn't make a move on her. But that was then.

Pat told himself that nevertheless, she was cute and into him, so that led to the one Dante didn't know about, which was after school sophomore year. Shannon led Pat behind the gym and she made out with him for a long time, maybe ten minutes. As awesome as it was, Pat felt so guilty, he avoided both Dante and Shannon, until Dante cornered him. Pat stammered that he did it because he was jealous because Dante was talking with Sophie Berger at lunch and Pat really liked Sophie, so... Dante didn't quite buy it, but what could he do?

Then, there was that kiss in front of Dante, at the beginning of the summer a few weeks before their car crash. It was after the graduation party for the class of 1983. Dante forgave him, maybe because it was the ensuing fight they had that got Shannon to realize Dante was in love with her. He hadn't yet told her for how long.

Pat gave him a full smile. "No way. That's awesome."

"Way." Dante couldn't help it. He grinned. His hand

went to his lip. "Ow, fuck, ow, fuck, shit."

Pat laid back down. "Dude, I can't hardly sit up."

"Do you need anything?" Dante noticed Pat's limp, unwashed hair. Typically for Pat it was a daily shower, feathered hair, tight jeans, and cutoff sweatshirt to show off his abs. Now greasy hair and a bloody T-shirt?

Pat went back to staring at the ceiling. "Nah. Maybe just more sleep. I am so fucking tired."

Dante thought of Pat's mom, the sound of panic in her voice. "Come on bro. I want some hot chocolate."

Pat sighed. "Fine." He sat up again. "Ow and fuckshit. But you gotta bring it here. My knee is all fucked up."

"Okay, but I cannot drink hot chocolate with your bloody shirt on full display. Please change it."

Pat's eyes grew wide. "Whoa...Straw — uh, dude. I just realized something."

Dante rolled to standing using his good arm. "What's that, Pat Bates?"

"I never even got a cut. So, whose blood is this on my shirt?"

That did it. They both started cracking up, punctuated with ow's, Jeezum Crow's, and assorted bad language.

Candice appeared at the doorway with a tray of hot chocolate with a look of relief on her face.

"You heard him, Patty. No cocoa until you change your clothes." She put the tray down on his nightstand and turned around to leave again. As she did, she looked pointedly at Dante and mouthed the words, "Thank you". Dante wanted to smile back at her reassuringly, but was afraid he'd curse again, so he nodded.

Pat had trouble sitting up and was struggling with his shirt. "Dude — get over here and help me. These clothes smell worse than you."

AT FIRST PAT'S DEEPER, more serious depression had everyone acting in extremes. His mother doted and coddled, endlessly asking things like, "What do you want for dinner, honey?" His dad, "You get down here right now and drive your sister to school, or else." Kitty was downright giddy as she tried to keep life at home centered around her.

No matter what the question or threat, Pat felt like all words were being pushed through a filter. When summer ended and he had to drive them both to school, Kitty started asking Pat, "Why are you being such a dick?", which became "What's up with you, anyway?", and finally, "Are you okay?"

Pat would just turn up the volume on the radio. Kitty was used to his incessant teasing — its absence felt like a snub. She eventually gave up, much to Pat's relief, and instead donned her Walkman earphones to block out Pat's Scorpions, Van Halen, or whatever he popped into the tape deck. Pat hardly heard the music — he'd kept it on as a way to shut her out and it worked. It wasn't that Kitty was worse than normal — he'd never minded taking her to school. He even liked hanging out with her sometimes. But now her words were cloudy and lacked meaning. That, and it took all of his focus and energy just to drive, to not let his thoughts drift to the gray bubble where they might get caught and end up wrapping them around a tree.

Everyone thought it was the trauma of the accident that led to Pat's heavy depression, the first of many. They were right, but they were also wrong. Changes had already been in motion.

2

1920: THE PANTS WETTER

"**O**lly Olly Oxen Freeeeeee!"

Once Giancarlo Donatelli gave the all-clear, kids from all sides regrouped for another game in the field behind Hopefield Elementary. This took some patience as legs were tired from pumping up and down in deep snow, attempting to either catch a kid from the other side or avoid being caught. It was the Jack Dempseys (flag represented by Ginny Swaggert's hand-knitted Christmas scarf from her grandmother) versus The Babe Ruths (their flag was Scotty Dupre's hand-me-down scarf from an older cousin), each flag tied to a branch stuck into the snow on either end of the field. The win went to the Babe Ruths after Clemens Bates pushed Danny Moran down hard into the snow and made a mad dash for the Dempsey flag.

No one knew how long it had been or how much longer the grownups would be standing around, talking and eating at the regular potluck that Pastor Anderson and his wife, Jolene, hosted at their yellow house behind the church following services. Since no adult had shown up yet to the elementary school field to whistle them back, they began the trek up the hill behind the school, dragging the sleds that some kids were allowed to bring to church for hill sliding after.

On the hill, you had two choices. You could take Easy Street, which started halfway up the hill and curved around a bush and a maple, landing you near the fence to the school yard. The other was the Pants Wetter, which began at the top and was a straight shot down into the field. The bump near the bottom of the Pants Wetter was still there from last week, hard-packed and icy. On the trudge up the hill, Clemens (in his new wool snowsuit) and his brother, Truman (in Clemens' hand-me-downs), stopped to pack more snow on top of it.

The girls usually peeled off at this point to take multiple runs on Easy Street, two squealing riders per sled. The girls scrunched up tight, the back-seater's legs wrapped around the front's waist, snow-encrusted boots heavy in the front-rider's lap. The boys continued to the top, deliberating about technique; should you slide face-forward with hands locked onto the front steer handle, or sit upright and steer with your feet. The boys never doubled up.

Scotty went first, sitting upright with sled rope in hand. His slide was smooth until the bump, which sent him flying off the path and narrowly missing a tree. The others scrutinized what went wrong and concluded it was his weight distribution — he should have been seated back more. Scotty decided to hoof it back up rather than finish the run, so Clemens egged on his brother, younger by a year, to go next.

"Come on Tru. What do you think? Face-forward sitting upright?"

Truman didn't like the Pants Wetter but didn't have much of a choice. The humiliation of going with the girls would have been unbearable. Clemens would have seen right through any claims of tummy aches or otherwise. Like most hijinks with his brother, he went along with it and most times it really was fun, at times even a thrill. Clemens seemed to need that more than Truman. For instance, Clemens would choose the course of action that would get him riding the fastest. Truman silently calculated which way he was less likely to get hurt. More control face-forward, but also more chance of cuts and scrapes from the icy snow if he did crash. Upright had less balance, but even Scotty only made it halfway down, unscathed. Then again, if Truman went all the way down, he could take his time coming up and by then, the grownups would probably have started their whistling and hollering to go home.

Face-forward it was. He lay down and centered himself, making sure the rope was tucked under his body so it wouldn't get caught under the runners and send him sideways. He said a silent prayer for protection as he pulled his cap down tight, then grasped the steering handle from his belly-flat position. The moment his hands were on the steering, he felt his brother (he just knew it was his brother) give his snow-heavy boots a push.

Truman picked up speed right away and before he knew it, he was soaring over the bump with a whooping cry and landing clean. He veered left all the way off the path and intentionally capsized near the bottom before anything bad happened. He rolled over in snow-encrusted victory and made a snow angel in celebration as a thanks to God for keeping him safe and to postpone heading back up the hill.

As he rested in his angel, he heard hollering from up the hill signaling the next rider was on his way. The next thing he heard was the whoosh of runners on snow and he picked his head up just in time to see the blur of Clemens' new wool snowsuit, the red of a runner, the blond wood of the sled and then nothing.

IT WAS HIS SISTER FELICITY, eight-years old to Truman's ten and Clemens' eleven, who came barging into the pastor's house, snow barnacles twisted into her long, brown hair. She stamped her way over to the Bates, flinging snow chunks in every direction from her snow-encased legs.

"It's Truman, *Maman*, Papa. Come quick — there's been an accident!"

Jolene Anderson handed them their coats and Henry and Emeline ran out the door, pulling on their heavy, wool coats as they tried to hurry through the slush of the road.

They could hear wailing as they got close. When they got to the crowd of staring, stunned children, Samuel, the youngest Bates at the time, stood with them. The sound was coming from Clemens, crumpled in a ball, his snowy rear-end in the air, head in hands, his body shaking with sobs. Beyond Clemens, there was a sled in the snow, red runners in the air. Emeline went directly to Truman, flat on his back, his head at an angle. Blood was spattered across his face and pink snow sprayed in the shape of a trumpet. She observed the flattened snow around him — angel's wings. He was perfectly still.

"*Mon Dieu*." Emeline put her head to his chest — there was breath.

Henry, color drained from his face, spoke in a quiet voice. "Someone get Doctor Hendricks here. On the double."

Dr. Hendricks was already on his way, knees pumping in the snow.

TRUMAN AWOKE IN A STUFFY, unfamiliar room. Someone was holding his hand. He tried to turn his head to the side, but his neck wouldn't listen. He shifted his eyes all the way to the side. He could only see a fuzzy outline of a person.

"Hello? Anyone there?"

"Oh! *Mon ange! Docteur! Docteur!*"

Truman relaxed — of course it was his mother. "*Maman*, my neck." Tears began to flow down his cheeks. "My head — it hurts real bad."

His mother laid kisses on his tears. "Tru, you must be strong. There was h'accident with sleds. But you are good! Now you are good, *mon chou...*" Truman, always confused by this particular endearment, had never been so glad to be called a cabbage in his life.

Truman had never been to the doctor's office; he had only ever seen the doctor in the Bates' own home when Dr Hendricks delivered Felicity and Samuel, and once for a scarlet fever scare, but the children only had the chicken pox.

When it was assessed that Truman was stable enough to be moved, they put him in the back of Jimmy Kleets' Chevy flatbed that he used for delivery; vegetables in the summer and fall, pine trees at Christmas, cords of wood throughout the winter, and milk all throughout the year.

Henry and Clemens were in the back keeping Truman covered in blankets against the gray February day. Clemens was numb from shock more than from the cold. Henry had his arm around him best he could, while keeping a hand on Truman to keep the blankets in place against the movement of the truck. Clemens couldn't stop looking at Truman's bloody mouth and his forehead, sliced open by the runner of his sled. It was bandaged now, but not before Clemens watched his brother's blood drain from his head and leak into the snow. And there were whispers that his neck might be broke. The truck was moving slow on the way to the hospital, for every jostle could mean paralysis, if it hadn't happened already. Clemens buried his head in his father's side and wept a river into the warm, scratchy coat.

3

1983: THE NEW KID, SLEEPOVERS, AND A DREAM

A few weeks after senior year started, Dante came home with Pat after school. No one talked about that it was to keep an eye on him. He was doing a little better, but still. It had become a routine since the accident — Dante would show up at Candice's request. Pat didn't seem to care if Dante was there half the time, but other times he acted halfway normal.

"Dude, do you remember your very first day at school?" Pat was reclined on his bed, arms tucked behind his head, well-defined abs revealed under his cutoff gray sweatshirt. His acid-wash jeans were tight all over as usual. He'd been wearing that same outfit, or some other version of it, since they started high school three years before. Dante now took it as "a good Pat day" when he was wearing his signature outfit.

"Are you talking like, this year, or like, before I moved here? Dante was reclined in his sleeping bag on Pat's drafty wood floor. Dante was glad Pat and everyone had finally stopped calling him Strawberry that summer, though he didn't like the fight it took to end it. It was Pat who gave him that name, on that very first day at Hope-field Elementary all those years ago, because of Dante's near constant blushing. He was better about it now, but not perfect.

"The day we met. You were such a skinny, nervous kid back then." Pat smiled, still looking at the ceiling. "Now you're just a skinny, nervous asshole."

Dante threw his pillow at him from the floor. "I don't know how the nickname Mighty Mouse slipped by. Oh, I know. It should have been Mighty Buttmunch."

The pillow came back fast, whomping him in the face.

DANTE THOUGHT back to when he moved to Hopefield and how he was not sure if Pat Bates was going to be a good friend to him, those first few weeks. But Pat hadn't given him a choice. It was like he decided what their relation-ship would be and until it was clear the friendship was going to stick. Sometimes Dante felt just along for the ride.

That first day, he remembered standing at the edge of the blacktop. The jungle gym was covered in kids that were deep into a game of their own invention. He watched and could only figure out that it had to do with aliens, lava and that no one wanted to touch the ground. It was pretty much like his playground from his elementary school in Brooklyn, except this one had a steep wooded hill next to it, playing fields beyond it, and a river beyond that — one that didn't come with warning signs telling people to keep out. And no black kids or brown kids — his best friend back home had been black, Elroy Jackson. Dante was white, although in that Jewish way, many were quick to point out in Brooklyn Heights. He stood there and wondered if anyone would be into comics the way that he and Elroy were.

Everything was new for him at Hopefield Elementary — faces, smells, classrooms, cubbies. His new teacher had long curly hair, was young and seemed to genuinely like kids, not like Mrs. Brockton from PS 81 in Brooklyn Heights — she was as old as a grandma (she probably was one). Dante had hoped Mrs. Brockton was nicer to her grandkids than she was to her students. He'd never forget the time she was looking over his cursive writing. He was sitting next to her on the conference bench that kids were summoned to for one-on-one time with the teacher. It had been snowing outside the window, the welcome kind that covered up the hard, sooty lumps that had built up over the curbs where the snowplows had pushed the earlier snows into any space that didn't have a parked car. He looked up at her thin, lined face, her sharp blue eyes, short silver hair and, from his position, up her nose. She had dry boogers suspended in the middle of her nostrils, which were flaring slightly with her breathing. Dante began to fear one would loosen on an exhale and land on his paper, his hand, or even his face. Then she gently took Dante's pencil from his hand, turned it eraser-side up, brought it to her mouth and licked it. Twirling it back around as quick as a gunslinger, she began to erase his words from the page, turning any lead left on the page into a gray, cloudy smudge. Dante remembered himself feeling erased. He never got higher than a satisfactory on anything in her class, and consistently received unsatisfactory in handwriting.

He had hoped Miss Devereux would be different and

he wasn't disappointed. She was still one of his favorite teachers to this day.

Pat grabbed a ratty baseball from the shelf next to him and began to toss it up and down from his reclined position. "Did you have, what do they call it... culture shock coming here?"

"I had no idea, like, zero, what it would be like when I moved here. What were we, like eight? Nine?"

Pat grabbed a ratty baseball from the shelf next to him and began to toss it up and down from his reclined position."I remember being so confused by your parents' store when they opened it. I was like, 'what do they even sell in here?', even after I went in that first time. I remember it smelled weird, but in a good way, that there were jars of dried leaves, books, and waxy wand-like things on the counter. I picked one up and I started jabbing you with it. What were they again? Ear somethings?"

Dante rolled his eyes. "Ear candles. God, don't you know anything?"

Pat made as if to throw the ball at Dante, who flinched.

"Don't be an asshole, Pat Bates, though I know that's hard for you. Anyway, that's when I began to worry. Like, will anybody here buy this stuff if no one knows what it is? Will we have to move again?"

Pat laughed. "Well, my dad says thanks to Greyson there's plenty of hippies with money around here, so you never had to worry about that!"

Dante sat up. "Did you know that I thought that's where we were going to live? At the store, because it was a house? We stopped there with the moving truck before we stopped at our actual house."

The Apothecary was just around the corner from the elementary school. When the Zuckermans bought it, it had been a one-story cottage with a peeling-paint porch. Doing almost all the work themselves, Ephraim and Darlene Zuckerman hung shelves, installed an industrial sink, built a glass-topped counter, and filled large glass canisters with orange, yellow, and green herbs. The cottage sat at the foot of the slanted bridge that had been built back in the eighteen hundreds over the Winooski River waterfall. The bridge connected Hopefield, located in the middle of Vermont, to Route 2, which, it turned out, you could travel on from Maine to Seattle, two lanes the whole way.

Dante still loved to look out the window of the back room of The Apothecary because it was eye level with the top of the waterfall. The Zuckerman's knew about the cottage, and Hopefield, because they had attended Greyson College, which from what Dante understood, specialized in subjects like growing things without chemicals, languages, keeping an eye on Uncle Sam, and natural healing, which had been his dad Ephraim's focus. His dad told him that he had fallen in love with the town of Hopefield during his college years, felt a calling to leave the city streets where he was raised to move to where the air was pure and the pace slow. To be where people believed in the earth and healing naturally. He fell in love with Darlene, too, who had studied Classic Literature and thought the idea of living in Hopefield was very romantic (she was from Queens). Dante thought romance was supposed to be about kissing and stuff like that. Nothing about Hopefield had ever felt remotely romantic to him.

Dante shook his head. "You know why I was so excited when we got to our real house? Because we had a second floor. Apartments in Brooklyn do not have second floors.

Brownstones, yes, apartments, at least in our neighborhood, no."

"Brownstone?"

Dante shook his head. "Never mind. You've really got to leave this village sometime."

"That first day I saw you standing at the edge of the playground, and I was like, 'Oh cool! New kid!' It's not like people move here a lot. I mean, how many new people since you came? Zero?"

THINKING BACK on that first day on the playground, Dante remembered standing in a patch of sunlight trying to keep warm in the frigid April air, tucking in his black curly hair that kept pushing up his blue and gray knitted hat. He had to keep stamping his wet Converse-clad feet to keep them from getting anymore numb.

He froze, not from cold, but from fear, when a kid left the group of boys he had been talking with and stomped over to him in moon boots — Dante recognized him from class. Unlike most other kids, he wasn't wearing a hat. He had shaggy blond hair, freckles, blue eyes and a cocked chin that made him seem ready for a challenge, anytime, anywhere. It also made him seem taller than he was, which was three inches shorter than Dante, easy. He had a large, faded red rubber ball under one arm.

"We're playing Smear the Queer. We need another kid. You wanna play?"

"Okay." Dante figured it must be a game he knew and they just called it something different up here.

He joined the five boys and together they walked around the other side of the fence to the playing field on the other side. Dante looked behind him — leaving the fenced yard would get you in trouble for sure at PS 81. The teacher on duty saw them but didn't do anything. Dante waited for the group to be divided into teams and for the game to reveal itself. Before he knew it, the ball was tossed to another kid, who had straight black hair under his red wool cap and was as freakishly tall as the blond kid was short.

Everyone started to chase him, so Dante did too. It looked like they were about to tackle him. *Oh! Football!* thought Dante, but then the tall kid tossed it to a chunky kid with brown hair and freckles, and then everyone ran after him. That kid got smashed under a dog pile, until the ball got loose. Dante figured the game must be about getting the ball to some goal or base, so he grabbed the ball and was about to ask whose team he was on when the freckled blond boy's face was suddenly two inches in front of his. He was slammed backward into a patch of snow-spattered mud. He heard himself say "oof" like out of one of his Batman comics and he couldn't breathe. He pinched his eyes closed.

He heard one of them say, "Way to go, Mighty Mouse, looks like he got the wind knocked out of him. Now we gotta wait." Dante panicked. He'd never not been able to catch his breath. He couldn't move or talk, but he opened his eyes and tried to communicate his distress with them as best he could.

Pat bent over and cocked his chin even farther out at him. "Hey, kid, don't freak out. You okay?"

All that came out was a squeak.

Already bored, the chunky boy asked the tall one in the red wool cap about the previous night's episode of Candid Camera. "Lyle — you see Candid Camera last night? Those people on the escalator going the wrong way." He lowered his voice to a whisper. "I thought my dad was going to pee himself he was laughing so hard." Dante would not be able to navigate that conversation, even if he wasn't winded and paralyzed — his parents didn't believe in TV.

Lyle smiled and nodded at the other boy – Dante had never seen such a wide mouth or such large teeth. "Oh — and that guy asking to park everyone's car in that grocery store parking lot. Wicked funny. When I can drive, I am one hundred percent going to do that. Oh, and Jer — what about the policeman that gave that girl a ticket in her own driveway?" The two boys cracked up.

Dante had gotten his breath back. The blond boy just stood there staring at him like he was daring him to get up. All the other kids had already drifted away with the ball and started kicking it around. The kid seemed to make up his mind about something and stuck his gloved hand out to him. "Come on, get up. You just stood there. Why didn't you run?"

Dante grasped his hand and let himself be helped up — he thought this boy must be made of muscle the way he gripped his hand and pulled him up so easy. In his embarrassment, Dante couldn't help blushing a deep red. In addition to strong emotions, blushing deeply was something that happened when he was caught off guard, called on in class, made to feel stupid, or didn't know the answer to something. His face burned. "I didn't know the rules."

Pat grinned. "Jeezum, you turned into a strawberry! Where are you from? You don't know Smear the Queer? There are no rules — you get the ball, you get chased and knocked down until someone else gets the ball."

"That's it? Oh." Dante paused. "How do you win?"

Pat looked at him closely. "You don't. We just play until we're bored or the teacher calls us in."

Dante hated to sound even more stupid, but he had to ask. "What's queer mean?"

Pat shrugged. "I think it means dumb, or weird, or something."

Dante craned his head to look around at himself when he felt muddy wetness along the whole back of him. "Am I going to get into trouble?"

Chin still cocked, Pat threw his arm around Dante's shoulders, which probably wasn't easy given Pat's small stature. "Nah, Miss Devereux's wicked nice. She keeps extra towels for us kids to sit on so we don't get the chairs all dirty. My name's Patrick Bates, but everyone calls me Pat Bates. What's yours?"

"I'm Dante Zuckerman."

"Okay, but I think I'll call you Strawberry. I never seen anybody turn so red before."

Dante froze, blush still intact. Was this Pat Bates kid being mean?

Pat dropped his arm and stuck out his hand. "Let's be best friends. Shake on it."

Dante hesitated. Elroy was his best friend still, wasn't he? He also didn't like this new nickname. As if an unseen force guided him, he said, "Sure." And put his hand in Pat's to seal the deal.

WHEN DANTE WOKE up the next autumn morning back in Pat's room, Dante was surprised to see Pat had gotten dressed before Dante had even woken up. It was good, though. Last night Pat just sat on his bed, headphones on, his Walkman resting on his stomach. Dante knew the routine by now. He was there, at minimum to try to cheer Pat up and at worst, to make sure Pat didn't do anything crazy. Dante didn't know exactly what that meant, but he would do anything Pat's mom asked. So now, when Pat got like this, he never talked to anyone, didn't come out for dinner, just laid on his bed and listened to Sabbath, play, flip, play, flip. The same tape over and over again. Now Dante could hear it was the song, "Wheels of Confusion".

In the mornings after Dante had stayed over, at least so far, Pat acted as if nothing was unusual, as if his best friend was always on his floor when he woke up on a school day. Dante never complained about being ignored all night. He had learned to bring his comics with him. He never mentioned that he was asked to come over. If Pat knew, he never let on.

IN THE KITCHEN, Pat took a slurp of cereal.

Candice bustled into the kitchen. "What about lunch today? Sorry, Dante, I guess it's peanut butter and jelly for you again. Patty, there's ham or bologna. Which one?"

"Bologna." Pat's mom proceeded to make his sandwich just how he liked it, then moved on to the pb and j.

Candice licked peanut butter off the knife. "You know, I remember the first sleepover you boys had here. Do you?"

Dante stood and brought his bowl to the sink. "Mr. Bates scared the crap out of me, that's my strongest memory of that night."

Candice touched his shoulder briefly. "You know,

teasing is just the Vermont way of showing we like someone!"

Dante rolled his eyes. "I wasn't born here, but I *do* know how Vermont works by now. And I'm still not convinced Mr. Bates doesn't hate me, you know, since that day." He wasn't sure he ever would since the hunting trip.

They all thought back to the disaster that was Dante's first and last hunting trip, with the Bates or anyone else. They all involuntarily shuddered at the thought of it.

Candice shook her head. "It was an accident. Nothing more."

THE FIRST SLEEPOVER was at Dante's house.

Pat came over to Dante's for a sleepover about a month after Dante had moved to Hopefield. Candice rang the bell. Dante's mom, Darlene, with Dante at her side. The nine-year-old boys immediately melded together into the kitchen and could be heard pounding up the stairs to Dante's room.

Darlene, wearing overalls, opened the door wide and stuck out her hand, long brown braids swinging and bracelets jangling. "Hi, I'm Darlene. Come in!" Candice caught a whiff of a perfumed smell that wasn't perfume and while she knew it wasn't marijuana, this scent was unfamiliar. It was a nice smell. Exotic.

Candice took her wiry hand and squeezed it softly with her doughy fingers, "Candice, but everyone calls me Candy. Thank you, I'll come in for just a minute."

Darlene indicated Candice should sit on one of the bench seats at the kitchen table and poured them both fresh-squeezed lemonade. Candice, large by even local standards, shifted her bulk onto a seat and took a sip. She tried, unsuccessfully, to hide a wince.

"Oh, I'm sorry, you'd probably like more sugar. Dante always puts more in, but Ephraim and I like it sour." Darlene made a move to get up.

"Oh, no, no. It's fine." She patted her stomach. "Probably good for me not to have too much sugar." She took another sip and smiled.

The mothers chatted about the Zuckerman's move from Brooklyn.

"Never moving again!" said Darlene, as she talked about their new store.

"Oh, I'll have to stop by!" Candice said.

"So great that Dante made a friend so soon! We were worried that he wouldn't fit in, everyone already knowing each other and all," Darlene confided.

"Oh, Hopefield is a real nice place — so friendly. You know, I've never moved? I still live in the house I grew up in!"

Candice had to ask. "Dante is an unusual name." Her eyes flashed to the Star of David weaving on the wall next to the refrigerator. "Is it Jewish?"

Darlene laughed, then caught herself. "Oh, no. We are Jewish, though more from our backgrounds than anything active now. We have opened up to other ideas about religion. I was a Classics major in college and I fell in love with the *Divine Comedy*."

Candice blinked. "Comedy?"

Darlene explained further. "Uh, not at all, actually. It was a poem written in the fourteenth century by Dante Alighieri. It's basically about how to get from Hell to Heaven."

"Oh, I wonder if my pastor has read that. Pat, short for

Patrick, you're going to think this is silly, is named after my favorite singer, Pat Boone." She laughed. "I don't know how my Bill let me get away with that one! Do you have any other children? We have one more — a girl! Kitty — she's younger."

Darlene shook her head and took a sip of lemonade, bracelets sliding down her arm. "I guess I just like doing things one at a time. Ephraim laughs and says I am the worst multitasker!" They both laughed at that.

Candice placed both hands on the table. "Well, I best get going. I no sooner get this one dropped off and I have the other to pick up! I'm nothing but a taxi anymore."

"Thank you so much for bringing Pat. I can bring him home tomorrow."

Candice considered that for a minute. "You know, we live out in Woodbury on a bunch of unmarked dirt roads. Call me tomorrow and I can give you directions, or maybe I will just come get him."

"Okay, great." Darlene got up and searched around in the small desk by the kitchen door. "Here we go — please write your number and I'll give you mine." And with two rips of notebook paper, the numbers were exchanged.

PAT DUG through his sleepover duffle bag. "I brought back a bunch of your comics. Thanks. One got ripped — I hope you're not too mad. It was my little sister, Kitty. She's the biggest pain. You're so lucky you ain't got sisters."

Dante was laid back on his Spiderman bedspread, a Hanukkah present from his grandmother last year. "Better not be a Spiderman one!"

"Nah — it was a Sergeant Fury — Eye for an Eye. It was wicked cool."

Pat sat on the rug and looked around. There wasn't much on the walls except a weaving of a rainbow and a Herbie the Love Bug poster. "Hey — you wanna go see the Herbie movie that's coming out?"

Dante's eyes grew large and he dropped his comic. "There's one coming out? Oh my God, when?"

"Pretty soon, I think. I saw an ad during Six Million Dollar Man."

Dante said, "Do not see it without me." He thought for a minute. "Wait, where's the movie theater?"

"Haven't you been to Montpelier yet? Or Barre?"

"I haven't been anywhere but here since we moved. My parents are too busy setting up the store."

"What do you guys sell in there, anyway?"

Dante shrugged. "I dunno. A lot of natural stuff, herbs, candles, books on vegetarianism."

Pat blinked. "Vegetari-whatnow?"

Dante flipped over onto his belly on the bed, legs bent, feet in the air. "Seriously?" Dante had been feeling so dumb since he got here; not knowing people's names, where things were, characters in TV shows or video games, how to use "wicked" in a sentence. Pat Bates never lost a chance to rub it in his face, either. Sometimes Dante just laughed when others laughed without having a clue about what was funny. Pat would look at him and whisper, "Nice try." Unsurprisingly, that would always make him blush.

"I can't believe I know something you don't."

Pat grinned. "Yeah, me either."

"If you came with me to the city, you wouldn't know

anything, either. Like how to ride the subway or hail a cab." He sat up. "I miss hot pretzels."

Pat said, "I been to Boston once, when I was a baby. I don't remember nothing about it. So, what is that word you said." It was more of a command than a question. Everything was with Pat.

"Oh — We're vegetarians. We don't eat meat."

Pat blinked. "Oh, like Noah and Eliza."

Dante shrugged and gave a small shake of his head.

Pat replied, "In our class? The twins? They both wear glasses?"

Dante replied, "Oh, yeah. I think they are coming over soon. My mom said something about a potluck."

Pat replied, "All they ever eat is peanut butter on celery, carrot sticks, and stuff like that, like you. Ever notice how Noah comes over all the time during lunch to ask for some of my chips? You don't ask for any. Why not?"

Pat was so bossy sounding sometimes. "Well, why don't you ever ask for some of my peppers and hummus. I dare you to try it next time."

Pat rolled his eyes. "No way! You know, there's a lot of people like you where my mom works. She works for Greyson College, and I went to visit her once for lunch and I couldn't hardly find anything good to eat. The baked potato bar was wicked big, though. What do you eat for dinner?"

The boys heard some movement on the stairs and a man's voice. "Come on boys — dinner!"

Dante and Pat looked at each other and cracked up — life was so funny.

~

DARLENE, Ephraim, Dante and Pat settled onto the bench seats around the cherrywood table. Pat's cocked chin barely cleared the edge of the table. The boys each had a glass of milk in front of them. Pat took a sip and recoiled, dribbling it down his chin. Everyone looked at him in surprise.

Pat wiped his mouth with his shirt. "Uh, what brand of milk is this?"

Darlene put her hand to her mouth. "Oh, Pat, I'm sorry — it's soy milk. We have cow's milk, too, let me get you some.". We have

cow's milk, too, let me get you some."

DANTE BLUSHED. What if Pat didn't ever want to come back again?

Darlene went to the fridge. She looked at Dante's reaction and picked up on his embarrassment. "Dante, do you want some, too?"

Dante glanced at Pat. "Yes, please."

Darlene replaced the glasses with fresh milk.

There were two pots on the table. Ephraim was seated at the end of the bench seat next to Darlene, facing Dante and Pat — he stood up and leaned toward the middle with a pronged pasta spoon. "Okay, boys, we have spaghetti squash with tomato sauce, and we have spaghetti spaghetti with tomato sauce."

Pat looked at the spaghetti squash. "Squashed spaghetti?"

The Zuckermans burst into laughter, Dante included. He couldn't help it.

Now it was Pat who turned pink.

Darlene patted his arm. "Oh, sweetie, We're sorry. It's

just, well, it was so cute what you just said. Here — have some spaghetti spaghetti."

Ephraim passed around a salad bowl. "Get your greens boys."

Dante took the tongs and put some salad on his plate. He passed it to Pat who put, at most, two pieces of lettuce on his plate.

The rest of the dinner continued with Ephraim and Darlene asking Pat questions about what subjects he liked at school and what he liked to do in his free time.

Pat shrugged. "School's okay. I like recess best. At home, I like boy stuff, I guess. 'Cause my dumb sister don't like what I like — video games, fishing, hunting." He glanced at Dante. "Comics, too. And my pop says he's taking me bow hunting next season."

Ephraim and Darlene looked at each other. Dante stared at Pat. "Oh," said Ephraim. "What do you do with the uh...deer, is it?"

Pat cocked his head sideways. "Of course, deer. My dad hangs 'em from the trees out back, butchers 'em. We have a venison freezer in the garage. My mom makes sausages."

The table fell quiet.

Dante felt pale and weak, imagining a deer hung by her feet, blood draining into the dirt. Pat squirmed in his seat, wondering if he had said something wrong, again.

Darlene looked a little pale herself and changed the subject. "How many sisters do—"

Ephraim interrupted. "Can you take Dante hunting?"

"Ephraim!"

Ephraim spread his arms wide. "This is the country-side! This is what people do — provide for themselves directly from nature, be it plant or animal. The balance of nature, God will provide. What an education to see what it's like to take a life in order to sustain another. It's all very regulated, right Pat?"

Pat's eyes were wide. It was clear he'd never heard anyone talk like that before. "I guess. You can ask my pop." He looked at Dante. "I'll ask if you can come."

Dante said it as best he could. "Wicked. Cool. Thanks."

After dinner, the boys played Parcheesi with Ephraim and Darlene, then Mastermind and Connect Four against each other. Pat kept saying he couldn't believe how many board games they had stacked up in the closet. Ephraim joked that they took up half of the moving truck, along with Dante's Hot Wheels. Pat had packed the few Matchbox cars he had into his overnight bag and after they were done saying how wicked cool each other's cars were, they spit-motored for a least an hour, building obstacles and crashing their cars around the tracks on the braided rug in Dante's room and racing their cars down the hallway.

They slept in sleeping bags on the floor, forcing their eyes to stay open and debating Disney characters.

Dante said, "Goofy's the best."

Pat replied, "Maybe. I really love Scrooge McDuck, though. I mean-" Pat yawned. "How funny is it when he gets mad?"

"Who do think is the worst?" Dante turned over in his sleeping bag.

"That's a cinch. Daisy Duck."

"Totally!" Dante closed his eyes.

"When you sleep over next weekend, we are going to watch so much TV. You have to come over Friday night so you can see Saturday morning cartoons. They are the best!"

Talking themselves to sleep, Dante forgot all about the talk at dinner about hunting, but that night had a dream about a deer that came to him in the forest. Dante held out his hand and she touched her nose to his palm. An antlered buck appeared in the trees behind her, one hooved foot stomping over and over, as if readying himself for a charge. Dante got the feeling he wouldn't charge if Dante showed he meant no harm. He held up his hands as if to show he had no weapons.

In the next moment, Pat was next to him, taller than in real life, taller than Dante, raising a bow. He shot an arrow, missing the doe, the arrow striking a tree. The buck snorted, charged, leaped toward Dante, its face inches from his, but it transformed into a human form mid-flight. When Dante awoke, panting, he could still feel the cold touch of the doe's nose on his palm and the image of Pat's face in front of his own.

BACK IN THE KITCHEN, Candice asked, "Do you boys have any big tests this week?"

Dante accepted his lunch sack from Candice. "I have a geometry test tomorrow, but that's it."

Pat accepted his lunch with a silent shrug.

Candice kissed Pat on the cheek and gave Dante's arm a gentle "thank you'" squeeze.

After they got into Dante's brown-pocked Tercel wagon, Dante debated if he should ask what he wanted to as he drove both Pat and Kitty to school. Candice had recently decided she couldn't stand the thought of another accident and with Pat acting so strange, she sometimes wouldn't let him drive himself or his sister to school.

Bill, her husband, didn't agree, but let it go. He was at work at the quarry too early in the morning to do anything about it, anyway.

Pat was looking out the passenger window. "I can drive next time, you know. Maybe we should even drive separate, so you don't have to drive me home."

Kitty piped up from the back. "I can drive, you know. Dad lets me drive the truck around our property."

Dante tried to be polite. "Cool." Pat stared straight ahead. Dante glanced at him. "Anyway, Pat, I'm just trying to help. You know, with your...I don't know. Condition."

Pat shook his head. "My what? Condition? Dude, that's the word people use to talk about Uncle Tru." Pat crossed his arms and looked out the window. "Fuck you."

Dante glanced at Kitty in the rearview. Her mouth was open. Dante needed to turn left, but he idled at the empty intersection in the middle of the woods. The trees all around them were a riot of red, orange, pink, and yellow. The woods looked on fire.

Dante knew he was the last person, except for maybe Kitty, that Pat would want asking him this, but fuck it. "Well, dude, are you? You know, hearing anything? Voices?"

Kitty couldn't stay silent. "Jeezum, for real?"

Pat turned to Kitty. "Shut up." He pointed a finger at Dante. "You're taking psychology with that weirdo Dupre, aren't you."

"Hey, it's got nothing to do with that."

That wasn't true. They were doing a series on signs of serious mental illness and the first was usually depression. And poor hygiene. Dante knew Pat hadn't taken a shower in a couple of days and he didn't bother to feather and spray his hair into place today. Everyone said he looked like Shaun Cassidy when he did, and he ate that up. He also changed into a regular sweatshirt this morning, not one of his innumerable cutoffs that showed off his abs. Dante had learned over the past few weeks what that meant.

"You know," started Dante. "Truman used to be pretty cool in our book."

Pat scoffed. "Yeah, when we were dumb little shits." Pat sighed and leaned against the door frame. "I am suddenly so incredibly, fucking tired."

And with that, Pat began to sob. Dante turned the car around and drove him home under the canopy of fire. Kitty, in a burgeoning flash of maturity, stayed quiet.

4

1920–1926: CLEM AND TRU

Truman returned home a few days later with nothing more than a few bandages and a tilted head. Dr. Hendricks said that over time, it would straighten out, but didn't want to force it. Truman was to receive physical therapy twice a week. After a couple of weeks, the bandages were removed to reveal that Truman had a puckered scar along his hairline.

"That looks jake, Tru. Real jake."

Truman beamed with pride. "Well, I guess I owe you one, then."

ONE YEAR LATER, it was Clemens, now twelve, who gave Truman, eleven, his first cigarette. They were playing hooky, the first of the new school year, to go fishing at Number Ten pond. They walked for three miles on the narrow dirt road under the peaking fall colors, stopping once to rest and speak about bait strategies. The lake burned with reflections of yellow, orange, and red leaves. Clemens had stolen a plug of tobacco and two papers from their father's supply on the top shelf in the pantry. Clemens had just been taught how to roll a cigarette the week before by John Stover, a boy two grades up, and was eager to show off.

They settled themselves behind the empty, clapboard Meeting House at the far edge of the lake. "You're doin' it all wrong, I bet," said Truman, watching his brother fumble with the tobacco and papers. "Pa's gonna kill you, too, if he finds out."

"Aw, he won't care. It's *Maman* we gotta look out for. She believes tobacco is the Devil's work. Anyway, I only took a little."

Clemens rolled the first cigarette so loosely that neither of them could get a drag and it fell apart in their hands.

Truman, disappointed that they wouldn't get a chance to do something they shouldn't, was also pleased that his brother was not too ahead of him in the realm of grownup secrets. "Told you so. You don't know how to roll."

Clemens dissected it and started over, dropping over half of what was left into the dirt. After Clemens successfully rolled the next one, he said, "Say it, Tru. Come on, say it."

Truman looked at him and blinked.

Clemens rolled his eyes. "Come on, Tru...You knoooow. When you want a smoke — remember, what that guy said in the bit about the doughboys in France in The Cuckoo Hour...?"

"Oh! I got it! Clem, butt me!"

The second cigarette was so thin and tight that both Clemens and Truman made puckering noises they sucked so hard to get smoke. They passed the cigarette back and forth, taking turns choking and cracking up. They finally gave up and went searching for their poles, which they had hidden in the hollowed-out pine tree the weekend before. They took the bread scraps out of their pockets, dug up some worms, declared a worm vs bread competition and put their poles in the water to catch some bass. The worms, Truman's bait, won out.

They couldn't very well bring home any fish, so they threw back whatever they caught. They knew their teacher would tell the younger ones to tell their parents that Clemens and Truman didn't attend school that day.

"What's it gonna be this time?" asked Clemens.

"Got me."

"Let's say some nutjob from Waterbury escaped and told us he'd kill us if we didn't help him."

Truman asked, "What's with Waterbury, anyway? I mean is the whole town nuts, or something? I mean, you heard about Willem Granger, right?"

Clemens nodded. "I think there's a place there for crazy people."

Truman said, "I overheard Willem's brother talking about it at the store, he said it was big, said they were surprised because it reminded him of a university, you know, the way it looked. A bunch of spread-out buildings, or something. I can't remember the word he used, like as... asy..."

Clemens started to laugh. "Ass? Is that where they're sent? To an ass?"

"Shut up. Oh, heck, you ruined it. So, is it like a jail, then? This place?"

Clemens shrugged. "I mean, what else are you going to do with them?"

Truman shuddered. "I wouldn't want to be the one to find out."

Clemens shook his head. "We better not tell too crazy of a story of why we skipped school, then maybe it'll happen to us!"

Truman nodded in agreement. "How about that we saw George Hobart get his wagon stuck in a ditch again on the way to school and one of his horses went lame and so it took us all day to help him,"

"No good. He works with Pa at the sheds. No, I think I got it. You got shanghaied by some older boys and got yourself thrown down the school well. I spent all day trying to get you out, which is why we weren't in class."

"They'll never buy that one. Besides, why do I have to be the one down the well?"

"Because you're the one all soaking wet!" Clemens grabbed Truman's pole out of his hand and shoved him into the frigid lake. To Clemens, the look on Truman's face was worth the trouncing he would receive. Truman hauled himself out of the lake, almost losing a boot, and jumped on top of his brother who was rendered helpless, shaking with laughter. They wrestled until Truman had victoriously pinned Clemens to the dirt and both were as wet as the fish in the lake.

TRUMAN LISTENED CAREFULLY to his father talk about the Granger boy that night over supper. Henry had said, "His pa told me that Willem stayed up straight for four nights. Imagine. Four nights in a row. Now listen closely, children, he fixed the roof of the barn during that time, banged out ten horseshoes, and pitched the barn full of hay. Then he slept for three full days."

Truman listened with rapt attention along with his brothers, sisters and mother, as they would any gossip about someone they knew. Truman was listening so hard he was ignoring Clemens' kicks under the table, who expected him to kick back and start the back and forth until one parent or another told them to knock it off. Truman's skin was prickling because he wanted to tell his own story about Willem.

Truman cleared his throat and raised his voice a bit so he would be sure to be heard over the din of the table. "Listen to this — I saw Willem's brother Chauncey at the store, and he had just come back from seeing him at Waterbury."

Henry raised his eyebrows and the table went quiet. Truman gloated at the reaction. "Uh-huh, and he said that the place was really big, looked like a college."

Henry shook his head. "So, Willem went to the nuthouse, huh?"

Emeline sat up straight. Her eyes darted around, taking in the reaction of her family.

Henry chuckled. "Well, the lesson to be learned here is that if any of you get in with the Devil like the Granger boy, go out back and dig us a new well!" Henry sat back in his chair and roared. Truman thought about the Devil. Is that what drove people insane? Or was it something else?

Emeline sat silent, thinking of her favorite aunt, whom she had not thought of for a long time. How one day she was her doting aunt and the next, a person she would have crossed the street to avoid. How *Tante Clémence* withdrew from her, spending time alone in her room, speaking to the others that had trespassed into her mind, twitching, and scolding invisible strangers, at times yelling at them to stop cooking because there was more than enough. No more hugs and kisses for Emeline, no more lazy walks visiting Montreal's multitude of *crêperies*, or games in the parlor on rainy afternoons. Emeline despaired at being more invisible than the intruders in her aunt's head. She had never told Henry about her, nor the children. Why scare them? That was the past, in another life, another country, and had nothing to do with them now.

TWO YEARS LATER, Henry got promoted to supervisor at the Rock of Ages quarry and the Bates bought their first car, a Model T. The kids, Clemens, now fourteen, Truman, thirteen, Felicity, eleven and Samuel, seven were besides themselves. It was more exciting than getting their own Silvertone radio the previous year. Clemens asked right away when he could drive it. Truman kept walking circle after circle around it, repeating, "So jake... so very, very jake."

Felicity wanted to name it something other than Lizzie, which she and Samuel argued about —just because it already had the widely known nickname Tin Lizzie, Felicity argued, didn't mean you couldn't call it something else. Samuel argued back that Felicity already got to name the family horse, a roan-colored Morgan. Until now, Daisy Chain pulling their buckboard had been their sole means of transportation. To name this next level of modernization was of crucial importance to them.

Felicity said, "How about Delilah?"

Samuel rolled his eyes. "Why does it have to be a girl's name?"

"Quit your quibbling and load up!" bellowed Henry, wearing his finest fedora. Emeline pinned her new, shapely wool hat into her hair and fluffed the pheasant feathers that stuck up jauntily. Henry's face nearly split in two from grinning. The kids piled into the back all at once and hierarchy was instantaneously established — two eldest, Truman and Clemens, got the windows, Felicity and Samuel smashed together in the middle. No arguments about fairness today- those would come later. A very pregnant Emeline was helped into the passenger seat by Henry and she, too, looked ripe to burst with excitement.

Henry drove immediately into town, where they circled the town square, which was made up of the church and its dooryard, both encircled by a waist-high stone wall. They waved and hollered to everyone on the street, who waved and hollered back as they went around and around. This is what everyone did when they finally got their car, a tradition that lasted for years after. Dizzy from the motion, Emeline had to ask Henry to pull over before she got sick and received a chorus of "aaawwws" from the back.

Henry put his arm around the passenger seat and looked back at them. "That's enough from the peanut gallery. Let's drive to the general store and get ice cream."

The store was exactly twenty-five feet from where he had stopped. Emeline, looking wan, stepped out heavily. With her hand on her swollen belly, she asked, "Anyone to walk with me?"

"No way," "Are you kidding," "What a wet blanket," and "Killjoy!" were the replies from the back seat.

Henry drove along slowly next to her, catcalling her to get back in, knowing she wouldn't. "Hubba-hubba! Look at the stilts on that tomato! Come on, be the Sheba to my sheik."

Emeline blushed and laughed and called back, "I will not get in that car for a million simoleons!" With her accent, the last word came out "seemoleens", which had the kids breaking up until they reached the store.

THE LAST WEEK OF SUMMER, Clemens and Truman had looked back on all the adventures they had had. One was playing ball at the elementary school- Clemens hit a foul tip that went so far behind him, it plunked into the Winooski River. Though they were lucky enough to be downstream from the waterfall, the ball, the only ball they had that day, was getting bounced along something quick. Truman, instead of running in a direct line to it like the other kids, took off downstream and waded into the river. Just before he got to the rapids, the ball floated neatly into his grip.

Clemens and Truman had also climbed the tallest tree in Hopefield, Piney Pete. They tied a rope around their waists so that they were attached to each other. If one fell, the other could hold on until the other recovered his footing. And if they went down together, sobeit. They made it up and over the top limb, one at a time, marveling over the view of Spruce Mountain in one direction and the church steeples of Barre in the other. They had a campout with Scotty, Giancarlo, and a few others at their house. Earlier that week, Henry helped them clear out a space in between the barn and the field for a bonfire, far enough away from each that neither would catch. In an anticipation of the bonfire, the boys had hunted hard for rocks that were small enough to carry, but big enough to make a solid fire ring until Henry was satisfied it was tall enough. Just to be sure the wind didn't carry an unnoticed spark, Henry stayed out there while they roasted hot dogs and marshmallows. He stayed until the fire got low, playing the few songs he knew on his out-of-tune fiddle and telling the numerous campfire stories he remembered from his youth. Though he couldn't play current songs, the boys seemed to enjoy the moldy oldies, as they called them. At that point, the boys couldn't believe it was near the start of school already. After the fire was out and the other boys were asleep, Clemens and Truman talked about how to scratch that final-adventure itch.

TWO NIGHTS LATER, just after midnight. Clemens jiggled the car keys in the tray on the table next to the door. "Shhh. You're gonna wake everyone," whispered Truman. "Do you have the tobacco?"

"Yes, now you shut up." Clemens tightened his grip around the keys and clutched them into silence. They crept to the kitchen and Truman opened the kitchen door, just as they had discussed, as it was the farthest from any of the bedrooms. They had practiced opening it slow enough that it wouldn't creak earlier that day until they got it right. Truman was better at it. They stole around the kitchen-side of the house under a half moon and light August breeze. They stopped at the large maple in the dooryard and paused, listening for sounds above the rustling of the summer leaves.

The brothers hunkered down low like the soldiers from the movie palace as they made their way to the front of the house. They approached the car according to their respective sides — Clemens was driving. They gently gripped the handles to pull the doors open and closed them softly. They tensed and waited. If they saw a light go on, they could slither out and pretend they were just goofing around outside. If worse came to worst, they could even stay in the car and just say they were pretending and hope no one noticed the keys missing until Clemens got them back in the tray.

Truman stared hard at the house, not daring to blink.

"Well?" asked Clemens, who was fiddling with keys to get them into the ignition.

"The coast is clear."

Clemens popped the stick into neutral like Henry had shown them during the lesson about getting the stick into the middle of the shifting box to orient before moving into the next gear. And how the car could roll after you turn the engine off unless you leave it parked in first gear.

"We're not moving," said Truman.

"I can see that." Clemens craned his body looking around for the answer.

Truman saw it first. "The emergency brake, nimrod."

"Oh, right!" Clemens pressed in the button at the top of the brake stick and pushed it down, keeping pressure on the button.

Still nothing. "Okay, Tru — open the door, get your feet down and push."

Truman did as instructed, leaning into the seat and pushing hard, given the flatness of the driveway. Grunting with effort, the car started to roll on its own after the slight incline at the curve of the tree-lined driveway.

"Oh, Jeezum. Oh God. Oh Jeezum," said Truman. He began to run alongside the car.

Clemens had a white-knuckle grip on the wheel and his breathing was ragged.

He pumped the brakes near the end of the driveway, and they stopped,

Truman ramming into the door. The house was well out of sight.

"Well, here goes the neighborhood." Clemens put his hand on the key in the ignition and paused, going through the steps in his mind.

Truman got impatient. "You gotta put your foot on the clutch, Clem."

"Hush up! I'm thinking." Clemens stretched his legs long and had to point his shoes to reach the pedals. He put one set of toes hard on the clutch, the other set lightly on the gas and turned the key in the ignition and the car started. "Shit — we didn't get any lessons about the lights."

Truman leaned over and peered at the dash on Clemens' side. "Look, that button, on your left."

Clemens pushed it and the forest lit up in front of them.

"Let's go!" Clemens released the gas instead of the clutch and the car stalled and jerked forward. "Shit!"

Truman put a hand on his arm. "Go slow — you did it the last five times we drove with Pa."

Clemens took a breath and glanced behind him through the dark trees. No lights from the house as far as he could tell.

Clemens tried again and the engine fired up. He simultaneously popped the clutch and stepped on the gas and the car jerked forward. He didn't dare change gears for fear of the loud grinding noise should he not shift correctly. They crawled along slowly and when they made it to the end of the unnamed road that led to their house, Clemens stopped and stalled, forgetting to put his foot on the clutch. "Jeezum H. Crow!"

"You want me to drive?"

"No! I got it. Just give me a minute."

Clemens went through the steps one more time, fired up the Tin Lizzie with more confidence and they made their way down the road.

After passing Number Ten, the Boisvert's, the Anderson's and the Tatro's, they reached Route 2, the only paved road in Washington County outside of Barre and Montpelier.

They sat with the engine idling, Clemens having remembered to keep his foot on the clutch.

"What now?" asked Truman.

Route 2 was pitch black and empty. "Maple Hill?" suggested Clemens.

"Nah, we'd have to go through town. I know! Bald Hill. We can go up and have a smoke."

"Jake idea."

They turned left onto Founder's Mountain Road and started the wraparound upwards drive around the base of the mountain. The boys arrived at the back entrance of Bald Hill a few minutes later. They still couldn't believe how much quicker it was to get anywhere. This would have taken them from sunup to sundown walking. Clemens pulled over to the side of the road where there was a turnout created after the last few years of increasing amounts of teenagers in cars parking there to head up the hill for some drinking or romance, or both. It was around one-thirty and at this point all the lovers and revelers had gone home.

Clemens put the keys in his pocket and felt in the

other for the tobacco pouch he filched from their Uncle Reggie who visited the prior week from Maine, on his way to a vacuum cleaner sales conference in Plattsburg, New York. His mother was dying to get one and he just so happened to have one in the backseat of his car. He couldn't give it to her free, but as his brother's wife, she got it for no more than he would have paid himself. She made sure to send him off with a basket full of sandwiches, muffins, and cheese for the rest of his trip.

Uncle Reggie patted himself up and down just before leaving with a basketful of sandwiches prepared by Emeline but couldn't find the pouch. "No matter," he had said. "I need to stop in town anyway and spread my business cards around. Hope you like the vacuum, Emmy! Gonna change your life!"

Clemens and Truman crossed a small field and then began the walk up the trail through the pine forest. They didn't think to bring a flashlight, but they had been up there enough times to walk it blindfolded. They crested the top after some time, and having walked past the tree line, stood on top of the hill, which was a large, steep field that rounded down and the bottom could not be seen. The view opened across the county overlooking Adamant. In the half moonlight, they could make out the shapes and outlines of familiar buildings and landmarks. They stood for a moment, feeling tall and important in the high, open space.

They walked around a bit and settled onto some rocks and Clemens handed the pouch to Truman. "I drove, you roll."

Truman was happy to oblige and commenced rolling. His technique had improved, and they sat back on the rocks, content, smoking and praising themselves for their accomplishment. Knowing their mother would be up before dawn, they put out their smokes and emptied their butts back into the pouch. They walk-ran back down the trail through the trees and climbed into the car. They passed one car in the darkness on Route 2, and there was a multipoint buck far off in the headlights once they got back on their nameless road, but otherwise they encountered no other living creature.

Clemens turned the lights off before heading up the drive, making sure he drove up the incline to where it flattened out at the bend before he cut the engine. Both he and Truman hopped out, pushing with all their might on the frame and opened doors, Clemens keeping one hand on the wheel. They rolled silently to the front of the house and Clemens hopped back in and parked the car, making sure to shift it into first gear and pull the emergency brake. "Oh, shit!" Clemens whispered.

"What?" Truman whispered back.

"The car! It's facing the wrong way! Papa always does a U-turn around the tree to make sure it's facing the road."

"Well, put it back in neutral and let's push it in a circle. You've got more room on your side, so I'll push harder — and keep that wheel cocked tight."

They didn't predict that the car would have such a large turn radius and the grill almost touched the house when Clemens whisper-yelled, "Stop! Back it up."

Breathing hard and sweating, both boys turned around and with the doors hitting them on their rears, they angled forward and pushed on the door jams, Clemens turning the wheel to line it up in the original position.

Before their last push forward, Truman pointed at the house. "Look!" A light was on in the back of the house, from the kitchen. They both knew it would be their mother.

Clemens wiped his brow. "Hurry!"

Car in position, Clemens yelled, "Get in!"

Truman thought he was crazy, but scrambled in. "Why are we in the car?"

"We're going to let *Maman* find us out here. We'll tell her we were goofing around, you know, pretending we were having a car chase and fell asleep."

"Shhh — I heard a door!"

Both boys, staying low, crawled around to the back — Truman lay on the floor and Clemens on the seat and closed their eyes. Less than a minute later, in the pale light of pre-dawn, the back door opened. "What is going on here, *mes chous*? Did you forget where to sleep?"

Clemens, the better actor, took the lead. He fluttered his eyes open. "Oh, goodness. Tru and I couldn't sleep, so we came out here to just play around." Truman rolled over and moaned.

Emeline put a hand over her small smile. "You two are *mes petits diables*. You do not tell your father!"

Truman pretended to sleepily push himself up as Clemens scooted out the open door. Emeline hugged him, then Truman, and sent them back inside.

They did not turn around to see her touch the warm engine or notice her head turn at the sound of Clemens replacing the keys on the table by the door. When school started up a few days later, they bragged to everyone about their joyride and how they got away with it.

~

ONE YEAR LATER, Clemens was legally old enough to officially drive with supervision. Truman would ride along with every lesson and Henry lectured them on how drastically dirt road conditions changed depending on the season. He showed them how to ride high on frozen ruts, downshift on washboard turns, and position planks of wood under their wheels should they slide on mud or snow and get stuck. He had Clemens drive them around miles of unpaved roads, pointing out which ones turned to mud stew come spring and which should be avoided entirely.

Clemens passed his driver's test, but Henry wouldn't let him take the car until he could change both a flat and the oil, which both he and Truman learned with ease.

Henry let the boys go on jaunts to the village on weekends for ice cream and to meet up with friends. That whole year, the boys came home with only one dent on the car and that was because Harold Ibey, whose family owned the general store, backed up into him in the town square.

His senior year, Clemens started asking if he and Truman, who had been practicing and would be legal to drive soon himself, could take the car to the movie palace on Saturday nights. By the time *Welcome Danger*, the first talkie to play in Montpelier, came out the summer after Clemens graduated, he had started meeting Ginny Swaggert in town after school. He wanted to take her to see it and he wanted Truman to double date with him.

Truman hadn't really had much luck with girls, but it was only a couple of days until the end of school, so Clemens cornered his brother during lunch. "Come on, Tru — imagine sitting with them in the dark. It's a talkie, dontcha know. Plus, it's got funny parts for us and lovey parts for them." He lowered his voice. "Think what that could lead to... Plus, Rebecca's the bee's knees, you know that."

Truman shuffled his feet. Having a crush on someone was new to Truman. For the first time, there was quickening of breath and squeamish anxiety when he was around Rebecca. He discovered he really liked the way she looked at him when he was talking, like she really cared what you were saying.

"I know, but what if she says no?"

Clemens angled his knees and spread his arms wide for dramatic effect. "No? *No*? Who could say no to those baby blues of yours? You know, I've always been envious of them."

Truman laughed. "You are one snake oil salesman. Don't you think you could just get Ginny to ask her to come and then, you know, I'd just be there."

Clemens shook his head. "You can't ride my coattails forever, Tru."

"Coattails? What in the Sam Hill are you talking about? Ginny's your first girlfriend!" But Truman knew what he meant — the things they had done, the trouble they had caused — it was almost always Clemens' idea.

Clemens laughed. "Still. You should just do it. School's going to be out soon and then where will you be? Calling up nosy Mrs. Osbourne on the party wire to connect you to the Sutter's house? She is Rebecca's aunt, you know, then everybody will know. Look — she's right over there, next to the water fountain. Come ooon, ankle on over there and ask her."

Truman looked at Rebecca and then at his brother. He smiled. "Twenty-three skidoo!" and he headed for the fountain.

Clemens couldn't hear but could tell by the look on her face that she said yes, just as he'd known she would because he had already asked Ginny to ask her to see what she'd say.

That double date was the first of many over the summer. Truman, finally sixteen, got his first fumbling kiss halfway into August in the back seat of their Model T. Clemens would remember it later as the last, best summer both he and Truman would ever have.

5

____

1983: A FOSSILIZED CHICKEN FOOT,
A POTLUCK, AND AN ENCOUNTER

The school counselor called mid-semester. Candice had just grabbed her purse on the way out the door to her lunch shift at the college cafeteria, but when she learned who it was, she sat her bulk heavily into a kitchen chair and turned toward the window, cord stretched behind her from the wall.

"Hello. How are you Ms. Tribault?" Candice replied.

"Well, I am fine, thank you, Mrs. Bates. It's Patrick I'm worried about. He has been missing some classes."

Candice stared out the window. It was still strange after all these years to be called "Mrs. Bates", which of course, was what her mother had been called. Funny how she married a man with the same last name as hers. Oh, the teasing they went through. Before that, she was teased about Truman, especially after the fire in the village. And Clemens. She was so little, but she remembers clawing at the fair skin of her kindergarten classmate. She could still feel the helplessness and rage caused by the taunts about her older brothers: the monster and the freak. She shook her head. Which was which? She couldn't remember anymore. God, she'll never forget the look of burned skin. She was so young then, she didn't understand. Just knew that everyone called her brother crazy and that the fire was his fault.

She refocused. "Is that so? He's been going every morning. He's driving himself now but had been coming in with Dante, too. Do you know him?" Bill insisted Pat drive to school again. He thought independence and responsibility would boost his confidence, his self-esteem. Now look what happened.

"I know the group of boys Patrick pals around with. I've had the other two, Lyle and Jeremy in my office, but I've never spoken to Dante. Anyway, Patrick is always reported present for the first few periods. It's after lunch, well..."

"I see. I didn't know that. He... well, I am at work when the kids get home. I really don't know when he gets home."

"How has his attitude been? He just doesn't seem, well, himself. I don't know him well, but as you know it's a small school and I... he looks different, is all. I am not trying to alarm you in any way. This is just a check in."

Candice nodded, then remembered she was on the phone. "Well, I... did you know the boys were in an accident last summer? It's been, well, a bit different for Pat since then. I figured it would pass, you know. But school. I didn't know."

"Well, students skip out on school for many reasons. I just wanted to let you know. I am scheduling an appointment for Patrick to come see me Friday morning."

"Should I be there?"

"No, not for this one. I want to talk to him one-on-one.

Try to build some trust. We'll have our own appointment soon after."

Candice's stomach tensed. "I see. We'll talk to him."

"Sounds good. And, Mrs. Bates, just to be clear, this isn't about Patrick being in trouble. I just... we, the school, just want him to be successful."

Candice didn't know what to say to that. She just wanted her Patty to graduate and then get a job, like everyone else. "Thanks for the call. Please keep me posted on his attendance."

"Okay, will do. Take care."

ONE DAY near the end of their third-grade year, Pat stayed after school with Dante instead of taking the bus home, which they had been planning because Pat wanted to show Dante something, but he wouldn't say too much about it. It was an easy arrangement because Dante lived in town and Pat's mom worked at Greyson, which was at the edge of town. She would pick him up at five-thirty. After the bell, Pat led them through the end-of-the-day bustle of backpacks and lines for the buses.

Instead of turning up the hill going to Dante's house, Pat led them to the middle of town.

They walked along the low, stone church wall that outlined the town square, passing the Zuckermans' Apothecary, which was across the street. The churning of the waterfall was clearly heard in the late spring afternoon. Dante saw a man wearing a dark gray hat and tan sweater perched comfortably along the other side of the church wall, across from the general store. He recognized him as the man he had seen on the wall almost every day since he'd moved to Hopefield a few weeks before. Dante smelled cigarette smoke as they rounded the corner.

Pat hopped up right next to the man, grandpa-old, with a yellow-stained beard and white hair sticking out from under a small, floppy hat. He was smoking and muttering to himself.

Pat cocked his chin at the man. "Uncle Tru, this is my new best friend, Dante."

Dante smiled at that. He looked at Pat and Truman together and a crazy comic book cover appeared in his mind with them on the front. He looked at Truman's cigarette and names flashed in his mind — Big Flame and Little Buck. Big Flame would stun bad guys with a puff of knock-out smoke. Little Buck would transform into a deer, but have Pat's face like in Dante's dream. He'd stand strong with his antlers aimed, bullets shooting out from the tips.

Truman Bates seemed to look past Dante rather than at him. Dante turned around to see what he was looking at. When he turned back around, Truman had his hand out. With jittery eyes still looking over Dante's shoulder, he said, "Nice to meet you, young fella." Dante took his gnarled, stained hand and shook it. After Pat, this was only the second person's hand he ever shook like that. He liked how people around here treated you like a grown up.

"Uncle Tru has a museum, dontcha Uncle Tru."

"Ayuh. You like fossils?"

"I saw a bunch at the Museum of Natural History. Have you been there?"

Truman's eyes squinted against the smoke under his bushy eyebrows as he took another drag. "Wherezat, now?"

Dante never met anybody who didn't know that

museum. "New York City. It's where I moved from, well, Brooklyn, anyway."

Truman nodded. "New York, pig pork."

Dante blinked.

Pat laughed. "Isn't it funny? He likes to rhyme stuff."

Truman's words were punctuated with smoke. "Patrick, wanna bring your friend here to the ComeSee?"

Pat nodded vigorously. "Yeahyeahyeahyeahyeah."

"Walkin' or ridin'?"

"Well, I ain't got my bike here, so we'll walk."

"Meetcha there."

Truman slid off the wall, the bottoms of his slacks hitching up to reveal his pale legs beneath. Dante noticed his socks didn't match. Truman took a moment to open a pouch he took from his cardigan pocket, open it, placed the butt of his smoke into it, then placed it back in his pocket. He ambled across the street.

"Come on." Pat hopped off the wall.

"Where's he going?" asked Dante.

"He's getting his car. The ComeSee ain't far, but he's old, so he doesn't walk there anymore."

"Why aren't we going with him?"

"My folks won't let me ride in the car if he's driving. Something about the pills he takes, but he drives wherever he wants, so I don't get it."

The boys crossed the street, running past Truman on the sidewalk through town as Pat shouted, "See you there, Uncle Tru!" They zoomed past the businesses that were housed in the long brick building along the river; Ibey's General Store, Maple Time Café, Suds 'n' Such Laundromat. Then the sidewalk ended just before a gravel parking lot. At that point, the road turned to dirt and started uphill. Just behind the gravel lot, Pat pointed to a two-story, L-shaped building with wraparound porches. The river that hugged the town rushed just behind it.

"That's where Uncle Tru lives. He's in the one on the first floor all the way on the end, on the right. See? My pop told me that this used to be a house of ill repuke, but it seems okay now." Pat stopped. "Listen. You can see and hear the river. It's really loud from his back windows, almost as loud as the waterfall."

After they were a little ways up the hill, Truman's powder blue Volkswagen Rabbit with rust spots passed them, spraying up some bits of gravel that pinged their legs. A few minutes later they arrived at a spare wooden fence on their side and a graveyard across the road on the other. The car was parked on their side next to the fence.

"Here we are!"

Dante looked around. "No building?"

Pat laughed. "Nope. What for?"

The boys entered through the opening. Truman was walking the aisles he had created out of barrels and crates, both wooden and plastic. The boulder-sized rocks were simply piled atop one another on the ground. In the middle of the exhibits stood a large stump, a bit taller than the boys.

"Wow," exclaimed Dante once he entered the labyrinth. He was genuinely impressed. "So many rocks. How long did it take you to collect them?"

Pat shook his head. "They're not rocks."

Truman turned around from the barrel he was sorting through. "S'right."

"If they're not rocks, what are they?"

"Fossils, a'course," replied Pat.

Truman came over with a specimen in his hand. "See

this brown one here? See the black stripe?" He handed it to Dante, who turned it around to see it from all angles.

"Yeah?"

"Chipmunk ear. From sixty thousand years ago."

Dante giggled. "Nuh-uh."

Pat grinned. "Yuh-huh!" Pat ran to a milk crate perched on a large rock. "Looky-here. These rust-colored ones? See how they're rounded and flat?"

"Okay..."

Pat whispered, "Fingernails." Then in a louder voice, "Isn't that right, Tru?"

Truman came over and picked one up. "Ayuh. We're all this color once. We changed when the solar flare came forty-three thousand years ago. Altered our genes."

Dante's jaw dropped. "Are you for real?"

Dante pointed to a wooden crate. "Alright, these speckled ones. What are those?"

Pat said, "Take a guess."

"Oh, okay, okay, ... fossiliiiiized..." Dante tried hard to see something other than the gravel in his driveway. "I got it! Bird eggs! From a species of mini birds that, um... the humans ate as crunchy snacks, like popcorn."

"Nice try! But, wrong. Trout scales. Thought that one was a no-brainer."

Pat brought Dante over to a rock-filled kitchen sink on top of a leaning barrel. "And these ones here, the small tan pebbles? Fossilized chicken feed."

"Huh?"

"Come on Tru, tell him the story."

"Alright, but you gotta get up on the leg."

"Leg? Where?" Dante swiveled his head around looking for it.

"Right here, a'course." Truman picked up Pat under

his armpits and swung him onto a tall stump. Truman looked at Dante. "You comin'?"

"Sure!" Dante tried to scramble up, but couldn't find a place for his feet, so Truman hefted him up by his pits, too. Dante almost gagged on Truman's smoker breath. When they were placed like double riders on a horse, Truman told them to look down.

"See that?"

All Dante could see were knotty, rough roots, four of them, splaying out from the bottom of the stump.

Dante didn't want to be embarrassed. "Of course!"

Truman smiled, revealing yellowed dentures. "Chickens used to be as big as bears. And they could fly."

"Really?"

Pat turned his head toward Dante. "And humans used to ride 'em and other dinosaurs, too! What you're on here's a fossilized chicken foot and those are its talons." Pat pretended he was holding reins and pumped his arms as if he were goading on the gigantic chicken.

Truman stood back, lighting a cigarette. "Okay, boys, time to ride. Heeyah!" Pat started wriggling in his seat and flopping his imaginary reins. Dante caught his excitement and began to whoop. Truman continued to cheer them on, "Higher now, Pat. Keep that chicken flying!" As if commanded, a breeze came up and began to blow into their faces and lift their hair. "H'yah! That's it. Like the wind! Almost to the clouds, boys."

After another minute of soaring between the beating wings of a prehistoric chicken, it was time to come back to earth. Truman took a tin box out from under the shade of a bush and opened it to reveal crackers, small bags of Chips Ahoy cookies that Dante had seen in Ibey's General Store, and wrapped hard candies. The boys helped themselves to the snacks and soon after, with waves of thanks, headed back down the hill.

When the boys arrived at Dante's house, Dante told his father all about their adventure. Ephraim smiled and kept repeating, "No kidding, really?" and when Dante was done spilling everything he had learned, Ephraim finished with, "Well, that really does sound like something to come see."

When Candice came to pick up Pat, she was told all about it, too. She laughed and said, "That's our Truman for you. You know, I didn't really grow up with him, we were born so far apart and plus, well..." She trailed off. "Let's just say he is a bit of a mystery to everyone, including me!"

It wasn't long before Dante had his own, unexpected encounter with Truman that left him wondering what was going on with Pat's uncle. This was the same night as the Zuckerman's first potluck and there was only one family that came that night, the Mosses, so that meant the other vegetarian kids from his class, Noah and Eliza, came, too. With them came Shannon, also in his class, who was having a sleepover with Eliza. He had never met anyone before who had two different colored eyes like Shannon did — one blue and one green. At dinner, Dante could tell that she was not a vegetarian by the way she kept asking Eliza what everything was and ended up just putting on her plate whatever Eliza did.

After dinner, the kids, Dante, Noah, Eliza and Shannon, asked to play outside. Being early summer, it was going to be light outside for at least another hour.

Ephraim waved them off with, "Sure, knock yourself out!" as Darlene poured more wine. The kids tumbled out the kitchen door and ran around to the back of the house, where Ephraim had put up a tire swing. The air was soft and warm under the green, sun-speckled leaves and Dante immediately started swatting at the tiny black flies that swirled around him. The other kids didn't seem bothered by them.

Dante thought Shannon and Eliza were really nice. Noah, on the other hand, kept whining about others taking too long on their turn on the tire swing, but then wouldn't get off when his was over.

Shannon peered into the trees. "Is that a path?"

Dante nodded. "Yeah — just goes down into the woods and then just kinda stops."

Shannon said, "You wanna see a really cool path? That you can ride bikes on?"

Noah said, "Aw, we don't have our bikes here. Not worth going all the way there."

Eliza got off the swing and Noah hopped on out of turn, again. "Come on, it's not far. It's just on the other side of the church yard."

A bug zipped loudly into his ear. Dante brought his hand up hard to his ear, which created a ringing in his ears that lasted for almost a minute.

"So, who wants to go?" asked Shannon.

Eliza and Dante raised their hands. "Me!"

Noah spoke up. "It's a railroad bed, which is why it's so big, and I been there lots of times."

Shannon said, "Come on, let's go!"

Noah pushed his glasses up his nose. "Nah, I can go there anytime. I wanna keep using the swing. If you swing fast enough, the flies can't land on you."

"Noah, tell the grownups where we are if they ask," said Eliza.

Noah shouted out to them as they were leaving, "Shannon has a crush on you!"

Shannon was behind Dante, so she couldn't see how red his face turned, nor could he see hers. Eliza, last in the line, turned her head and shouted, "You weren't supposed to say anything!"

The three adventurers walked down the street, around the church yard. Dante looked over at The Apothecary before turning the last corner around the wall to Main Street and he could see someone standing on the porch directly in front of their cigar store Indian, which, to hear Darlene tell it, Ephraim stole from Greyson College. To hear Ephraim tell it, he liberated it from a trash heap of political correctness.

THEY ALL HEARD the story that night at dinner before the kids disappeared outside. Darlene recognized the dual playfulness of his father's mouth and tilt of head whenever he told a story like this — where he was the Hero. The Instigator. The Rebel.

"I couldn't believe it. I mean this statue, legend has it, used to sit on the porch of a tobacconist shop. There was a fire, here, right? About fifty years ago? Burned half the street down?"

The Mosses shrugged. They had only lived in Hopefield for a few years.

"Anyway, no one knows how it ended up at the college, but for years it lived on top of the roof of the college library, right at the entrance, and when things got boring, we'd scramble up there and slap another sticker on it."

Darlene said, "I've always had mixed feelings about it. I mean, it's exploitation, right? But it's a relic, too." She shook her head.

Peter Moss laughed. "Well, I hear ya, but I just love the stickers all over it. 'Make Love, Not War.' Classic."

Ephraim plopped another spoonful of Andrea Moss's baba ghanoush on his plate. "Anymore pita?"

Darlene passed him the last piece.

As he worked the spread onto his pita, Ephraim went on, "Well, some..." He mouthed the word "assholes... Got on the Board of Directors and pushed hard to get Greyson away from its so-called hippie reputation into a more respectable direction and took the statue down. But I guess no one could quite throw it out, either. I mean, Darlene and I were walking through the campus soon after we moved back, reliving it all, wham! There it was behind the Smoker, which of course was one of our favorite places to ah..." He glanced at the kids. "You know, hang out between classes." So, we liberated it into the back of the Subaru that same night!"

Darlene laughed. "And now I get to experience mixed feelings about it multiple times a day whenever I walk by it. What an opportunity to practice patience!"

～

Eliza squinted down the street, too. "Is that Pat's uncle? The weird one on the wall all day?"

Dante could feel his face turning red, this time from anger. "He's not weird. He's... I don't know. He's nice."

Shannon moved a step closer to Dante. Dante was

wondering why she was looking at him like that, all soft. He looked at her eyes for a beat too long. She had one green eye and one brown. They were beautiful. She put her hand on his arm. "Yeah, he's nice. He always says hi back when I say hi first."

Eliza sniffed. "He talks to himself."

The trio continued, Dante glancing back every so often to see if Truman was still there. He continued to stand face-to-face with the statue.

The railroad bed path started soon after the Rose Garden Apartments, where Truman lived, the entrance hidden by overgrowth. The project was abandoned decades ago, and no train tracks were ever laid. There was a chain-locked, triangle-shaped gate one hundred feet just beyond the tangle of bushes. Dante tripped on a rock and pinwheeled into some bushes. "Dante, look out!"

It was too late. He stood up and looked around. "What?"

Shannon and Eliza looked at each other. "Uh, poison ivy, hello?" said Eliza.

Shannon pointed to the shiny leaves at Dante's feet. "At least you're wearing jeans," she said, "but I bet it'll be all over your arms."

Eliza said in a singsong voice, "You'll be scratching like crazy before bedtiiiime..." She giggled. "Now your arms will be as red as your face, *Strawberry*."

Shannon folded her arms. "Eliza, that's not nice."

"What? His best friends call him that."

Dante felt his face flush and wondered when he would ever be able to stop it from doing that. "It's okay, Shannon. Maybe I deserve it." Dante wondered how a girl could have a crush on him. But the more he talked with Shannon, the more he liked her, too.

The gate seemed to have been built to keep out cars, but they easily walked around it. Shannon was right, it was a big, dirt path. It was very wide, so they walked side-by-side. The wind rustled the trees — the sun had gone down a little bit and the path was partially in shadow.

They walked under the sun's orange glow peeking through the canopy overhead, chatting about school, debating about who they'd like to have for a teacher in fourth grade. They all hoped for Mr. Lytton, the only male teacher in the whole school, because he was so funny.

Pat had been bugging Dante about hunting, trying to convince him that it was a cool thing to do. Dante thought he'd ask Shannon about it. He already knew what Eliza would say.

"Shannon, you eat meat, right?"

Shannon laughed. "Yep. My family would about die if I came home and said I wouldn't eat it anymore."

"Meat's gross," said Eliza.

Dante ignored her. "What about hunting?"

"Hunting's even grosser."

Dante rolled his eyes at Eliza. "I'm asking *Shannon*." He silently agreed, but part of him thought it *was* cool, like the guys in movies with guns sometimes were. The thought of hunting with Pat made him flutter with excitement and his stomach hurt at the same time.

Shannon said, "My dad hunts. Venison is wicked good."

"That's what Pat says," said Dante.

"You don't want to try meat?"

Eliza shook her head. "Nope."

Dante shrugged. "Maybe. When I was at Pat's house, it was so funny. His mom had no idea what I would eat — they were having some kind of casserole that had everything all mixed together and it had chicken in it." Dante started to laugh. "And then she said, 'Oh, chicken counts?'"

He and Eliza cracked up. Shannon laughed along, too. "Why are you guys vegetarian anyway? Are your parents health nuts, or something?"

Dante said, "Well, that, plus raising beef is bad for the planet 'cause you gotta cut down so many trees for grazing." He continued reciting what his parents tell anyone who asks. "And chickens are kept in crowded pens and start pecking each other from the stress."

Eliza chimed in, "Baby cows are kept in cages and never allowed to run and that's how veal is made. Geese are shoved in boxes and force-fed to make them fat."

"Stop!" They hadn't seen that Shannon had started to cry.

Dante and Eliza both put their hands on her arms. "Hey, Shannon, don't cry," said Dante.

"Yeah, I'm sorry," said Eliza. "We didn't mean to scare you."

They paused, looking up at the now dusky sky. Dante ran his hand through his thick curls that he obviously got from his father. "Time to turn around?"

They turned around and stopped dead in their tracks. Coming up the now fully shadowed path was the figure of a man. He was wearing a hat, a sweater, and he appeared to be smoking. Dante could see the red glow as he inhaled. Fireflies began to appear, swirling and signaling.

Eliza inhaled sharply. She whispered, "It's Pat's uncle. He's coming toward us!" Her voice went up in pitch to a whisper-whine and she began to shake her hands at her sides, as if she were trying to dry them quickly. "He's so creepy."

"No, he's not, watch." Dante waved to Truman who was getting very close. Truman was holding a flashlight and he clicked it on. Dante dropped his arm.

Eliza started to whimper. Shannon whispered, "Don't be such a baby."

Eliza bolted into the woods. They could hear her panicked sobs as she crashed through the thick underbrush.

Truman was almost to Dante and Shannon. They could hear him talking. "No, sir, no flames here, sir. Nobody's gonna flame me. No more Vienna sausage. Mr. Indian told me to come. He protects the flame."

Shannon had a tight grip on Dante's arm. Truman stopped and loomed over them, flashlight in their faces, blinding them. He said, "You been to the cabin, aintcha."

Dante shook his head. "N-n-n-o. I, we, haven't seen any cabin. We're going home."

He raised his voice. "Well, don't go there! It ain't safe. I'm gonna clean it, see. Scrub it. Don't never go there! Brunella-Newtella, rest her in peace." He went silent as his eyes fixed to a point over their heads. He lowered his flashlight.

Through the spots dancing in front of his eyes, Dante looked at Truman's hands and didn't see any cleaning supplies, just a crumpled paper bag like the ones they used at The Apothecary. Truman continued on, leaving them alone, light-blind in the near darkness. Eliza came crashing back. "Oh, noooo, I think I got poison ivy!"

~

WHEN ELIZA, Shannon, and Dante spoke of their encounter with Truman, Ephraim didn't seem to think much of it, nor did the other adults. The Zuckermans heard Shannon announce to Eliza's parents on their way out the door, "I'm going to be a vegetarian."

Ephraim and Darlene looked at Dante, "A convert! Well done!"

Dante was thinking so much about Shannon that he forgot about his run in with poison ivy until right before bed and when it started to itch. Dante's arms soon became so inflamed and painful that he started to cry. Darlene covered his arms in apple cider vinegar compresses and stayed with him until he went to sleep, secretly happy that this had happened. This was why they came — poison ivy instead of poison fumes, walking in the woods instead of dodging taxis, getting spooked by a strange man who was no stranger after all. She couldn't put her finger on it exactly — it's not that living in the country would make every problem disappear, it was that the problems here were more innocent. At least for now.

Dante couldn't wait to see Shannon again but had to wait until the start of fourth grade. She didn't seem to have a crush on him anymore, but Dante figured it was just a matter of time. She was so nice, even though she didn't stay vegetarian for long. Still, she always made a point to say hi to him, all the way through elementary school, and for a long time after that. He wanted to ask her out but kept putting it off. What if she said no? What if he blushed so much around her that it became permanent?

AT THE NEXT sleepover at Pat's after the potluck, Dante was telling Pat about his encounter with Truman.

"Whaddya mean there's a cabin? In the woods, by the Rose Garden?" Pat crossed his arms. "Then how come I don't know nothing about it?"

Dante shrugged. "I don't know, he's your uncle."

"And what, crazy to boot? That's what that Eliza and them say. Go ahead, if that's what you think. He's the smartest man I know, what with all his knowledge of fossils and such."

"Think your mom would know?"

Pat leaped off his bed. "Mom. Mom! Mom!"

Candice came out of the kitchen, wiping her hands on a dishtowel. "What, Patty. My goodness!"

"Do you know anything about a cabin in the woods, you know, off the railroad bed, by Uncle's Tru's?"

"What, by the Rose Garden Apartments? Well, if it's the same one you're talking about, I know a little something. What's all the fuss about it?"

Dante appeared at Pat's side. Candice smiled and said, "Come on, let's get some chocolate milk."

Candice mixed up the milk and handed the glasses to the boys while editing the information in her mind to make it rated G. "Well, I was still very little during the Depression."

Pat took a sip and left a cocoa-colored strip on his upper lip. "'Pression was when there wasn't no money. Even the government ran out." Dante waited for Pat's grammar to be corrected. When it wasn't, Dante thought Pat's mom was the coolest mom in the world.

Candice nodded. "That's right. Luckily, our family has always been in the quarry business, which can last through any situation. After all, everyone needs construction and grave... oh."

Dante's eyes got wide. "Gravestones? Wow! Your family made gravestones?"

Candice nodded. "Well, families like the Spinellis made them – Rock of Ages just procured, and still does, the raw rock. But we didn't own the quarry, you see, so my brothers got cut from their jobs, even my father, who was a supervisor, got his hours cut." Candice stopped and looked out the window, hugging herself. "It was not a nice time. That's also when Truman, um, moved away."

Pat rolled his eyes. "Mom, the cabin?"

"Oh, right. I know about this next part from school. During the Depression, the government made a program called the, uh... let's see, C-C-C, what did that stand for?" She put her finger to her lips in thought. "Civilian Conservation something, that's it. Anyway, I remember Clemens — that's Pat's eldest uncle whom Pat never met, joined the program. They got paid to build public works projects. They were building a railroad to join up Montpelier to Augusta. It never did get finished, which is why it's just a railroad bed and not a railroad."

Dante finished his milk. He didn't know where Augusta was but didn't say anything.

"And?" Pat raised his hands in impatience. Dante was getting used to Pat's bossiness by now, but he was surprised to see him act like that with his own mother. Dante thought if he were like that to his mom, he'd be on the receiving end of a week-long lecture on respect. Pat's mom, on the other hand, didn't seem bothered.

"And, that's it. They built a cabin as the railroad bed got longer and longer, probably as a place to store things, take breaks and get warm, that kind of thing." Candice left out the rest of it and how Clemens got caught spending a lot of time there, even after he was married, back when the Rose Garden was more than just an apartment building for single moms and Section 8-ers like Truman. She remembered going by it when they went to Barre and how her mother would suddenly start pointing out the window the opposite way so they wouldn't glimpse the lingerie on the line behind the building.

WHEN BILL GOT HOME that night after Ms. Tribault's call, Candice handed him a beer and sat him down at the kitchen table. Candice saw his face tense as she told him the news about Pat's absences. She explained that Pat had an appointment with the counselor on Friday.

"Well, maybe he's not in trouble with the school, but we better find out what he's doing, or there could be more trouble than we could ever want." He picked at the label of his Bud.

Candice blinked. "You think he's with a girl?" She scoffed. "Patty hasn't even been brushing his teeth. I hardly think he's the cock of the walk right now."

Bill ran a hand down his face and took a long drink. "God help me, I wish it was a girl problem. If I go in there right now and see him lying in his bed again in the dark with those goddamn headphones on, I might just lose it."

Candice laid a hand on his arm. "I could call Dante and maybe he —"

Bill landed the bottle on the table harder than he intended. "Dante, as nice as it is for him to come play nursemaid, isn't the answer. We need help. Real help." He tipped his head back and finished his beer.

Candice kept silent about the thoughts that were rolling around in her mind — that she was thinking of

Truman. That the Vermont State Hospital in Waterbury, then called the Vermont State Asylum for the Insane, is where he called home after the...incident. She shook her head. Fire. Hunting. Sleds. Cars. So many accidents for one lifetime, all happening around her. What would the next one be?

Bill gave her a questioning look. "What?"

Candice did her best to give a reassuring smile. "I'll go talk to Patty now."

6

1929–1930: THE WIND AND THE
BIRTHDAY PARTY

The year of The Crash, Henry Bates was told he could keep his supervisor position at the Rock of Ages, but with a cut in hours and pay; the local construction business was holding its breath waiting for the New Deal programs to reach central Vermont — and no one was spending precious dollars on headstones or crying angel statues anymore. Clemens and Truman had now both finished high school — Clemens had been able to grab a few hours at the quarry, and also a few hours farming for Jimmy Kleets. Truman followed suit when he finished school. The boys settled into a dull routine of too little work and too little money. They fished for hours on end, cutting holes in the ice in the winter, played endless card games, horsed around with the little kids, and picked up smoking. Between contributing part of their paychecks to the household and their new tobacco habit, Clemens and Truman didn't have enough money left over for much.

Even so, Clemens had started courting Ginny in

earnest. Clemens had tried for weeks on end to get Truman to continue double dating with Rebecca Sutter, but Truman would have nothing to do with her. It was like one day the light went out. Started claiming to be too bushed to go out, or some such. Truman had begun sleeping more and more, only getting up to go to work the few hours he could get. The family, including Clemens, chalked it up to boredom and lack of enthusiasm, what Emeline called *ennui*. Everyone in the household was dealing with the lack of opportunity and economic hardship however they saw fit. Clemens focused on his courting, Felicity pored over her books, Samuel took up hunting with their father and so had become the new favorite, while Emeline was kept busy with the babies, on top of her baking for barter. When Henry worked a week with few hours, it wouldn't take much for him to blow a fuse over what used to be small infractions, like not shutting the door all the way to the ice box, leaving a dirty plate on the table, or not sweeping in the corners.

THEN THE WIND CAME. It blew in Truman's head. It got so that he couldn't even hear conversations at times. The first time, when he was eighteen, he asked the already tense dinner table if anyone knew about the storm that was coming and everyone stopped mid-bite to stare at him. Truman chalked it up to then newly installed pneumatic drills at the sheds, which were mind-numbingly loud. He told *Maman* they must be making him deaf.

Clemens and Truman used to talk together from their beds at night, but now it was Clemens who talked and

Truman who listened. Since Clemens was the one out still living life, it was natural he had more to say, so he took Truman's silences with a grain of salt. What Truman hadn't told him yet was that listening was getting hard for him. Almost as hard as talking.

Clemens was in the middle of a story about the Harvest Fair in town and how it wasn't as big as previous years, for obvious reasons, but they still had the log rolling competition, and that Clemens had never been so close to winning.

"Maybe if you'd been there, cheering me on, I would have won."

Then Truman asked out of the blue, "Clem, you having trouble with your ears?"

Clem turned on his side to look at him. "My ears? No, don't think so. Why? Is that what's going on with you?"

"I don't know Clem. I just don't know what's wrong."

Clem turned back onto his back. "Tru, when these hard times is over, let's us go on a trip. Like, to the ocean. Wouldn't it be fine to see the ocean?"

Truman shrugged from his prone position. "I guess. Right now, I just want normal, you know? Things to go back to the way they were."

TRUMAN HAD STOPPED GOING to work. Emeline tried to make as many excuses as she could to Henry, who was becoming more outraged every day. He would march over to Truman's bed and holler about laziness and ingratitude, free lunches, and how idleness makes the Devil's work, the last time grabbing his feet and yanking him out of bed, Truman's head bouncing hard on the hardwood floor. Clemens ran in and pulled Henry out of there, dragging him past the other children frozen in place in the parlor.

The next day, after Henry and Clemens drove their car to the quarry, Emeline had Truman hitch up Daisy Chain and he drove them both in the buckboard to Dr. Hendricks in town. He gave him a brief hearing test and said Truman was fine. He asked Truman if he wouldn't mind helping unload some medical supplies that were being delivered and Truman obliged. Dr. Henricks took Emeline aside and quietly suggested that there might be another problem. That he had seen other cases like this, where the men in particular were getting down and out with too much idle time on their hands. He asked if Truman had been sleeping more, isolating from the family. Emeline nodded, guilty that she had noticed, but had hardly done a thing about it.

"But he is still teenager, *non*? Maybe he needs some push."

Dr. Hendricks shrugged. "Everyone reacts differently to extreme times such as these, and melancholia is one unfortunate side effect."

"*Mélancolie, mon dieu.* His father will not understand."

On the ride home, Truman's hands shook as they held onto the reins and he kept on the lookout for hard, mud-caked ruts on the road. He couldn't face his father with a broken wheel or broken horse along with the doctor's diagnosis of "nothing is wrong with him." His mouth opened and then closed wordlessly.

Emeline looked carefully at her son. "*Qu'est-ce que c'est?*"

Truman confessed. "I hear the wind, *Maman*. I hear it something awful. It comes and goes when it wants. Everyone at the quarry speaks to me two and three times, the same sentence. They are the ones who convinced me I am going deaf. I hoped I was."

Truman continued in a voice-cracking whisper, "I think it is something else. I didn't tell the doctor this, but..." Emeline waited as her eyes searched his face and discovered that his terror was real, and it was deep. Truman swung his head to search his mother's eyes. He saw his terror reflected. She touched his arm and he leaned back hard on the reins and stopped Daisy Chain short. Truman and Emeline turned to face each other. "I think it's the Devil. I think he is following me like a cat watches a field mouse. I look over my shoulder twenty times a day if it's a dozen. Someone has a grip on me, and it is *forte*." Tears streamed from Truman's eyes.

Emeline gathered him into her arms as best she could. Truman allowed himself to crumble into her embrace and weep. Emeline cast her gaze up to God and silently asked him if he could be so cruel as to make her suffer through such a thing, all over again. She had loved her aunt deeply, but remembered how the invasion of her spirits, as her own *maman* called them, had pained the family. She had been so frightened by the unpredictable behavior — walking naked through the village, silently weeping for hours, coming into Emeline's room at night, screaming about the people clawing at her legs. How could she watch her son lose his tether to the world, to her, and to convince an increasingly hard-headed and stressed husband to have patience with him. And they needed every paycheck.

When Henry got home that night, Emeline sugar-coated the story as much as possible, but Henry heard "melancholia," grabbed Truman by the collar and pulled him straight out the back door to the chopping block. Henry forced the angled ax up and out of its resting spot in the block and blindly tossed it to the side. Forcing Truman to his knees, Henry bent him in half over the block. Truman felt his father's hands at his waist, fumbling with his belt. Henry stripped the belt from its loops and commenced to lash his son as a master to the slave.

Emeline was at a loss. It all happened so fast. Clemens had been dropped at Ginny's house after work, so it was up to Emeline to defend Truman. She was pushed to the ground as soon as she grabbed her husband's arm. Henry, while never a gentle man, was not *sévère* before The Crash. Her frenzied pleas had no impact. When it was over, Emeline ran to the well and filled a bucket with water. She rushed to the chopping block with a cloth and the bucket. She called to Felicity, who had run back inside with the other horrified children as soon as Henry turned back to the house. Felicity had come out the side door to avoid passing her father.

"Baking soda, *rapidement*." Felicity did as she was told, tears streaking her cheeks. Emeline fell to her knees and lifted Truman's head off the dirt, cradling it in her lap. She unbuttoned his shirt and peeled it away from his skin before the blood could congeal and join the cotton and skin together as one.

Truman spoke a steady stream of torment, "*The Devil, he squeezes. My heart, I can't hold it. The Devil wins for those who sins. The Devil is in the wind.*"

Whether he meant the spirits within or his father, she could not tell. Emeline turned Truman gently onto his side and bathed him in baking soda and water and as she did, murmured sweetly to her son in French and English and told him everything would be like it was before. All they needed to do was to pray, have patience, and forgive; for only then would the Devil let go his tight-fisted grip. Clemens was beyond consolation when he came home to find his brother lying face down on the bed, unable to move without screaming from the pain of the bloody welts on his back. Clemens didn't talk to his father for a week. Eventually Henry declared that while did not believe that melancholia was any sort of medical diagnosis, he agreed to lay off Truman and instead, like all other family members, pray for him every night.

THE FIRST TIME Truman heard an actual voice, one that no one else in the world could hear, was three months after his beating, when he was almost nineteen. It sounded like Calvin Coolidge, who became president when Truman was a boy; he'd never seen images of Coolidge but had heard him the summer he was ten after President Harding had been shot. This was news that prompted a need for social contact, so the family rode into Hopefield on the buckboard and he gathered in among the throng in front of the radio at the general store the day after Coolidge's middle-of-the-night emergency inauguration in 1923.

Inside the store on that sweltering August day, Truman stretched and craned his neck, reading the faces of the grownups so he could make some meaning out of the recent tragedy. Some faces, like Johnny Ducharme's father's frowning face, told of serious matters, of worry, of change. Emma Holt's mom stood with her thick, doughy hand covering her gaping mouth and her eyes were wide. Coolidge was a Vermonter like one of them but unlike himself and everyone he knew, Coolidge was well-educated, a politician who amounted to more than being the boy down the street who would die of stonecutter's TB one day. Hank LePaige's face had a small smile on it and his thumbs were hooked into his belt loops. It took him a bit, but Truman finally figured out it was an expression of pride. Needless to say, the event and the reactions to it left an indelible impression on Truman and it was something he'd remember clear as day for the rest of his life.

CLEMENS HAD BEEN SPENDING LESS and less time at home. His time was taken up courting Ginny and convincing Mr. Swaggert that he could provide for his daughter, not to mention being a devout Christian. It was not lost on him that he was filling his time with activities he and Truman used to make fun of, like socializing at the church potlucks. He tried to joke with Truman about it, but more often than not, was met with a blank stare. With his increased visibility and eagerness to please the Swaggerts, Clemens was asked to volunteer his time doing things like building sets for youth plays, repairing equipment for the schools and the like.

He tried eight ways from Sunday to include Truman — arranging double-dates that Truman never went on, leaving Clemens to think up excuses quickly, not wanting to let on the bad shape his brother was in. He invited him on picnics with their old friends, thinking some laughter might cheer him up. When he could, he tried to get him to go fishing, just the two of them, like they used to, but the hours of sullen retreat and under-his-breath mutterings won out. If Truman wanted to sit in a dark room by himself, so be it. Clemens hoped to God it was just a melancholia of a teenage variety. Maybe best to let him stew in it until he couldn't stand himself no more and he'd snap out of it.

Clemens, did, however, manage to get Truman back at the quarry in an attempt to keep the peace between Truman and their father. Henry talked with his superiors, who agreed that given the family history with the quarry, they'd give Truman another try, though they would have to split the hours Clemens and he worked between them, especially if they had to work the same shifts. Clemens was not happy about the cut in hours, but if this was what it took to get Truman back to his old self, then so be it. Clemens had to wake them up extra early because Truman's lethargy made getting ready an hour-long process.

The first words that only Truman could hear sounded as far away as the end of a child's tin can telephone. *They can see you*, said Coolidge. *They will vote against you.*

Truman was outside in the pit trying to clear a path for the carts to come in and carry newly carved granite blocks from the walls of the quarry to be processed in the sheds. In late winter, was a tradeoff between the cold, dust-filled, ear-splitting shed and the cold, wet, back-breaking quarry. He stopped shoveling slag and dust so he could hear it better. For a moment, Truman only heard the drills in the nearby sheds. He looked around. There was no one. *You could be president.* Truman dropped the handle of his shovel.

He took a few steps back. "Come on, you guys. Cut it out," Truman yelled to the workers scattered around the quarry, hoping they were pulling one over on him. *Listen to them cheer! It's a parade.*

Truman squeezed out a laugh, "What the hell are you guys doing? Are you trying to drive me crazy?" The only replies were puzzled looks. *Listen, Truman, they scream.*

Truman's knees began to shake. His voice wobbled, "You're all a buncha screwballs. Don't you got nothing better to do?" Truman turned heel and ran into the clatter and hiss of the drills in the sheds. No one looked up from their work. Except for his wide eyes, Truman looked no different from the other dirty, sweaty men covered in granite dust. No one could even see his shaking from the vibrations of the machines that sent tremors through the building. The voice stopped, but Truman's terror lingered.

Over the following days, Coolidge got bolder and the only thing that would shut him up was the sound of the deafening drills. Truman didn't dare tell a soul. Instead, he asked his father to get moved into the sheds where he couldn't hear the voice, but Truman wasn't slated to apprentice carving monuments until next year. Those were coveted positions and given Truman's recent poor performance, on that they would not budge. Truman, never before swayed by Sunday sermons, began to pray daily. It was no use; he became besieged by Coolidge and then a woman, Aimee, who would only talk dirty to him.

The world in front of him became too bright and colorful to see clearly. Truman retreated inside himself, and he spoke to no one at work. He could only see the faces in the high quarry walls, towering above him and closing in from the sides. He could hear the rocks protest the slicing, the drilling, the sectioning of their granite bodies and it filled him with nausea and remorse. He began to disappear more often, which everyone took for laziness, everyone saying he was a no good dewdropper.

No man at the quarry dared mention Truman's increasingly bizarre behavior to Henry, who would not discuss his son, even with his wife. But they did ask Clemens, who tried to make light of Truman's odd behavior, saying he's just a teenager, he'd been not feeling well lately and so on. Clemens learned that some workers drew straws to see who would be forced to partner with Truman hauling slag. Truman's hands slowed and lost their grip on the shovel over time. He finally let his shovel drop to the ground with a clang and he stood still. And listened. And he began to speak openly with the people who plagued him from the inside. Much to Henry's humiliation, he had to let Truman go. He had to fire his own son.

Despite Henry's protests about spending money on someone who wouldn't appreciate it, Emeline organized a party for Truman's nineteenth birthday. Clemens invited Ginny and had fleetingly thought of asking Rebecca to join, but knew it was out of the question. Truman had lost interest in her and anything, really, though she kept asking after Truman.

The day before the springtime birthday party, early enough in the season to have spots of muddy snow on the ground, Clemens walked into their bedroom where Truman was laying on his bed in the dark. He tried to convince Truman to take a bath before his party. Truman had been avoiding all sorts of hygiene of late and Clemens could hardly stand to be in the same room with him. "Tru-what is going on with you? I mean, you're protesting a bath like a little kid. Don't you want to look good for your own party?"

Truman mumbled something unintelligible and turned over. Clemens sighed. "I don't know what to do anymore, Tru. I-I... I miss you. I just want you to know that. I don't even know if you know what I'm saying anymore. Or if you care. Or when I ask you a question, you're answering me, or whoever that is in your skull." He waited for a response and when he got none, he left, disappointed but not surprised.

Clemens sought his mother in the kitchen. She was wearing her usual simple cloth head covering to keep the oil, milk, blood and whatever else out of her blonde hair. The cake had just come out of their wood-fired oven and was cooling while she prepared chocolate icing.

"*Maman*, do you remember when I hit Truman in the head with the sled all those years ago?"

"*Mai oui, mon chou*. It was 'orrible day. Poor Tru, laying in his snow *ange*. Why do you ask this now?"

Clemens sat on the only chair in the kitchen, a dark, high-backed chair that Emeline used for the short breaks she took between baking bread, churning butter, plucking chickens, stoking the fire, cooking, and scrubbing.

"Do you think..." Clemens put his hands on his knees and looked at the high tin ceiling when he spoke. "Do you think that accident caused Truman's...spirits?" This was the first suggestion from anyone that the problem could have a physical cause. Both Henry and Emeline discussed the possibility of the Devil's influence on Truman. Emeline still hadn't told anyone, not even Dr. Hendricks, about her aunt, for fear of a similar fate for Truman — the asylum. Clemens continued, "I mean, could I have triggered something, damaged or let something loose? Cut some wires?"

Emeline kneeled in front of her eldest. She knew Clemens was taking Truman's *changement* as hard as she was. She saw the anguish on his face and it nearly broke her.

It was time to tell Clemens, the only other one who loved Truman as much as she. "I had *une tante,* a favorite aunt. Her name was *Clémence.*" She waited a beat to let this sink in. Clemens looked at her searchingly.

"*Oui,* you are named for 'er. She was the youngest sister of *mon mère* and she also went through such a change. It was so 'ard to see and not to do anything. She would talk to no one or scream, just scream. It was when she walked *nu* in the streets — without the clothes. She said the clothes, they..." Emeline stopped and used her hands to make an open and close gesture.

"Squeezing? Like a boa constrictor?"

"*Oui.* It was then she was sent away *a l'asile.*"

Clemens shook his head.

"To the place where the persons who are sick here." She pointed to her head.

Clemens turned white as a sheet. "An asylum? For the insane? *Maman,* no, no, noooo..." and with that Clemens sunk his head into his hands and wept.

TRUMAN'S BIRTHDAY cake was hiding in the kitchen until after supper. It was tall and round with smooth chocolate icing accented with white and pink roses. Emeline had gotten quite a reputation at the church potlucks for her baked goods, which had given her the ability to add a small income to the household by bartering or outright selling her cakes and muffins in town.

Henry came into the kitchen. "Emmy, you've outdone yourself." He wrapped his arm around her, showing her he'd softened about the expense of the party.

Emeline flushed with pleasure. "You h'always say that."

"Clemens is bringing Ginny, did he mention that to you?"

"*Mai, oui.* It will be nice to 'ave a guest. It 'as been so long."

Henry nodded and put his hands into his pockets. Emeline knew this meant he had something serious to say. "No one has really seen Truman since he, uh… took a turn for the worse. Do you think it's wise to have a visitor?"

Emeline grew hot. "H'are you worried about Truman or your reputation? Truman is still your son and we will celebrate him like the others."

Henry knew she would defend Truman. He also knew this family was being tested — why, he couldn't say. Henry confided in Pastor Anderson, who consoled him by saying God didn't give us more than we could handle, and Henry wanted very much to believe that.

Henry brought a finger in close to the icing and Emeline slapped it away. "You are like a child."

Henry brightened. "You know, it will be nice to have a party. This will be a proper good time. I'm looking forward to our guest and some good conversation."

~

CLEMENS BORROWED the car to pick up Ginny and returned an hour later, as she lived clear on the other side of Hopefield. Slushy snowbanks were melting on the side of the road. Clemens got stuck in the mud on the outskirts of town. He slipped some of the tree bark he always had in the trunk under the back tires and encountered no more problems after that, though it was embarrassing to show up at the Swaggerts with mud on him from the knees down. They all laughed about it and waved them off, asking them to give Truman their best on his special day. Clemens wasn't sure even how Ginny was going to react when she saw how Truman was these days.

When they got back to the Bates' home, Clemens excused himself to change his trousers. He had begun to sleep on the parlor sofa because Truman's muttering kept him awake all night, but kept his clothes in there. He found Truman in the room, freshly dressed, though his hair was unkempt. He knew this was his mother's handiwork and that she had done her best. Clemens knew his mother was a saint but wondered how much more she could take. Clemens found himself only talking to Truman to give commands — come for supper, pick up your clothes, brush your teeth. He snapped at him as often as not anymore and for this Clemens was ashamed. He learned to leave some things alone, like Truman combing his hair. It was his birthday, anyway, so let him do what he wanted.

Emeline and Felicity propped open the swinging door that led to the kitchen so they could go back and forth the multiple times needed to bring out the birthday dishes. The table was set with care, Felicity having folded the napkins into little hats and an extra chair had been brought in from the kitchen for Ginny. Everyone was excited for the party and to have a guest made it all the merrier. Baked beans, roasted potatoes, mashed sweet potatoes, Indian pudding, biscuits, and a small ham that Emeline had acquired after a fierce round of bargaining at the butcher's, which included Emeline's promise to bake a birthday cake for his wife next month. The girls kept stealing glances at Ginny, who looked very pretty with her new, short haircut and her drop-waisted dress.

After saying grace, led by Henry, dishes were politely passed around the table, unlike the usual melee of grabbing and complaints of who got more than they should have. Emeline asked after Ginny's family and about her studies (she was taking classes to become a nurse) and she might have been the Queen of England for the rapt attention she received upon her answers.

Truman was going along with the rhythm of the plate passing when Aimee, the dirty girl, began to demand Truman's attention.

I want you to lick, to suck it. Put it in, anywhere you can find. Wet river, sticks in my mud. Nookie! Go someplace now only I can deliver my bubs no bug-eyed Betty. No weevils in snatch only on the others. Winter snow melts, snakes run down, pull your flesh, flay the day away, so keep it dry. Don't you want to lick it?

"I will lick you." Truman was passing the sweet potatoes to Ginny. Emeline dropped her fork with a clatter. The little ones thought Truman was pretending to be a dog and Candice, barely talking at this point, barked and burst into laughter, while the older ones' jaws dropped. Henry's face was red as he tried to keep his composure. Clemens grabbed Ginny's hand under the table. He may have told her about Truman, but it was nothing like hearing him directly.

It was Henry who spoke. "Truman, we have a guest. You need to stop that talk."

"Poke it, I will poke it," Truman continued. "Nookie!" Emeline and Henry and others saw at the same time — Truman had his hand down his pants and he was playing with himself.

Samuel's jaw dropped. "Christ!" No one bothered to comment on his swear.

Henry slammed his fists on the table, crushing any vestige of the festive mood. "The Devil has entered this house, Emmy."

Ginny covered her open mouth with her free hand. Clemens caught her eye and motioned with his head that they should go. Ginny shook her head no. Clemens loved her even more in that moment.

Emeline stood behind Truman and she tried to simultaneously put her hand over Truman's mouth and pull his hand out of his trousers.

Henry stood and roared, "He's going to goddamn Waterbury, that's where he's going!"

Emeline thought of how they had wrapped her aunt's limbs around her body in the cruelest of buckled vestments. "*Non*, 'Enry. Never!"

Clemens dropped Ginny's hand and rose from his seat. The children cowered, until Felicity ran from the table, Annabelle close behind. Samuel continued to stare, mouth still agape, while Candice started to cry in her highchair.

Truman continued, "Put it in, it's all we want. Just to put it in."

"Enough!" Henry bellowed. "Clemens, get him the hell out of here," though Clemens was already on his way. Henry went on, spit flying across the table in his fury. "He will sit anywhere but at this table made holy by the saying of grace. I will not put a curse on the little food we have left. He eats in the kitchen, or he will not eat at all. And we'll see who is not going to Waterbury!"

The subject was closed. Clemens and Emeline managed to stand Truman up and they each took an arm, hand still down his trousers. "Let me lick. Weee..." They pulled him into the kitchen, the door swinging wildly behind them.

Clemens returned immediately after sitting him in his mother's resting chair next to the stove, not wanting to leave Ginny alone with his father. Emeline stayed with Truman until her shame overwhelmed her and she fled through the back door into the cool evening dusk. Arms wide, she pleaded directly to God, hidden in the overcast sky, "No more of the Devil in my house. *Libère mon coeur.* Do you hear me? Do you care? No more!"

When she came back, Truman's face was smeared in chocolate — he had found a fork to dig into the bottom half of the cake on the counter in front of him. She sighed and using a knife to slice the unsullied top half of the cake, she placed it on another plate.

Emeline kissed her now quiet son on the top of his head and left with cake. Emeline called Felicity and Annabelle back to the table and Emeline sliced and handed out cake to everyone. The table was silent, except for when Ginny complimented Emeline. Clemens' cake remained untouched in front of him as he sat with tears in his eyes until it was over.

~

As a last attempt to free the family of Truman's affliction, Emeline, a devout Catholic, invited a priest to perform an exorcism. The incense was lit, the incantations uttered, laying on of hands performed, all to no avail. Truman settled into the rocking chair on the porch and began to smoke incessantly. He left the porch only to relieve himself and to eat. He refused to bathe, and a black beard grew down to his chest.

7

1983: NICKNAMES, A FIGHT, AND THE CABIN

Dante didn't have any good answers for Mrs. Bates when she called and asked him about where Pat was going during school hours. "We don't have any afternoon classes together. He's been driving most days now, so I figured he just took off right away after class."

He didn't tell her that after school, he didn't even look for Pat anymore. He and Shannon were finally going steady. They often went driving around the back roads, or back to one of their houses, whoever didn't have parents at home. Fooled around. Her blonde hair and two different-colored eyes made him crazy. Her soft skin, firm boobs, wet—

"Dante, do you think he's coming straight home on the days he drives? Or, leaving early and going home? Or somewhere else?"

Dante refocused. "I really don't know, Mrs. Bates. But I'll find out."

"Thank you, Dante." Candice hesitated a moment. "You know, I used to wonder if you and Patty's friendship was going to last, what with you both being so different and Patty, well, so bossy and name-calling. Does he still call you Strawberry? I never really liked that he did that."

"No, Mrs. Bates. Not anymore." He didn't tell her about the fight that finally put a stop to it at the end of junior year, the one over Shannon. "And I didn't know either, to be honest. When I first moved here, that first day at school. I don't know, he just demanded my friendship. It has taken some turns since then, but he's my brother, Mrs. Bates. In that way that you can't choose family, but you can't shake them either."

She laughed. "Maybe that's why he chose you. You know, for this time...Well, we are all so blessed to have you in our lives, Dante Zuckerman." Dante wasn't so sure how awesome he was being these days. Maybe he needed to do better.

"I wasn't the only one with a nickname, you know."
"True enough, but the others weren't so...you know."
"I know."

EVERYONE SEEMED to get a nickname by the end of elementary school, even Shannon. Some stuck and some didn't.

The Strawberry nickname for Dante caught on with Lyle and Jeremy after it was obvious Dante turned red for almost any reason and stuck all through elementary school. Next was Lyle's turn. Even as a tall, stringy boy, he had large pillowy lips that could have easily led toward his nickname going in another direction after a certain rock star. But in the end, it was his towering height and consistent Halloween theme ever since fourth grade — Zombie

Lincoln, Vampire Lincoln, Frankenstein Lincoln — that won out and he had been "Lincoln" to all the kids ever since.

Of the group, Jeremy Ibey was the last to get one, if Pat's always being called "Pat Bates" could be considered a nickname. Dante had never liked his, but as far as he knew, it wasn't up to him to change it.

Jeremy's nickname popped out of Lyle's mouth during a sleepover at Dante's house, the summer before that first year of middle school. The night started with all four of them sitting on or laying in sleeping bags, nowhere near tired, spread out on the Zuckermans' living room floor. The room was decorated with spider plants in macramé holders, indigenous weavings, and tribal art. There was a wicker chair hanging from the ceiling with rainbow cushions and a red lava lamp surrounded by Buddhist-themed incense holders, which accounted for the faint scent of nag champa. Ephraim Zuckerman's guitar case was in the corner and Darlene's yoga mat was rolled up by the door that led to the backyard. The Zuckermans didn't have a TV or home video games, or what they called "corporate snacks." Jeremy always made sure to pack a bunch of chips, cookies, and soda from his family's general store because the only kid-food at Dante's were rice crackers and dried apricots.

They had finished with talking about who saw Star Wars the most when it came out the previous year. Jeremy won by a mile at twenty-one times, and then moved on to talking about what middle school was going to be like when they started next month.

Jeremy started with, "It's going to be far out, I mean, we'll be one step away from high school. Thank God I won't have to see Lisa at school. She's always calling me a spaz in front of other people. She's such a phony. *She's* the spaz — on the phone all the time talking with her friends about who likes who. I mean for *hours*."

Lyle smiled, showing a lot of teeth. "Yeah, but your sister's hot. Like, Farrah Fawcett hot."

"Oh my *Gawd*, I can't believe you just said that." Jeremy threw his pillow at him.

"Thanks, dude." Lyle began to snuggle it. "Oh, Lisa, you know you want it. Come here, baby."

Pat and Dante threw their pillows at Lyle, too shouting, "Shut up! Gross!"

Jeremy started ripping into his knapsack and pulling out his pajamas, underwear, socks and whatever else wasn't food. "Okay — we're stocked. Cokes for me and Strawberry, Yoo-hoo for Pat Bates, Moxie for Lincoln. Aaaaannd — check this out. Twenty, that's right, twenty packets of Pop Rocks. We're all set for our Pop Rocks contest later."

Lyle clapped his hands together. "Let's get moving!"

Dante inwardly froze. He'd been half hoping the guys would forget about the plan to go to the cabin at midnight. They were at his house, so according to the unwritten code he had to give his okay. His thoughts tumbled. Why did sneaking out seem like such a good idea when they talked about it at school? But this was Hopefield, not New York, wherever they went, what could possibly happen to them?

Dante decided that what Ephraim and Darlene would freak about is if they didn't know where he was. Dante stage-whispered, "Hey, keep it down. Okay, we can sneak out easy without my folks knowing, but I gotta leave a note."

The other three cracked up. Pat whispered back,

"What kind of dork breaks the rules and leaves a note about it?" His voice got louder in a poor imitation of Dante. "Oh, uh, Mom, Dad, sorry to uh, wake you, but, uh, we're gonna sneak out and I uh, just wanted to let you know." Everyone but Dante had tears from laughing.

Lyle grabbed Jeremy's knapsack and started digging through it.

"Hey Lincoln, you D-bag, what gives." Jeremy lunged for his knapsack.

Lyle remained silent. He sat back and rolled his eyes. "You forgot my Cheeseballs, you nimrod."

"Oh yeah — sorry." Jeremy grabbed the bag back. Will five packs of Hubba Bubba make up for it?"

Lyle flashed a big smile under his shaggy black hair. "Almost, but not quite, because I like it when you owe me."

Pat, who had been laying back, rolled onto his side, head propped up by his hand. "More like 'blow me'."

Jeremy made a move toward Pat, but Lyle grabbed him by his arm. "Wait. Waaaait." Lyle ripped a loud fart into his sleeping bag, immediately slithered out, and pounced on Pat, pulling the sleeping bag over his head.

Jeremy pulled the bag down while Dante hugged Pat's kicking white-socked feet. The chant began, "Fart lock, fart lock, fart lock..."

Dante left his note next to the lava lamp to the disapproving chorus of his friends.

"Wicked lame."

"Pussy."

"Buttmunch."

Dante ignored them and they left out the back door. They each grabbed their own bike and they started riding toward Main Street. There was no moon and they soon grouped together in the inky dark. They raced down the road until the forest gave way to the churchyard and the town, dimly lit under low buzzing streetlights. As they passed the stone church wall, Dante and Pat instinctively looked up to see if Truman was on the wall out of habit. He wasn't there. There was no denying he had some strange habits, but none of them included being out at midnight, as far as anyone knew.

Pat and Dante had hardly visited Truman on the wall or at the ComeSee anymore, ever since they had grown out of thinking fossils were cool and that perhaps, after all, there weren't really any fossils. It made Dante feel bad, maybe because he lived in town and saw Truman on the church wall every day. Dante brought it up to Pat once, that maybe they should just go say hi, but he just mumbled something like, "I just don't want to, that's all."

The group turned right at Sawyer Street. The boys didn't say much on the way there for fear of attracting attention. Once they passed the Rose Garden—Truman's light was off—and got to the entrance to the railroad bed, they loosened up. The triangular bar blocking the widest portion of the path looked like it was made of pipes welded together. There was a chain link lock wrapped around one end. The boys bumped their way over the rough opening next to the gate that was wide enough for people, bicycles, and winter recreational vehicles. Moonlight blinked through the forest canopy as they started down the wide swath of the railroad bed.

"Speaking of Star Wars," said Lyle, picking up their earlier conversation. "Did you hear they are making a holiday special coming out this Christmas?"

Jeremy nodded. "I bet it will be cheesy, but, shit, you gotta watch it, right?"

Lyle said, "This Christmas, I am asking only for Atari games."

Dante sighed. "You're so lucky. If I asked for that, my parents would just give me books about how to light campfires by rubbing sticks."

Jeremy shrugged. "At least your parents are chill, Strawberry. Mine are sooo uptight. The other night, Lisa came home a pubic hair after nine on a school night and she got grounded for two weeks."

"Speaking of books, Strawberry, are you done yet with The Silmarillion?" asked Jeremy. He raised the pitch of his voice to a falsetto singsong and continued, "I've been waiting for, like, eveeer."

"Two more chapters, I swear."

"I do not get the whole hobbit thing," said Pat. "I mean, do you wanna read about a bunch of ground-dwelling furry buttmunches, or dream about Loni Anderson in that new show about the radio station?" Pat brought up his hands in front of his chest and made a large breast gesture.

Lyle nodded. "I'm with you Pat Bates. Oh! Did anyone see The Hulk this week? Well, we know you didn't, Dante." Lyle put his arm around Dante's shoulders. "Sorry, your life's so retarded, Straw. You know you can come over to my place and watch the boob tube any old night. Hey, is that why they call it that? Because you can see boobs?"

Jeremy leaned over and punched him in the arm, nearly toppling over in the process. "Dumbass."

～

WHEN THEY GOT to the cabin, Dante, Jeremy and Lyle let their bikes drop to the ground. They all stared at the dark structure with its gaping, glassless window. Jeremy asked, "Why haven't we checked this place out before?"

"We didn't know people had sex in it before, that's why," Lyle replied.

"Yeah, you can thank my sister's boyfriend's cousin's grandpa for that info."

"Ew, you heard about it from a grandpa? That's gross." Dante shook his head to get the image out of his mind. "So, it all happened, like fifty years ago, or something?"

"The guy didn't have *details* or anything, it's just that he worked with Pat's other uncle is all, the one he never met." Jeremy lowered his voice to a whisper. "Pat did not like hearing that his relative visited a whorehouse regularly and this cabin in particular. The way the guy said it, he knew that his uncle...what was his name?"

Dante turned, "Hey, Pat Bates, what—" But Pat wasn't there.

Dante got back on his bike. "You guys go on in." He turned and rode his bike back to Pat who had stopped pedaling a ways back. When Dante caught up to him, he tried to see Pat's face in the dark.

Pat shook his head. "Do you know how weird this is for me? We are going to check out a cabin where my dead uncle that I never knew had... you know. And my current uncle, according to you, comes out to it to clean it, or something."

They turned to the crunching of wheels on dirt. Lyle and Jeremy pulled up. "Sorry, too creepy to go in there without everyone. And say that again? Dante knew what?" asked Lyle.

Dante said, "It was years ago, like the first year I lived

here. I was walking down the path with some other kids — Shannon was there — and we saw Truman. It was getting dark and he kind of freaked us out. He was carrying a paper bag, I think from my folks' shop, he comes there for stuff, and said the cabin wasn't safe. That he was going to clean and scrub it, or something like that." Dante shrugged. "We don't sell cleaning products, so I don't get it."

Pat continued, "We asked my mom about it back then, but she didn't know much, or I guess because we were so little, say much. Wish maybe I didn't know anything else."

Jeremy lifted his hands in the air. "What's the big deal? Everyone knows your uncle's loopy."

Dante's head shot up. "What kind of thing is that to say?"

Pat shook his head again. "Well, shit, it's true, right? I wish he was somebody else's crazy uncle."

Dante was shocked. He'd never heard Pat talk that way about Truman.

"Okay, is the therapy session over? I wanna try to find a condom wrapper, or something," said Lyle.

Dante put his head in his hands. "A fifty-year-old condom wrapper?"

Jeremy shrugged. "Who knows if they even had them then. Or maybe they weren't the only ones who found the Secret Cabin of Love." He waggled his eyebrows while everyone groaned.

Jeremy lowered his voice to a whisper, "My folks are talking about stocking, you know, rubbers, at our store. You know, for the college kids."

Pat laughed, a sign he was readying into the adventure. "Let's hope they do it by the time we get girlfriends."

THE MOONLIGHT through the leaves was only so much help, but it did help outline the large bulky shape.

Dropping their bikes in a pile, Jeremy fumbled through the snacks to get to the flashlight, the only one who had one. He flicked it on and moved the beam around the side facing the path. The beam flashed through the vacant window into the interior. All they could see was the back wall.

"Wicked," said Lyle.

"Where's the door?" asked Dante.

Pat went around the left-hand side. "Here it is. It's open, like open, open."

The boys were immediately disappointed when they went inside. There wasn't a stick of furniture and nothing on the walls. Not even a stray leaf on the floor. Dante caught a scent, one that was vaguely familiar. Because there was no glass in the windows, the insects were as loud when they were outside, and the air was as muggy as outside.

"Man, when Truman said he cleaned this place, he really meant it," said Dante.

"Well, might as well make ourselves comfortable." Pat sat on the floor and the others followed suit. Jeremy placed the flashlight upright so the beam shone on the ceiling, allowing a bare amount of illumination.

TEN MINUTES LATER, Jeremy crushed his empty Coke can in his hand and tried to throw it out of the hole in the roof where a wood stove must have been. "Do you think there'll be a lot of homework next year?"

Pat shrugged, "Probably."

Lyle smiled. "More boobs, too. Did you see Scaron at Number Ten yesterday? She's got titties!"

He was referring to Shannon. Lyle gave her the nickname after she wore mascara for the first time. It was near the end of last year. It was a hot day and after recess, she came in with streaks of gray and black down her face. After everyone was seated, the teacher gave a startled look and asked Shannon if she was okay in front of the whole class. Not knowing what had happened, she ran, head ducked, to the bathroom, while all the kids snickered.

Anyway, the "Scaron" nickname lingered at recess and after school until the year was over. After that, Lyle was the only one who called her that anymore, even after Dante confided in everyone that he *like* liked her.

Dante tried to figure out how to shut him up. It wasn't easy for him to do. He never seemed to know how to shut any of them up when he wanted. Maybe because he always felt a little bit on the outside. He was the only one whose family here didn't go back generations.

"I think she has a crush on Pat Bates," said Lyle. He glanced at Dante, looking for a reaction.

"Shut up, Lincoln." Pat made as if to throw his Yoo-hoo bottle at him, then thought better of throwing glass. "You don't know anything."

Dante smiled at Pat defending him.

"Oh, yeah? Then why did I see Pat Bates and her alone at the end of The Point?" asked Lyle. The Point was a piece of the shoreline at the lake that jutted out one hundred feet into the water and, like most of the shoreline, except for the large green spot where everyone laid their towels, was overgrown with bushes and trees.

Dante, who had been fidgeting with the tab from his soda can, lifted his head up. "What?"

Pat got up from his spot on the floor. "Hey, what do you think this was for?" He grabbed the flashlight and shined it on a square outline cut low in the wall, almost touching the floor.

Dante looked at Pat and then at Lyle. "What did you see?"

Lyle flicked his long bangs. "I don't know. I could just make them out through the trees."

Jeremy laughed. "Yeah, cuz they were making out."

Dante stood up. He felt his face burning and was glad it was dark so no one could see. The last thing he needed right now was to be teased. "Is that true, Pat Bates?"

Pat sighed and turned around. "Sorry, Straw. It just happened. All we did was kiss a little and —"

Before anyone could stop him, Dante pounced on Pat, knocking him over. Never having done this kind of thing before, Dante didn't know what to do next, so just hung on to him and wouldn't let him out of his grip. Pat sputtered, "What the heck, dude?"

Pat squirmed out of Dante's grip and stood again. Dante got to his feet and pushed Pat so hard he sailed backward out the gaping front window and hit hard on the ground by the bikes.

Dante jumped out after him and they began rolling, the dirt of the path crunching under them. Pat yelled "Let go!" Dante was filled with anger he didn't know he'd had. The bossiness, the nickname, feeling like an outsider with his own group of best friends. And, God, that cursed hunting trip that still haunted him. And now Shannon. "Stop!"

The fighting boys crashed into the parked bikes. Jeremy yelled from the glassless window, "Cut it out, guys, you're gonna—"

Pat drew back his arm and punched Dante in the face.

Lyle swung out the window, long legs first, and grabbed the bike that had toppled on top of them. As he dragged it off, Pat rolled onto his back. The chain got caught on his shirt and scraped across his stomach.

"Ow! Fuck, dude!"

Then it stopped, Dante and Pat panting on the ground and Lyle holding the bike like he was afraid to do any more harm.

Pat spoke first. "Jeezum, Straw..."

Dante was breathing hard and looking up at the strip of stars visible through the divided canopy on either side of the wide path. He had never seen stars before he moved here. Now they blurred and he blinked his eyes, trying not to cry, adrenaline still pumping. His voice shook when he spoke, "I am sick of that nickname. I'm sick of not feeling like I fit in here." Dante peeled himself off the ground. "And I can*not* believe you kissed Shannon." He thought of what Pat said about his uncle. When did Pat become such a jerk?

Lyle chuffed. "Don't be such a baby, Straw. It's just a nickname."

Pat said between breaths, "I'm sorry. Really. It just happened. I was helping her look for her stupid sandal and the next thing I know, we were kissing."

Dante sat up and wiped his eyes. "Whatever, but you knew I liked her. That's the messed-up part. But it's not just that. I don't know what I need to do to feel like I'm in the group, you know?"

Pat looked surprised. "Seriously?" He lifted up his head off the ground. "Ladies, is Strawberry in the group or out?"

Lincoln dropped the bike and raised his hand. Jeremy said from the window, "We're not in class, dipwad."

"I'm voting, D-bag. In my humble opinion, he is most definitely in."

"Of course, you are, Straw. Don't be such a girl."

Dante's voice had calmed. "At least Lincoln is Lincoln because he's tall, which is a good thing. I'm called Strawberry because I blush every two seconds. That sucks, it's like, like... it just sucks. And why don't you have a nickname, Jeremy?" He reached over and poked Pat in the chest. "And is calling you 'Pat Bates' even a nickname?"

Jeremy, putting on his best Rodney Dangerfield voice, called from the window, "As for you, you don't get no respect. In fact, I'd say that was the last straw...berry." Lyle laughed. Dante couldn't help it; Jeremy's impressions always cracked him up, but he repressed his smile into a smirk. Pat, on the other hand, tried to laugh, but just ended up groaning and clutching his stomach, red and black from cuts and chain grease.

Dante said, "Roll over on your side."

Pat looked at him with narrowed eyes but complied. Dante called over to Jeremy, "Dude, throw me a soda."

Jeremy just took a second to grab one from his backpack stash, then threw a Coke through the window. Dante popped it open and poured it onto Pat's sideways belly.

"What the—"

Dante was clearly enjoying this. "Well, we don't have

any water, but there's probably gross stuff in there. You can clean it better when we get back."

SEATED AGAIN in a circle on the floor in the cabin, Jeremy shone the flashlight into Dante's face. "Straw, that's a shiner like you read about. It's like, massive."

Lyle leaned over and peered closely. "You can say that twice and mean it. Wicked color."

Dante delicately touched it with his fingers. "It's growing by the minute. I think my eye is closing. So may I say, fuck you very much, Pat Bates."

Pat laughed, then put a hand to his stomach. "Ow. Don't forget, I'm the one with gear grease and soda pop in my guts, thanks to you, and numbnuts over here." He turned a thumb toward Lyle.

Jeremy dumped his knapsack upside down and divvied up the packets of Pop Rocks so that each of them had two — the rest would be divvied up accordingly dependent on ranking.

Jeremy announced, "I am the reigning champion. Who's going to take me on?"

Pat shot his hand up. "I will."

"Three, two, one, go!" Lyle said. "And may the belch be with you."

Pat and Jeremy simultaneously ripped open the Pop Rocks and poured them into their mouths, initiating the fizzing sound. They each pulled the tabs from their sodas and began to chug.

Dante couldn't help but be a little worried. "You guys, what if it's true?" The rumor was that doing this could make your stomach explode.

Lyle gave him a shove. "Dude, everybody but you has already done this like five times. Even your parents gave their whole explanation that it's just carbon dioxide being released, so all it will do is give you gas. In fact, they're the ones who made me think of this brilliant idea."

"When they see our blue tongues tomorrow, my mom will probably make us drink a special candy-detox potion. And it won't taste like soda."

Pat and Jeremy continued to stare at each other, waiting. Pat started with a small belch, then a deeper, more impressive one. Jeremy answered in a series of small burps, then ripped one long and low, topping Pat's easily with length and depth.

Lyle and Dante applauded. "The champion reigns supreme!"

"That Ibey kid is unstoppable!"

Next was Lyle's turn and he lost as well, producing only a small series of burps. He clutched his stomach. "The gas isn't coming out. Maybe I *will* explode."

Finally, it was Dante's turn.

Lyle started the chant. His large teeth gleamed in the dark as he grinned his famously huge smile. "Jer-Bear, Jer-Bear, Jer-Bear."

Pat joined him. Lyle and Pat chanted all the way through the final round, which, unsurprisingly, went to Jeremy. And with that, "Jer-Bear" was born.

Pat gave Dante a light punch on the arm. "See, we're all the same now."

Dante gave a small smile. "You're still an asshole. And stay away from her."

"Alright, but there wasn't even any tongue. And I don't even think she knows you like her. You gotta, you know, *talk* to her."

Lyle started crawling toward a corner. "Dude, I need the flashlight."

Jeremy got up and brought the flashlight over. "What?"

Lyle sat up. "Check it out — weed!"

"No way!" Jeremy and the others crowded around Lyle and looked at the brownish-green bundle on the palm of his outstretched hand.

Lyle shook his head. "Wicked."

Pat picked it up and sniffed it. "Smells like weed."

Dante grabbed it from him. He thought back to the night he saw Truman on the path clutching the paper bag. He started to laugh. "You guys are the biggest idiots. It's not weed, it's sage. Must be from Truman. I bet he left it here."

Pat lifted his hands. "Why?"

"Well… It's supposed to cleanse out any, you know…"

"No, I don't know, what?" Pat was clearly annoyed.

Dante willed his blushing to stop with limited success. Sometimes he was very embarrassed by what his parents believed in. "Spirits. Bad Energy, that kind of stuff. Remember when I told you Truman said the cabin wasn't clean, wasn't safe, remember?"

"Whatever. He is crazy, after all."

Dante crossed his arms. "A lot of people buy it from my parents, you know. Maybe you gotta give your uncle a break, here."

Pat took the flashlight from Jeremy. "Hey, I want to check out what I saw earlier." Pat got on his knees and felt around the edge of the low square cut in the wall. His fingers got hold of an edge and a small door swung outwards. The flashlight beam revealed a small space, square, like a box had been attached to the outside wall.

Jeremy, "Dude, I think I know! My Grandpa Provost has something like this at his camp at Island Pond. It's cold storage, you know, for in the winter. He doesn't have any electricity."

"Check it out." Dante reached to a back corner. "Pat Bates — here." Pat shined the light on two circles in Dante's hand, both embossed with a small, wood-cut shape: a rose.

Immediately after that, there was a whoosh, and an owl flew in through the open window. It swooped and dove around the boys' heads, causing them to panic and climb on top of each other as they tumbled out the window. They hopped onto their bikes and started pumping hard back the way they had come, yelling to each other about ghosts and close calls.

JUST AS THEY got back to the entrance to the railroad bed, a flashlight beamed in their faces, stopping them dead.

"Stop right there, boys. Let's see who we got." They couldn't see past the light in their eyes, but Officer Eastman was a familiar voice to most of them. "Jeremy Ibey, won't your father be pleased." His flashlight turned up to shine on Lyle. "Lyle Laguerre, or should I call you Stretch Armstrong?" Officer Eastman knew their names, not from being in trouble, but from church. Though Dante had gone a couple of times with the Bates after a sleepover, being Jewish meant he wasn't well-known with the church crowd.

"Pat Bates, what happened to you? You look like you've seen a ghost." His flashlight moved to Pat's midriff. "And fought with one."

The light moved to Dante. "Don't know you." His flashlight bounced back and forth between Pat and Dante's ruined clothes. He put the light back on Dante's face. "Quite a shiner. A little trouble in paradise, boys?"

Dante didn't know if he was expected to say anything or not, so he kept quiet.

"What's your name, son?"

The boys joked with him later how he looked like a deer in headlights, frozen but ready to bolt.

"D-d-dante, sir. Zuckerman."

"Dante? That's a name? Okay, Mr. Zuckerman, land all of you. Leave your bikes here, let's all get into the cruiser and we'll go give your parents a call from the station. You can pick the bikes up with your parents." He swung the flashlight away from their faces and they headed back to the parking lot, where the cruiser was waiting, headlights shining toward them.

"Um, sir, uh, what law are we breaking?" asked Jeremy. Lyle gave him a small

"shut up" shove.

The flashlight swung back at them. "Curfew."

Officer Eastman trained the light onto their faces again, making them squint. "Wait a second. Open up your mouths, boys." They did as instructed. "Why're your tongues all blue? You kids aren't huffing toilet bowl cleaner or some nonsense, now, are you?"

Jeremy cleared his throat. "Pop Rocks, sir." Officer Eastman lowered his flashlight. Dante thought he could see an amused look on the officer's face through the after-image of light dancing in front of his eyes.

Jeremy apparently didn't know when to stop. "How did you even know we were here?"

They had walked far enough they could see Officer

Eastman's face under a streetlamp. They saw his eyes flicker toward the Rose Garden. "Just a concerned citizen."

They piled into the back of the cruiser. Dante, pressed up against the door, noticed it first. "Whoa, no door handle. We are totally locked in!"

They were suddenly excited at what was happening. They gave each other low fives, out of sight of Officer Eastman, though he could hear then chattering about what they were going to tell the kids at school. The station was two miles down Route 2, next to the middle school-high school campus, where the boys would be starting very soon.

After making them each recite their phone numbers and all the sleepy parents were called, the boys sat on a bench across from the only cell in the station and were given a talking to by Officer Eastman. He told them how they had broken curfew and how that was a serious offense because if something happened, no one would know where they were. The boys looked at each other — none of them had known there even was a curfew.

Dante and Jeremy's fathers arrived first, as they both lived in town. Officer Eastman gave the groggy and upset fathers the rundown and said he'd let the boys off with a warning, then did the same routine with Pat and Lyle's dads. Jeremy got grounded for a month with no TV or video games. Lyle got grounded for two weeks and no TV but there was no mention of video games. Pat didn't get grounded or lose TV privileges, but had to do his, his sister's and his parents' laundry — washed, dried, folded, and put away— for three weeks.

Dante and his parents sat together at the kitchen table, each in the spots where they would normally sit during meals. Dante held the bag of ice his mother had given him over his bruised and swollen eye.

Ephraim started the conversation. "Are you okay?"

Dante was not expecting a question like that, and tears came to his eyes. Darlene reached across the table, bracelets jangling, and laid her hand on his. "What happened? Not about curfew, but to you..." she glanced at Ephraim. "And maybe Pat?" "

Dante sniffed and wiped his eyes. "We got in a fight."

Ephraim leaned back. "Wow, your first fight."

Darlene gave Ephraim a sharp look. "What was the fight about?"

Dante shrugged. "Nothing, really, I guess. They were just, you know, bugging me and Pat was in on it, too."

Darlene considered this. "But you didn't fight with the other boys."

Dante shook his head.

"You know, I hear Pat call you 'Strawberry' sometimes. Did he give you that nickname?"

"I guess, yeah. Because you know how red I get."

Darlene let go of his hand. "How do you feel about this nickname?"

Dante did not understand why these questions were coming now but was glad he was not getting yelled at. He decided to keep quiet about Shannon. He wasn't even sure if that was a big deal anymore, anyway.

Dante shrugged again. "I don't know. It's just a thing. We all have nicknames now. It doesn't mean much. There's not much I can do about it anyway, so..."

"I think it does bother you," Darlene continued. "When you fought — did you pick the fight?"

He wished this question hadn't come from his mother. Dante nodded, blushing yet again. If it were from his dad, it would have felt more like a detective piecing together an incident, not his mom feeling out if she should be disappointed or not.

Darlene sighed. "I think this fight was more than about what was happening in the moment. If you ask him, and all of them, to stop calling you that nickname, they will, if they really are your friends."

Dante nodded that he heard her but didn't say that was exactly what he did, and that it was no use. He knew if he brought it up again, the boys would just say he was whining. Plus, what if they gave him a new, worse nickname because he couldn't handle the one he already has? After all, he did turn red all the time. Maybe *that's* what needed to change.

As for his punishment, not having any TV or video games to take away, Dante got off with a hug and a lecture about how he would devastate his parents if anything happened to him because he was all they had. His parents said they saw his "sneaking out note" after the wake-up call from the police, and while they weren't happy about him leaving in the middle of the night, they appreciated him leaving the note.

At school, everyone told him how lucky he was that he didn't have to worry about his parents. They were just the coolest. This was the first time Dante was in any kind of real trouble and he had to admit, his parents were being pretty okay. But perhaps that's what made him feel worse than if they gave him a punishment, which honestly, he thought he deserved.

Before school on Monday, Dante stood in front of a mirror by the front door and put on the Band-Aid eye patch his mom had given him. He knew he didn't need it, but his eye was puffed closed and he thought the eye patch would help him look less idiotic. As he stared in the mirror, he got an idea. Digging in the stationery drawer in the desk under the mirror, he found a black Sharpie and began to draw an eyeball on top of the patch. The eye was drawn half-shut. Everyone at school told him it looked like his eye was stoned, which got a lot of laughs. This, on top of the fact that the boys got busted by the police, gave them all a bit of a reputation, which they thought was an excellent way to start middle school.

Shannon asked about how he got the black eye and, fighting back the blushing, he told her Pat and he were messing around and it was an accident. Pat had agreed to tell the same story.

"Shannon, um, do you like comics?"

Shannon shrugged. "I don't know. I've never read one."

Dante reached into his bag. "Here's a Spiderman one. Tell me what you think when you're done." And looked deeper into his bag. "Oh, here." He took out one of the rose tokens from the cabin and gave it to her. "Found this over the weekend."

Shannon's eyes grew big. "Wow, thanks. It's pretty." Later that day, she had looped a piece of string through it and was wearing it as a necklace. Someone in wood shop must have put a small hole in it for her. When Dante saw it, he was surprised and happy, and he asked who helped her.

"Pat Bates."

Dante was not sure what that meant, but he was sure that he did not like that answer.

~

THESE DAYS, Pat didn't seem to even think about girls, much less his attendance. Dante, at Candice's request, started collecting homework for Pat twice a week and often ended up staying the night.

On this particular day, close to Christmas, Dante hadn't put on his winter tires yet, but it was only flurries coming down that day, so Dante knew he could make it. Pat was lying in bed, listening to Black Sabbath and flipping the tape over and over in his Walkman, completely oblivious to Dante. Dante went to get a soda and Candice and Kitty were in the kitchen. Kitty exited after handing her mom a photocopied list of things she needed to get before the next cheerleading practice. Candice had looked at the paper and sighed. "We'll get it done, but maybe not all by then."

"Okay, thanks." She wrapped her arms around her mom's large, soft body before bouncing away.

Candice rolled her eyes. "'Try out for cheerleading!' I said. Well, I knew she'd be good at it and now, we have to pay for it. Literally." She put the list on the table. "It's good, though. It will help her keep from thinking too much about Patty. She doesn't let it show, but I know she's worried."

Dante only saw Kitty as annoying and self-centered, but mothers knew best, he imagined.

"Mrs. Bates, I uh, don't know how to say this..."

"Go on, Dante. I'm all ears."

"Do you ever think, I mean, does, uh, Truman ever cross your mind? You know, with Pat's, uh, thing."

Candice turned away abruptly and grabbed dishes that had been sitting in the dish drainer and began putting them away. "Sometimes, yes. I was so young when Truman, well, changed, I don't know him any other way.

But I knew my eldest brother, Clem, loved him very much. He changed, too, after the fire." She looked at him a beat. "Do you know about the village fire?"

Dante shook his head.

"Well, that's another story, but what I'm trying to say is that Clem lost the sparkle in his eyes. For a long time, I thought it was what happened to him, to Clem, that devastated him. He was badly burned in the fire, you see. But as I got older, I realized what had really got to him was that he lost Truman, who was no longer the brother and best friend he had before the... change." She sighed and continued putting dishes away. "I can't imagine."

Dante sincerely hoped that none of them would have to.

8

1931: BIG FLAME

Clemens Bates, dirt-encrusted and dusty, climbed the slate steps up to the side entrance of the house. He heard the floor model Silvertone radio blaring, The Shadow, from the parlor on the other side of the house before he even opened the door. The narrator was encouraging all to send a penny to the folks at the Blue Coal Company for a free magazine episode. There was a time when Clemens would have jumped at the chance for a piece of junk like that. Before.

He shook off his work boots in the mudroom and hung up his wool coat on top of the layers of all the other coats. He put both hands on his lower back and arched, hoping for some relief. He'd pulled a muscle shoveling the rocks and dirt being cleared for the railroad tracks, due to be laid down in a year's time, if all goes well. Another year. Clemens wished he could turn back time. Get his quarry job back. That was a tough job, too, but he'd be apprenticing right now for stonecutter if things weren't so bad.

At least Henry was able to hold onto his position and keep his foot in the door for when the quarry was in full swing again. These New Deal construction projects were a help, but Clemens prayed nightly that he'd get back to the quarry sooner than later. Lord knew he could use the higher pay, too. Then he could finally ask Ginny for her hand before someone else did.

How that flatlander Daniel Riley got around the town regulations to get a cathouse up and running was beyond Clemens and many others in town. Rumors flew while it was being built about how it was to be a hotel, Hopefield's first, in anticipation of the influx of visitors the railroad would bring. Others thought it was another government project for the Civilian Conservation Corp, which Clemens and his fellow workers were members of, to build affordable housing for the now countless indigents. No sooner was the last nail hammered, then the rooms were all filled with girls from out of town, the likes of which many had never seen.

The CCC workers were set up in tents along the slowly constructed railroad bed. A cabin had been built, too, two miles east of Hopefield, for the two supervisors. Not much more than a shack, for it would be torn down and rebuilt farther along when enough progress was made. It housed a bunk bed, a woodstove, a table for spreading out blueprints and a couple of chairs.

That Riley fellow, from Connecticut, went to every tent that first week, placing a wooden token with a rose stamped on it. At first there was much confusion because no one ever said directly what it was for, but it didn't take long for the young, hard-working laborers to start giving those ladies on the edge of town their roses in exchange for a bit of their time and talents. The system was easy; a man who worked for Riley, nicknamed The Florist, would check the tents each day while the workers were out. If there was a dollar on the inside of the door, The Florist would take it and leave a rose-stamped token to be used at the young man's discretion.

The Rose Garden, as it got to be called, was set back by the river at the far edge of town. It was, however, close enough to keep the church ladies enormously busy. Not allowed to vote on town council matters, they filed petition after petition. The county officials feared what would become of the town if those CCC workers, who were from God-knows-where, raised with God-knows-what-values, did not have a way to "recreate." So, they responded to the petitions with restrictions on "visiting hours at any and all hotels and multi-residential dwellings," but that was all. At some point, a train station was slated to be built on the same property, as Hopefield would be the second stop on the Montpelier, Vermont — Augusta, Maine (Capitol to Capitol!) Rail, so that was made official as well. As soon as the train station was built, the Rose Garden would have hotel zoning only, no residences allowed. Brothel or no brothel, folks were hoping the railroad would bring more visitors to the area, putting Hopefield on the map.

Clemens, as one of the local boys who went back home every night, was not able to receive a token in a tent — so a worker he made friends with, Stubby Gleason, went ahead and setup a two-token system for his own tent, which he arranged one day as a surprise for Clemens for his twenty-second birthday.

At this point, Ginny's father had been inviting another suitor around for dinner, Howard Proctor, son of a local banker and part of Hopefield gentry, if it could be called that, as it was Howard's granddaddy that founded the town. This, on top of Ginny's nurse-training at Central Vermont Hospital, meant a lot less opportunity for courting. One or the other of her parents typically answered the phone anymore and Clemens got the distinct impression she was not getting his messages. She had called a few times, but Clemens was never home at the time of her calls, which made him think she had no way to use the phone when her parents were home. The times he stopped by her house after work, filthy and reeking, the door was no longer opened all the way, much less an invitation to enter. After all the church potlucks he had attended, all the work for the Ladies' Auxiliary.

He lost his job and his girl, this on top of losing his brother and best friend. Now breaking his back earning peanuts for the government program, Clemens had never known that a person could feel so low.

And with prohibition having just been repealed, any reason would do to put together a liquor-fueled celebration. So Clemens let Stubby put together a party for him at the tents, followed by a parade of token-holding fellows marching off to the shiny-white clapboard building. They each stood by a door: four rooms on the top story, accessed by a set of stairs on the side, and four on the bottom. If there was a scarf tied on the doorknob, which was the case on almost all the doors given the time of night and new freedom to drink, they would have to wait their turn.

The men leaned on the white porch railings that lined the two stories, passing hooch, smoking, and listening to the rapids of the Winooski River rushing by on the other side of the building. Clemens had never been with a woman — it was only proper for him and Ginny to wait until marriage. And look what proper had gotten him. He wished to God that things were such that Truman could be here by his side at the crossing over to manhood. He missed him so very dearly, but Truman was gone, replaced by a greasy, raving lunatic that could make Clemens' stomach turn with the things he said and did.

As with all virgins, Lady Brunella refused Clemens' token, but not his liquor, and invited him to come back as soon as he could. Clemens obliged.

Clemens wanted nothing more than to tell Truman all about Lady Brunella. About how he was no longer a virgin, and how he finally felt like a man. One evening when he got home, he crossed the parlor in stocking feet after removing his boots and pushed open the swinging door to the kitchen. He reached for the metal water pitcher, beaded and waiting for him, and poured himself a glass. His mother was rolling out the dough for dinner biscuits. She accepted the just-got-home kiss from her son on a tilted, floured cheek. Clemens gulped down his water. With a flannel-sleeved wrist, he wiped his mouth dry and by so doing, wiped away a layer of fine dust, leaving a flesh-colored streak around his mouth.

Clemens reentered the parlor, which was empty — no surprise given the ear-splitting volume of the radio program. He didn't know how his mother could stand it, but he knew it was the only thing that kept Truman calm. Clemens crossed the room in wide steps and switched off the radio, cutting off a panicked damsel in mid-sentence. He opened the screen door to the porch and stepped out. He walked down to where Truman was rocking and talking. Clemens slid up onto the porch railing across from his brother and then followed Truman's gaze to the gigantic maple, in the dooryard, a fiery orange and yellow. Beyond that was a dusky sky over the barn and field nestled in among an outline of pines.

Back on the porch, Truman replied to a "spirit," as his mother called it, in a low tone, "It needs to be on the stove. Everyone knows that, Mr. President."

It is clean. It will scrub your soul. Coolidge had reminded him of this before.

"If I get you some fire, Mr. President, will you go away?" Truman pleaded. "I got some important information to relay to Truman."

When I go away, you are gone, too.

"Then it ends, Mr. President?"

Yesssssss.

"Well, who'd ever think my screwball little brother would have an audience with the president?"

Startled, Truman focused his eyes on his brother through his stringy, black hair, unwashed for at least a week. It had been that long since his mother rounded up Clemens and Samuel to take Truman out back and scrub him down with a bucket of soapy water and a rough sponge. Truman howled about the snakes running down his sides.

"Well, Truman, do you want the good news first, or the bad news first?" asked Clemens. Truman waited. Clemens had the fire.

"The good news is that I popped my cherry." Clemens looked at Truman for a reaction. Truman continued to stare at the maple in the dooryard and mutter to himself. "With a beautiful, experienced woman. Her name..." Clemens sighed remembering the feel of her tongue on his skin. "Her name is Brunella."

"Brunella-Newtella."

Clemens barked out a laugh. "Ha! You are listening, you crazy bastard." Clemens paused. "I'm sorry. I didn't mean that, Tru." He put a hand on his brother's shoulder, which caused Truman to recoil and rock faster in his chair.

Clemens ran a hand down his face. "Here's the bad news. I am almost out of tobacco, what you call your precious fire. This means *we* are almost out of tobacco since I am your supplier. Now, I don't know if you remember, or care, but my shitty job and my shitty little paycheck don't count for much and besides, I don't get paid for another three days and I am out of dough." Clemens didn't mention that he spent his last dollar on Lady Brunella. "But I got a plan. A real doozy, and I need you to pull it off. Only fair, right?"

Clemens nestled one of the porch beams between his shoulder blades. He pulled his Prince Albert tobacco pouch and papers out of his shirt pocket and began hand-rolling a cigarette. After Clemens had taught Truman how to roll cigarettes, Truman used to buy and roll his own like other men. Since the spirits had come and settled into his mind, Truman not only lost his income from the sheds, but also the coordination in his hands. Most everything he did now was quick and graceless, like his was the body of a man freezing in the dark, dropping his matches again and again, never able to light that warming fire.

Clemens knew Truman was pining for his next cigarette. He wished he could tease Truman about it a bit, like when they were kids. That raucous love was gone and Clemens couldn't explain what he felt, but he thought it might be grief. But now he had to use Truman like Truman was using him. He rolled matter-of-factly, simply acting the provider.

First Clemens cleanly yanked a paper out of its packet and with his free hand, pinched a brown clump out of the pouch and placed it in the paper. His and Truman's eyes focused intently on his handiwork, Clemens positioned both sets of fingers alongside the back of the paper and anchored the front with his square thumbs. Truman fidgeted with impatience. Clemens rolled it up, followed by a shake of his head as he licked along the top section of the paper and neatly closed the cigarette with his thumbs. Truman leaned forward. Clemens painstakingly tore off the dangling tobacco bits and put them back in the pouch. Finally, Clemens leaned over and snatched the box of strike-anywhere matches off the table next to Truman and, scraping a match along the railing, snap-pop-hissed the match awake, bringing the lively little flame to his cigarette. Truman fell back, clutching the rocking chair arms. Clemens simultaneously shook out the match and inhaled the first drag.

Truman gripped the chair harder to keep himself from springing on his brother. He had tried not to smoke his ration of five cigarettes that Clemens had given him so quickly. To make the cigarettes last, he smoked half of one and then put it out, then smoked it again when he couldn't stand it anymore. "Mr. President is really angry, and he wants me to hurt you. He wants the flame." Truman said. He felt near to bursting watching his brother blow out the smoke.

"Well, tell that bastard I am going to hurt him. He's

been hanging around a lot more than ever, right little brother? Shame you're not visiting with that dirty girl as much. We could swap stories." Clemens leaned forward and made as if he were giving the cigarette to Truman. He dropped it to the ground before Truman's trembling fingers could grab hold.

"Whoops! Sorry, Mr. President."

Clemens watched as Truman lunged for the still-burning cigarette on the floor, then sat up shakily and inhaled the smoke. Clemens felt shame rise in his throat. He wanted to piss off the "President," but he only managed to fill his eyes with tears at the sight of his brother scrambling like a chicken after feed. It was no one's fault — except maybe the Devil's. Clemens wiped a hand down over his face, sighed, and resisted the urge to cry. He started to roll his own smoke. "Sorry, Tru," he said, voice constricted by sadness. "Anyway, it's like I said, we're almost out of tobacco. Now you sit back, and I'll tell you and that old fucker Mr. President there the plan."

Now that they had the flame, Truman and Coolidge could focus and smoke and listen.

CLEMENS WAITED until the next day when he knew his father would drive his mother into Hopefield and possibly into Barre in their now questionably reliable Model T to barter eggs, milk, and Emeline's locally famous Cheddar cheese muffins for flour, lard, and kerosene. The Bates had been able to hang onto their buckboard and horse, which allowed Clemens some independence, at least to get back and forth to work. It was easier to feed the horse then to put gas in the car, at least while they had hay left in the barn, so there were few restrictions on taking her out.

Clemens had Truman put on his warmest coat and they both donned wide-brimmed hats. Daisy Chain, despite her age, clopped along sure-footed and well-paced, huffing white breath in the morning air. Clemens drove Truman along the wooded five miles of familiar turns, dips, and loose patches of dirt into town. Well, almost into town. They hadn't passed a soul on the road, which was perfect. Clemens didn't want anyone to know he wasn't at home. Harrison's Feed, the first store on that edge of town, was barely in sight when Clemens stopped the rig and hopped off, leading Daisy Chain and a still-seated Truman five-hundred feet into the woods onto a logging trail. "Okay, Truman, just like discussed. I'll meet you back here as soon as we're done."

Truman rubbed his frozen hands together and nodded his head in understanding. Under his wide-brimmed hat, his long, stringy hair hung down around his ears like dank river grass.

"We need a flame for the road," Truman said.

"Alright, alright, don't get your presidential knickers in a twist. But this is your last one and even I only have one more after this, so let's do it right."

After Clemens warmed up his hands in his armpits, he rolled Truman a cigarette. Truman climbed down off the rig and began walking down the road, smoking and muttering to Calvin Coolidge and telling him to leave him alone, he'd do it better without him. Besides, did Coolidge want the flame or not?

Coolidge was relentless and berated Truman the whole walk into town about how stupid he was and how he should just let Coolidge do it himself. Truman puffed out a continual cloud of steam. His muttering became near to shouting as his and Coolidge's arguing grew more heated.

After tying up Daisy Chain to a low branch and carrying a burlap sack, Clemens slinked his way along the road, parallel to his brother, invisible to any passers-by. His movements were silent, the only noise being when he stepped on a dry twig or once when he slipped on a debris-buried rock and landed hard on a pile of dried leaves. Truman gave no indication as to whether he heard him over Coolidge's barrage or not. Truman and Clemens both stayed straight on course. When Truman got to Main Street, Clemens remained stealthy and unseen behind the buildings. Luckily, the general store, or anywhere else their folks could be, was on the other side of town, near the waterfall and entrance to Route 2. Their target was the recently combined Thompson Tobacco and Haberdashery. No one was spending good money on new hats anymore, so Earl Thompson bought the tobacco shop when the proprietor, Garrett Sundry, passed on. Truman turned in a mechanical fashion to face the entrance and Clemens tip-toed to a stop in back of it.

Truman and Coolidge were arguing at fever pitch now. Clemens could hear Truman's side of the argument all the way from the back of the building and tensed. "I don't need your help. The flame calls to me. It is you it despises. It is mine to deliver. Let go!"

Clemens became alarmed at these last words. Did somebody grab Truman? Clemens glued himself up against the wall and slowly peered around the corner, trying to observe with one eye. Truman was alone on the street. Clemens watched Truman shake his arm as if to loosen someone's unwanted grip. This invisible assault was a first for Truman, as far as Clemens knew, but he didn't see how it could affect the plan. Dotty Holt, an elder in the church, hurried by Truman with wide eyes.

"Go on," Clemens whispered to himself. "Come on, Truman. Go in."

Truman dropped his arm and in silence, walked up the porch steps. Clemens didn't like the silence, but couldn't see him anymore to confirm if he'd gone inside or not.

Clemens then heard a low murmuring, something about "Mr. Indian". *Christ*, thought Clemens, *he's greeting the Indian statue that's next to the front door.*

Truman was meant to be going on like he does; in fact, that was pretty much the whole plan. Truman goes in muttering and shouting, knocks some merchandise off the shelves — on purpose, though he'd probably do it by accident, anyway — and gets thrown out. Then Clemens waits for Thompson to move the commotion onto the front porch, which is Clemens' cue to go into the backroom and grab as many cans of Prince Albert tobacco and rolling papers as possible, stuff them into his sack and then return carefully through the woods to meet Truman back at the rig.

Adrenaline tensed his muscles as Clemens, hand on the back latch, waited for the noise and the chaos. Silence. Nothing. What the hell was going on up there? Did Truman suddenly go sane? Did he think that the Indian statue spoke to him, and told him to call it off?

Clemens waited five more minutes in the same position. He took his cramping, frozen hand off the latch and paced back and forth for two more minutes. Maybe Truman got muddled and left. Maybe he got sidetracked and went to the café for coffee. Should he just go back to the rig? What if he goes back to the rig, but Truman never shows up? He could make up some lie to his folks about Truman wandering off; that would be an easy one to swallow, then he could come back and get him.

Clemens smelled it before he saw it. Smoke. He looked around — was someone burning trash behind another store? He turned back around, his hand flying to his mouth. Smoke began to billow from underneath the door. It smelled like the store's whole supply of cigars was burning.

Clemens felt as if he had been punched in the throat. "Truman," he squeaked. He sucked in an involuntary breath.

"Truman!"

Clemens raced around to the front of the store. Smoke was pouring out from every crack of every window. Mr. Thompson burst out the front door, gasping and confused. He tripped and came rolling down the wooden steps, taking his cigar store Indian statue with him. Clemens realized that he was still holding the burlap sack and let it drop. He checked Mr. Thompson, not knowing what to do even if he was hurt, and then, stepping over the Indian, pushed his way through the smoke to find his brother. He ducked low the best he could and raced around the aisles, knocking over hat stands and tobacco supplies. No Truman. His eyes burned and his lungs filled with what felt like a thousand tiny needles. Clemens lurched behind the counter and forced his legs in the direction of the back room. Where was the smoke coming from? Where was Truman?

The door connecting the storefront to the back room blew open with a wave of flames and smoke. Clemens was overcome. He fell choking onto the rough floorboards. He didn't see Truman run out back, using the storeroom door where Clemens had been waiting moments before, clutching five cans of Prince Albert.

"I've got the flame! I did it, Clem — I burned the old fucker out! Coolidge can't hurt us now. We're safe!"

9

1984: SLEDS, RAVINES, AND ROSES

As unsure as Dante was about how Mr. Bates felt about him, there was no questioning his loyalty to his kids. But Dante was under the impression he also had loyalty to a certain mindset. Bill's reaction to Pat's depression thing he was going through worried Dante. Bill was a pull-yourself-up-by-your-bootstraps kind of a guy.

From what Dante could see, Bill was keeping his distance. Whenever he was over, he didn't see Bill except at dinner. If Pat was able to get himself out of bed to pick at his food, Bill wouldn't look at him straight on and avoided any topic that would circle back to Pat. Which didn't leave much for Dante to talk about — school, work, cars, girls — Pat's topics were his topics. This left it wide open for Kitty, who took full advantage. Her topic was cheerleading. Candice would ask appropriate follow up questions, Bill would nod at the answers, Dante would try not to yawn, and Pat would quickly eat his food, eager to get back to his room. Dante wondered how this whole thing must be affecting Kitty, too. She was becoming less annoying, but she was still only fourteen. What did she think about her brother?

He ran into her in the kitchen late one night during one of his stayovers. Sleepover didn't quite seem like the right word anymore — sleepovers implied fun and Dante stopped expecting fun ten stayovers ago. Dante was way past needing to ask permission to go into the cabinets at the Bates' home.

"Oh, hey." Kitty was eating Frosted Flakes at the red, square kitchen table and flicking through pages of *Teen Beat* magazine without reading. She must have been there for a while because the soggy flakes were mush stuck to the side of her bowl, the milk almost gone. She flopped back in her chair. "You should just move in at this point."

Dante smiled. Leave it to Kitty. "Very funny."

She crossed her arms. "Do you think it helps? You know, you coming over so much? I mean... isn't it all kind of...Isn't he kind of..."

Dante opened the snack drawer and took out a package of Keebler Fudge Stripes. He leaned against the counter and took one out. "Crazy?" Dante wished he had chosen a different word because Kitty's eyes immediately filled with tears and her nostrils started to flutter.

Kitty wiped her nose with the back of her hand. "I mean, we're not close or anything, but he..." A sobbed escaped. "He's my brother. But I can't even talk to him or tell him all the usual stuff, like what a jerk he is, but that's because I never really mean it, we never do, but now —" She took a sharp breath in and exhaled loudly. "Now it's all so wicked *serious*."

Dante pulled out a chair next to her. "Kitty, I don't know if it was the accident, or what, but Pat is really going through something right now. It's bad." Dante popped a cookie in his mouth and threw his hands up. With a mouth full, he said, "I don't have a flippin' clue if I'm helping." He swallowed and continued, "I do it because your mom asks, and I would do anything for her. And for Pat."

Kitty looked at him, eyelashes dark and wet. Dante thought that this was the first time he didn't see her as the brat that used to get on their nerves all the time. "They're talking about sending him somewhere. Dad said it wasn't right to keep using you like a nurse, or whatever. That he needs to see someone." She lowered her voice to a whisper. "Or go somewhere."

Dante felt his face grow red with anger. "Like where? What, just send him away, let someone else fix him? They won't know him like we do."

There was movement in the doorway. Now there were tears in Bill's eyes after hearing what Dante said.

"Son, how are *we* helping? We're not doctors. Pat needs a doctor. His mother, well..." He wiped a hand down his face. "Dante, I love that you are here for him, for us. Truly. You are the best friend Pat could have. But it's not fair to you, either. To make all this effort, for what? He goes in and out of this thing, and it's only gotten worse. I don't know how much longer we can simply watch and hope." He sighed. "It's just talk now, anyway. The school counselor is setting up regular appointments with a psychologist."

Dante stood up, the chair scraping behind him. "Mr. Bates, I'm sorry. I didn't mean what I said. It's just that, it makes it all so *real*." Bill walked toward Dante with his arms outstretched. He wrapped his granite strong arms around him, which somehow allowed Dante's own tears to finally flow. Bill, whom Dante thought hated crying, began to sob even louder than him. Dante didn't know when it happened, but Kitty crumpled into their huddle, too.

When Dante went back in Pat's room, Pat was a silhouette in the dark, standing and peering through the window. "Do you see it?"

Dante, glad he was finally being acknowledged, walked over and stood next to him. It was noticeably cooler next to the window. The glow from the light over the kitchen door created a golden circle like on a stage, the woods made dark beyond it. Together, their breath steamed the frosted window as they looked into the night. "What do you see?"

"Remember the buck, Dante? The one from the hunting trip?"

Dante turned to look at him. Still emotional from the encounter with Bill and Kitty in the kitchen, tears sprung to his eyes. That damn hunting trip. The accident that was his fault.

"What about it?"

"He's here. He wants revenge."

Dante laughed. That sounded more like Pat; he was fucking with him, reminding him of the day Dante almost got Mr. Bates killed. He played along, wiping the tears away. "I don't see him."

Pat took a step back. "He's gone. Wish I was on a snow machine right now. I'd chase down his ass and that would be that."

Dante looked more carefully at Pat and was suddenly alarmed. There was something unfocused in his eyes. Fear. Unfocused fear.

Dante watched his eyes as it cleared, like an actor shaking off his role. There was almost a sparkle in them again. Pat said, "Dude, remember the first time we rode the snow machines on the railroad bed?"

Dante's head was spinning. He didn't know what was happening, all he knew was that for this moment in time, this minute in time, Pat was back.

"Totally. That was wicked nuts."

Pat considered this as he sat on his bed. Dante was glad he was away from the window. Dante was a little shaky as he sat down, unable to make sense of the fear he saw in Pat's eyes. Was that part of depression? Or... oh, shit.

Pat absently picked up his baseball that had always lived on the shelves next to his bed and twirled it in his hand. "Hard to believe that sled trip was only a few years ago. What were we, fourteen?"

That snow machine trip was the first time Dante had seen an actual hero in person and it was Pat Bates, saving his life.

THAT SATURDAY MORNING back during the winter of their freshman year, Dante and Pat stomped their way up the steps to Dante's house, each pausing to tap their boots against the door frame to knock as much snow off as possible. They had just come in from shoveling the Zuckerman's steep driveway. They stood in the doorway, pulling off their boots. Their jeans were soaked from the knees down.

"I am wicked thirsty," said Pat, his wet socks slipping on the floor as he crossed the kitchen for a glass, his snow pants making a swishing sound as he walked over to the sink to get himself some water.

Pat got some water from the tap and started to drink. Dante gave him a small shove, making him dribble water down his chin.

"Oh no, Pat Bates, it looks like you have a drinking problem." They had just gone to Barre to see *Airplane* and were reciting as many lines as they could. They had also recently seen *The Empire Strikes Back*, which they both agreed was better than the first one, so cool about the Darth Vader-Luke father thing. They disagreed about *Caddyshack* — both thought it was funny, but Dante thought Airplane was funnier. They also disagreed about *Superman II*. Dante thought it was a real snooze fest — Lex Luther wasn't near evil enough.

Pat wiped his mouth and said, "See if you can guess what I am now."

"Oh, no", said Dante, seeing that Pat had moved on to *Animal House*. Pat filled his mouth with water.

Dante backed away, hands in front of him. "No, no, don't do it, dude!" Dante backed up into the fridge and had nowhere to go.

Pat got right up in his face and pushed his cheeks, forcing a spray of water all over Dante. "A zit, get it?"

"Oh, man. That sucked way worse than what I did to you." They laughed while Dante wiped his face off with a dishtowel. Pat continued to stand in front of the fridge, looking at the flyer held up by a peace sign magnet. "Class of 1984 fundraiser dinner — Senior Trip."

"Man, already raising money for our senior trip in four years. That's crazy."

Dante shrugged. "Think it will be Montreal or Boston?"

"I hope Montreal."

"It would be so cool to take you to New York someday.

Now that my grandma passed, I don't know when we'll go back. I'd love to see you on the subway."

"That would be awesome. Hey, you ready to ride?" asked Pat.

"Surely, you can't be serious."

Pat looked at Dante's smirk and replied as expected. "I am sure. And don't call me Shirley."

THEY CHANGED THEIR JEANS, put on snow pants and winter gear and, snow pants loud with the usual swishing sound as they walked, they made their way over to the Rose Garden. Pat having stayed the night at Dante's, Bill had towed the sleds to the village, parking them next to Truman's VW Rabbit, which was half buried in plowed snow, after he and Kitty took a run. Bill left the keys with Truman and said he would come back later to tow them home.

Pat knocked on Truman's door, but there was no answer. Pat shrugged. Dante was glad that Pat seemed to get over being embarrassed by his uncle. Maybe it helped that Lyle and Jeremy stopped teasing him. Dante guessed they were all starting to grow up.

The door opened, just wide enough for Truman to show his bushy white and yellow beard. The warm smell of ashtrays and unwashed clothes rushed out, which was not unexpected. "'Lo boys."

"Hi, Uncle Tru. Can we get the keys?"

Truman stepped back and let them in, smoke trailing behind him. It looked the same as always — greasy counter tops, yellowed walls, filmed up windows. Dante had to shut the door behind him to keep out the chill of the gray, winter day. Truman muttered as he walked to the other side of the kitchen table, where the keys were resting next to an overflowing ashtray. Bill and Kitty probably stayed for a few minutes, to be polite. It wasn't that Truman was to be avoided, necessarily, but his apartment was. Pat never said anything, but Dante always had trouble breathing in there.

Truman took a drag of his cigarette as he exhaled, Pat and Dante heard words like "Coolidge, voters, flame."

Pat elbowed Dante. Pat had told him to bring the wooden token they'd found that first time in the cabin, the one that matched the one Dante gave Shannon. Pat had shown it to his mom, but she just blushed and said, "Oh, how cute. Maybe it was used as decoration for something." The only one who could answer at this point was Truman.

Using his teeth, Dante pulled off a glove and with the bare hand, unzipped his jacket pocket. "Check it out, Truman." He held his palm out that held the rose-stamped token.

Truman took it with no comment. He held it up to get a closer look. "A rose for the garden, make it rise. Brunella-Newtella. A rose for Clem."

Pat and Dante looked sideways at each other.

"What's it for?"

Truman held the keys out and Pat took them from him. Truman curled the token up in his other hand.

"A rose to make it rise. Soothe it and stroke it, the brow and the shaft."

Pat looked at Dante, who shrugged. Pat sighed. "Well, thanks!" He mumbled, "for nothing" as he turned toward the door. "Come on, Straw—"

Pat felt a vise grip on his arm that spun him around.

Truman's face was inches from his. His ash-laden breath poured out as he spoke, his voice as soft as his grip was hard. "Back to the cabin. The rose belongs there."

Pat was surprised, but not scared. Crazy as he was, Pat hadn't been scared of his uncle a day in his life. "'K, Uncle Tru. We'll bring it back." Pat took his glove off and tucked the token into his jacket pocket and zipped it up. "See ya later."

THE BOYS CLIMBED onto the snow machines. The entrance to the railroad bed was clear as the overgrowth was buried under the snow. There was plenty of room for snow machines on the sides of the locked gate, where they found Bill and Kitty's, and perhaps others' tracks. When Dante saw them for the first time and called them snowmobiles, Pat gave him a dead arm and told him to stop being such a flatlander. The sleds, as they were called, were mostly used behind the Bates' property, where the trails led all the way up to the Northeast Kingdom. They had never ridden them on the railroad bed, which linked up to a dozen or more paths, including ones well-maintained for the sugarmakers to check their taps during the winter. They decided they wanted to see where the railroad bed ended, which no one had been able to tell them, so that's why Pat had asked his dad to trailer the sleds into town so they could run it, plus there was a great set of jumps on one of the paths they had heard about and wanted to try them. His dad had never ridden the trails either, so was more than happy to tow them and go out for a spell with Kitty, who sat behind him, too young to ride solo. Even the boys weren't legally old enough to go out without an adult, but they had been riding for a couple of years on their own without incident.

They saw ski and snowshoe tracks, mixed in with footprints that stayed within the flattened track lines. They had no doubt some of those tracks were Truman's, going to the cabin to "clean" it. They stopped at the cabin and Dante waited while Pat put the coin back, as promised.

They went another mile, turned right at the lightning tree Pauly Miller had told them about, the one with the deep black split down the length of it. Soon after they came across the two-foot jumps, the foundations of which were different combinations of tree roots and rocks. There were three jumps separated by fifty feet or so, enough to get air, land, repeat. Pat went first, whooping when he felt the ground drop away beneath him. He finished all three, but the best air was off the first one. Next was Dante, who got no air at all, which was fine by him. He caught up to Pat, who had taken off his helmet and leaned up against his sled with a disappointed look on his face.

"Come on, Strawberry, live a little!"

Dante took off his helmet and laughed. "Whatever. I wasn't born on one of these things like you were."

Pat rolled his eyes. "Let's go a few more times, then see where the end of this path goes. We'll head back after since it's still getting dark early."

By the time they finished their runs, Dante had gotten air on that first jump.

AFTER A FEW MILES, they switched places so Dante could lead for a while. They agreed on twenty more minutes, then they'd turn around. It started to snow, a few flakes at first, but then it started to really come down. Pat lost sight of Dante ahead of him. He expected Dante to stop, being the admitted pussy that he was on a snow machine, so Pat kept going at an even clip so he wouldn't ram into him. Pat didn't see Dante, but saw tracks veer to the left, off the path. He revved his engine three times, their signal to stop, not that it worked every time. Pat turned off his sled to listen for Dante's engine. Silence. He got off and followed the tracks a few feet until his foot slipped over an edge he couldn't see in the falling snow. Looking down, he saw the tracks disappear over that same edge. Dante was nowhere to be seen.

Pat whipped off his helmet and threw it to the side. "Strawberry!" Nothing. "Straw!"

Pat turned sideways and began to clump slide down the steep incline. Following the tracks was easy. Stopping once he started sliding was more difficult and he sought out rocks sticking out to allow him to stop so he wouldn't roll out of control and end up in who knows what condition. After he was down about fifty feet, Pat stopped and called out again in the falling snow. He looked around and all he saw was white dotted with trees plunging out of the snow. A few boulders were large enough that their rough edges made some black-lined contrast. He realized they were in a ravine that was too steep to ride a sled back up, if Dante's sled was even operable.

"Dante!" He slid again until his feet landed on a stump, or rock, or tree root, it was impossible to tell what was under the snow. Snow was jammed up his jacket sleeves and his wrists were starting to burn with cold. He looked below his buried feet and saw red and black; the color of the sled Dante was riding. "Dante! I'm coming!"

Pat slid recklessly the rest of the way. Once he got to

the bottom, he fought through snow that was at least three feet deep. His blond hair was matted with white clumps. He reached the sled and instantly formed a shovel-shape with his thickly gloved hands and began digging. "Dante, where the fuck are you?" Once he cleared enough snow, he saw that the sled was upside down. "Ohfuckohfuckohfuckohfuck."

He dug all the way around. Nothing. He looked up and saw a black shape a short distance away. "Dante!"

Pat lurched through the hip-high snow and began to shovel again. Dante had been thrown clear from the sled and, hopefully, had a soft landing in the thick powder. Dante's body was angled sideways, and his helmet was fogged. Pat was so relieved he began to cry. He got Dante's head onto his lap and pulled off his helmet.

"Dante. Are you okay? Fucking talk to me, man."

Dante groaned. "If you're calling me 'Dante', I must be pretty fucked."

Pat laughed through his tears. "No way man, we're gonna get out of this. Do you hurt anywhere?"

Dante struggled to sit up and moved his limbs. "Ow. Here, my ribs, ah... my shoulder. I think I landed on it."

Dante sat up straighter and looked at Pat. "Wow. *You're* crying?"

Pat took off his snow-crusted glove and wiped his eyes. "Fuck you a lot, you ingrate. You know you should have broken your neck."

Dante looked up at the steep incline through the thickly falling snow and fading light. "Shit, it's getting dark."

Pat shook his head. "That's not the problem, unless we can't get up the ravine. Then I'm going to have to cut open a Ton-Ton and stuff you in it to stay warm."

Dante started to laugh, then put his hand to his side. "Ow, fuck, don't make me laugh, for real."

"What happened, anyway?"

Dante shook his head. The snow started to really come down, so I figured we were going to head back. It looked like there was a wide enough spot to turn the sled around but guess what I didn't see."

"The edge of a steep-ass ravine."

"I was going slow for the turn, you know, so I just started..." Dante shrugged and flinched. "Ow. That hurt... I just started sailing down the slope. I tried to stop, but it was just too steep. I'm not sure what happened — I think I endo'd."

Pat nodded. "Probably." He pushed himself to standing. He shivered. The temperature had dropped considerably. "Shit. Can you lift your arm?"

Dante tried to lift his left arm. "Halfway."

"You go first."

Dante stood and hugged the slope. He lifted his right hand up, digging around for something to grab. He scrabbled his feet up and held himself awkwardly. "Dude, this is hard one-handed."

Pat got himself under Dante's boots. "Stand on my shoulder and get another handhold." That strategy worked for the next two moves and then they both slid back down ten feet. Dante reached farther to the right to get on a new pathway, and they began again.

They made their way up the snow-crusted slope, up some-down some, sometimes sliding backwards enough to lose significant progress. Night fell along with the temperature. After two hours, they rested, clutching snow-buried roots in complete darkness. The temperature had dropped to the point where it was too cold to snow. Pat, who had seen his cousin's fingers after he got frostbite, got them moving again.

They flung themselves onto flat, snowy ground at the top and lay there panting, throats raw with frigid air. They were both sweating and had numb fingers and toes. "We're going to have to armpit it," said Pat. They took off their gloves and unzipped their jackets. Dante knew what that meant. Unzip your jacket and stick your hands in your armpits to warm them up. He had learned that from Bill years ago, back when they were on wooden sleds. He was surprised to see Pat taking off his boots. "What the fuck...?"

"You do it, too. You're not going to like it, but we have to stick our toes into each other's armpits until they warm up a little. Put your gloves behind your head and lay down."

Dante did as he was told and let Pat arrange their bodies on top of the snow.

"Unzip your coat." Both reclined, ass-to-ass, Pats stretched his legs over Dante's body and tucked his thickly socked toes into his armpits. "You've got longer legs, so you go on the outside." Dante complied. "Now stick your hands down your pants and into your crotch."

Dante raised his head. "Wait. What?"

"Trust me. Armpits and crotches are the warmest parts of your body. You wanna get frostbite? Fine, don't do it. First pull your neck gaiter up over your nose. That is not going into anyone's pit or crotch."

Dante did as instructed, then lay back down and stuck his frozen hands into his snow pants, under his long underwear. "If you start beating off, I'm suing."

"In your dreams."

"How long?"

"I don't know. Five minutes? Think about something not sexy."

They laughed and settled into their awkward positions, eyes closed to the snow splashing and melting on the exposed parts of their faces that were still flushed from climbing. Though it would have helped, Pat didn't even try to look for his helmet in the dark.

Dante said, "I'm thinking about the time Jer-Bear blew chunks at your twelfth birthday party because he ate, like, half the cake and drank five cokes."

"That was pretty awesome."

"Yeah, but too gross to think about for too long. Let's name superheroes."

"Incredible Hulk."

"Spiderman."

"I was going to say that first, but knew you wanted it. Superman."

"Wonder Woman."

"Aw, you should have known *I* wanted that one."

After about fifteen superheroes each, they decided they could feel their digits enough to get going. They pulled their wet boots and gloves back on, then climbed onto Pat's sled. He turned over the motor, clicked on the lights and they made their way through the frozen night. Pat accelerated when they got to the wide railroad bed. He almost passed the cabin but stopped. There was a light coming from inside.

They got off the sled and peered in the open window. A sputtering candle burned in a lantern hanging from the ceiling, too low to last much longer. They inhaled — there was the sage, almost all ash, burning on a dish under the lantern. There were wet footprints on the floor. They looked at each other and shrugged. Truman.

As they crossed the threshold from the path to the Rose Garden Apartments, they saw Truman's door closing. They needed to use his phone to call Bill to come get them, and so Pat parked and knocked on his uncle's door. They started to brush the snow off of themselves and each other the best they could.

The door opened. "Hello Patrick."

"Hi Uncle Tru. Okay if I call my dad?"

"Go ahead." Truman stepped back to let them through. Pat and Dante jostled in the doorway while they took their boots off, leaving them on the step outside, walked in and closed the door. The warmth felt so good the stench didn't matter. Pat went into the living room to call home.

Dante stood by the door, took off his gloves and unzipped his jacket. He saw that Truman's boots were wet by the door and he still had his fedora on. Dante could hear the radiator hissing from the next room. He gingerly felt along his left side with his right hand.

Truman stared at him, mumbling under his breath. Dante was used to it and knew to talk to him like he would anybody else. Pat had said that his mom told him that the doctor told her that Truman's mumblings were about the fact that his brain never seemed to shut down, not that he wasn't paying attention. It was soon after that revelation that Pat started to be okay with being around his uncle, once he understood his behavior better.

"Guess what, Truman."

Truman broke off his mumblings, again about the flame and a president. Dante pictured a TV series in Truman's head, rerun after rerun.

"What to what." Truman continued to talk about voting. He sat down. "Sit down. The President is curious."

Truman dug around in the pockets of his lumpy cardigan and pulled out a packet of tobacco and matches. The ritual never failed to mesmerize Dante. Pulling out a paper from the tobacco pouch, Truman shook a pinch of loose tobacco onto the paper and began to tamp and roll it between his fingers, lifting it up to seal it with the flick of his tongue. He lit it and began to smoke. He stroked his beard, which was yellow to the point of almost orange around the mouth, with his other hand. "The Keeper of the Flame brings the fire. Match it and burn it and fire it and scrub it."

"I think I broke a rib."

Truman's expression didn't change. He tapped his cigarette into the ashtray. "Rib to bib, splinter, say now go see Doctor Hendricks."

"I go to Doctor Fletcher."

Pat came back into the kitchen and pulled out the chair next to Truman and sat down. "Thanks, Tru. He'll be here in twenty." Pat looked out the smeary kitchen window that let the light in from the parking lot.

Dante asked. "Is your dad going to freak about the sled?"

Pat shook his head. "Nah, he'll find a way to tow it back up. It might be just fine, really. Hey, Uncle Tru, guess what."

"What to what, now."

Pat pointed his thumb at Dante. "Slick here ran off the edge of a ravine on the sled. Can you believe it?"

Truman's eyes went wide. "Sled? Bed? Doctor Henricks, I say." He closed his eyes. "*Maman*." He shook his head. "The bringer of the flame, when he was a spark. Right here." Truman pointed to his forehead. "Pants Wetter. I wanted Easy Street."

Pat glanced at Dante. Neither of them had a clue what he was talking about, though it seemed to be about the scar he'd always had near his hairline.

Pat decided to just go ahead and ask. "Uh, Uncle Tru? Were you at the cabin tonight?"

Truman took a last inhale and stubbed out his cigarette. He began to pick through the butts and roll them back and forth between his forefinger and thumb so the tobacco remnants fell out of the tiny wrappers and into the ashtray.

"Brunella-Newtella, flame and the rose. Scrub it. Keep it clean."

Dante's eyebrows lifted. "Hey, that's what you said to me all those years ago. That you were going to clean the cabin. Is that why you burn sage there?" Dante swallowed. "Is there a spirit there? Ow!"

Pat had kicked him under the table. "Dude, really?"

Dante shrugged. "Well, why not?"

Pat rolled his eyes. His leg started to jiggle under the table as he looked at Truman. "What can you tell us about the cabin?" He had asked before because he knew his mom wasn't telling him everything, but Truman had only given his "word salad" answers. That was a term his mom had learned recently from Truman's doctor.

They had already heard about the Rose Garden being a former brothel and that the cabin was used by the workers sometimes for sex, but Pat and Dante really wanted to know more about Truman's connection to it. Why the sage? Was it really Truman that had called the cops on them three years ago that first night they went there? What was he protecting?

Truman pulled out another paper and began to roll a new one from the blackened tobacco he had collected in the ashtray. "My brother, Bringer of the Flame, asked me a favor 'for he died. There was a rose." He pointed around the room, possibly indicating the apartment, or the whole building. "The votes were cast, the fire was brought, and she was alone."

Pat and Dante looked at each other.

"This Rose, was that a woman? Was that her name? Was she a... oh Jeezum, can I say it?" He mouthed the words, "a whore?" asked Pat. "I mean, it was a *job*, right?"

Truman went on. "Newtella-Brunella. Specialty of the house. Clemens of the secrets, rose, flower, and thorn."

Pat knew virtually nothing of his uncle Clemens who died long before he was born. Except that there was a fire, the one that got Truman sent to the hospital, and that Clemens was disfigured as a result. And that he was married. Dante and Pat were silent, each trying to decipher the words. Pat asked, "She was special to Clemens? And her name was Brunella?"

"Cast out of the garden, drowning dry. Cough, coffin, cough, coffin. Voters never had a chance, tricksters, every last one. Burn it out, clean the air. Single rose. The garden died. Don't tell Ginny." Ginny. That was the wife's name, Clemens' wife's name.

Truman lit the cigarette. "You don't go there, boys. Don't disturb her. Keep it clean, smoke it out." He rubbed his hip. "Jointer-disappointer. Tough to clean and scrub. Fewer and farther."

Not quite understanding it all, but not sure what else to ask, Pat and Dante passed the rest of the time lighting matches and throwing them into the ashtray for points. Truman didn't seem to mind, even though more than half landed on the kitchen table and left a speck of brown.

There was a knock on the door, startling all of them.

Bill Bates opened it without waiting for an answer. "Hi Tru. Boys." He nodded at Dante. "You alright?"

"I think so. I'm sorry, really. I can pay to fix it and stuff."

"Ahhh, don't sweat it." There was a noise behind him. Candice poked her head around Bill. Keeping a hand on Bill's shoulder, she pulled off her boots with her free hand and walked in.

Bill gave a salute. "Tru, I'm going to shovel you out." And with that, he closed the door.

Candice pursed her lips at the closed door. She pulled out the last chair, placed her tote bag onto the floor, and sat down next to Dante. "I'd prefer he didn't. I mean Truman, have you renewed your license lately? What about insurance?"

Truman coughed in response. "The President takes care of the votes."

Candice shook her head. "Well, we'll get the call someday. Anyway, how are you two? I didn't get too much info except that one of the sleds needs a tow?"

Pat smiled. "Wow, dad didn't tell you sh-, uh, anything."

Candice unzipped her coat. "Well? You two look okay, unless...?"

"Well, Strawberry?"

Dante cleared his throat. "I, uh, kind of launched it, the sled I mean, and, uh, me, over the edge of a, um, ravine."

Candice turned to face Dante. "A ravine? And you're fine? Mercy, you must have angels on your side."

"Well, mostly fine. My ribs feel a bit banged up."

"Let's have a look."

Dante took off his jacket and lifted up his sweater,

along with the long john shirt underneath it. Pat and Truman leaned over in tandem to have a close look. Dante tried not to laugh. Big Flame and Little Buck, together again. He suddenly got a jonesing to crawl into bed and read comics.

Candice sucked in air through her teeth at the bruising. "Did you call your mom yet?"

Dante shook his head. "I can just walk from here."

"Well, I want to take you so we can all talk about what happened. So it won't happen again."

Pat said, "Mom, before we go, can you help with some things Truman is saying? Like 'Doctor Hendricks' and uh," he glanced at Dante, "'Pants Wetter'?"

Candice shrugged. "You know, it's funny I didn't know Truman at all growing up and now, I am his interpreter. Anyway, if he is talking about Pants Wetter, it must be because you two just had an accident on a sled, although a very different sled. Anyway, way before I was born, Clemens and Truman were sledding next to the elementary school and from what I know, Clemens ran over Truman with the sled. By accident, of course, and they were on the Pants Wetter trail."

She got blank looks from the boys. Truman said, "I wanted Easy Street. The spark and the Pants Wetter, together forever."

"I guess no one calls it that anymore. The steep sledding trails, you know, next to the school. There's one that's steep and the other is nearly vertical?"

Pat and Dante simultaneously said, "Ooooh." Pat said, "The A-bomb and Stayin' Alive."

Candice laughed. "Well, every generation has its time."

Dante turned a little red. "Brunella?"

"Brunella-Newtella. Rose of the garden." Candice reached out and put her hand on Truman's.

"I always wondered if you knew, Truman. It all happened while you were, uh, getting well."

Candice sighed. "I guess you're old enough. The story was that she was Clemens', um, paramour, for lack of a better phrase. I actually saw her, once. I was in the car with Clemens, Ginny, before they were married, and Felicity. They were taking us to get dresses for the Maypole Festival. We were driving by here and there was a woman standing outside." She turned and pointed. "Right out there. She was wearing a delicate looking, antique rose-colored dress. Clemens nearly ran off the road staring at her. I remember Ginny laughing and saying, "Gee, honey, you wanna stop by right now?" Candice looked at Truman. "Clemens must have told you. She was real special to him, I think even after he was married." She put her hands up into the air, opaque from Truman's cigarette's. "Don't know what happened to her."

"Cast out of the garden, drowning dry. Cough, coffin, cough, coffin."

Candice thought it out. "TB! Tuberculosis. So many people got it in those days."

Bill popped the door open, letting in a whoosh of frigid night, which had started up again. "Alrighty, let's get going. That tuna casserole isn't going to eat itself.

Oh! That reminds me." Candice reached down into the tote bag and pulled out a small casserole dish covered in plastic wrap. "Here's some for you, Truman. It's warmish, but give it a few minutes at three-fifty, should you need it." She placed it on the table.

They said goodbye to Truman, Candice giving him a peck on his whiskered cheek. They went outside and saw that Bill had already loaded the snow machine onto the trailer. Getting into the Bates' truck, Candice explained to Bill why they had to stop at the Zuckerman's first.

Brunella would not be mentioned again until the cabin was visited for the last time, over three years later. That last time, it was Big Flame that cleaned and scrubbed it for good. By that time, Pat was no longer Pat. He had become Little Buck.

DANTE, though distracted by talking about the sled disaster, was still shaken by Pat's hallucination, or whatever it was, and was caught off guard by what happened next. Pat clicked on a light, punched him lightly on the arm, and said, "Sorry I suck these days. I wish I knew what the fuck was wrong with me."

He had promised Candice, and this seemed like his chance. "Where do you go, you know, when you're supposed to be at school?"

Pat got quiet. Dante waited. "I come home."

"That's it?"

Dante followed his gaze as Pat turned toward the window again. "Pretty much."

Dante knew now that wasn't the whole story. Not after what he witnessed just then. He didn't know how he was going to break it to Candice that Pat was seeing things, feeling fear. They had covered that in psych class and he had been able to put a name to what Truman had, what the Bates had never named, not even Pat. Maybe he never knew — Uncle Tru had always just been what he was. The condition was schizophrenia. A disorder characterized by delusions and paranoia, and other stuff he couldn't remember. It tended to run in families.

Dante suddenly pictured Pat that first day at Hopefield Elementary, all three-foot-nine of him pulling Dante up from the muddy snow after knocking him down, then flinging his arm around his neck.

"Let's be best friends."

The echo of that small voice created tears that filled Dante's eyes and rolled down his cheeks. Pat looked over at him with smirk. "Don't cry. It'll make your mascara run."

Dante smiled as he wiped his tears. "Fuck you very much, Pat Bates."

10

1931: COMMITTED

Henry and Emeline Bates were taken into an airy office with large windows. The showpiece of the room was the gleaming mahogany desk, behind which sat the supervisor of the Vermont State Asylum, Dr. Stanley, in a rolling black leather chair. The Bates were seated in the smaller, upholstered chairs for guests. One wall housed shelves of intricately bound books, the thickest of which was *American Medical Association's Standard Classified Nomenclature of Disease*, in addition to numerous volumes of *American Journal of Psychiatry*, *The Journal of Nervous and Mental Disease*, *Journal for the Healing and Diagnosis of Pathological Mental Disorders*.

Emeline ogled the stately office, wondering just how much had changed since *tante Clemence* was taken away all those years ago. While she wore her town dress for her trips to see Clemens at the Central Vermont Hospital burn unit, for this visit, she wore her Sunday best. She expected to be greeted by scowling, uniformed officers, but instead her hand was warmly grasped by Supervisor Stanley after they were ushered into his office in the administrative wing of the asylum. Both she and Henry were offered glasses of water, which they both refused. Emeline now wished she hadn't — the steamy heat of the radiator was making her perspire, but she didn't dare take off her wool hat for fear of making a bad impression. The large window behind Dr. Stanley had no bars and she could see men doing nurse-led exercises in a large green quad. The grounds were edged with bursting fall colors of early October maples that nearly hid the chain link fence that lined the trees. From what she could see driving up, *l'installation* was much, much larger than she could have imagined, able to hold three times the population of Hopefield. She was expecting an imposing prison facility, not this Victorian-styled multi-building campus with trees and grass.

It was the police who brought Truman to the asylum and the Bates had not been allowed to visit before now, leaving Emeline's imagination to run rampant with images of her son in a straitjacket, surrounded by screaming lunatics and brutal guards. Though Truman had not caused any sort of serious problems in town, other than making other residents uncomfortable with his mutterings and odd gaze, the police knew Truman well enough. As it was, Truman was only brought to town to see Dr. Hendricks, who was getting too old for house calls. Dr. Hendricks had been recommending that Truman be brought to the asylum for months, ever since the spirits appeared and it was clear he was not simply suffering from the temporary *ennui* of teenagers, coupled with the long winters and economic hard times.

Emeline started to feel dizzy and stared at the floor, while Henry looked directly at Dr. Stanley, who was explaining about Truman, who, as they must understand, is a patient committed by the state of Vermont and as such, is required to follow all rules and treatments without question.

Dr. Stanley pushed his fingertips together. "We had to first determine if your son is truly a danger to himself or others. For example, did he intentionally start that fire? Was he trying to hurt anyone?" He leaned forward. "As I understand it, your other son was burned quite badly."

Emeline closed her eyes at the mention of Clemens. Every bandage change was a brutal exercise, his eyes revealed the agony of raw nerve endings touching the air, despite the large amounts of morphine administered. His ruined mouth and his slurred words. *Dieu Merci* for Ginny. She was Clemens' angel of mercy in Emeline's eyes.

Henry passed a meaty hand down his face. He was in his wool Sunday suit and was about to sweat through it. Henry wanted no part of any of this. It had been two weeks of explaining what had happened, town folks asking after Clemens, awkward silences when no one asked after Truman. Henry had already been missing too many days at work, not getting paid, running up credit. The humiliation of his son nearly burning down the town and almost killing his own brother made it difficult to go out in public, like he had a choice. Clemens, his firstborn — half of his face melted off, his left arm useless, lungs scorched. How was he expected to forgive this foul-mouthed Truman of late, who only took up space on that porch rocker and caused trouble for Emeline. He thought of the precious gas it took to drive all the way to Waterbury and back and it made his stomach clench.

"Yes, Doctor. Our Clemens is in a bad way," Henry replied. "He'll never be one hundred percent, but he'll be okay." Henry hoped he made it sound like that part of this mess, at least, was under control.

Dr. Stanley gently placed his hands, fingers spread open, upon his desk. "We observed, for lack of a better term, multiple markings on Truman's back. Can you account for this?"

Henry glanced at Emeline, who continued to look out the window. Henry knew this was his to tell. "Back when this all started, you have to understand, we thought it was insolence of some kind. We... *I*, thought it could be whipped out of him." Henry was anxious to take his wife's hand at that moment, but her hands had turned to white-knuckled fists in her lap. "I am truly regretful."

Dr. Stanley shook his head, though whether in sympathy or admonition was hard to discern. "I know it's difficult, but you need to realize that it wasn't *Truman* who committed this grave action, it was his *insanity*."

Emeline audibly moaned to hear it stated so plainly. Henry reached over and laid his hand on her arm. Dr. Stanley pushed a button and a voice responded. "Two waters, please."

"So, it's true, Doctor, Truman is crazy. It's not the Devil," Henry said. Dr. Stanley's secretary carried in two waters and placed them on the table between Emeline and Henry. After a moment, Emeline drank some.

"Crazy is not a word we use here, but rest assured what has happened to your son, as disturbing as it is, is nature at work, not the Devil. We have diagnosed him with dementia praecox, or in more recent journals, schizo-phrenia. Do you know what that means?"

Henry shrugged. "I only know what I see and hear, which isn't normal by any stretch of the imagination. I can't even let him sit at the table with the girls for fear of his shameful acts and words."

Dr. Stanley nodded. "Let me break it down. One behavior is hallucinating, for example seeing a person or an object that no one else sees. Or having delusions — paranoia — thinking that someone is 'out to get them', so to speak. Emotions are blunted. Perhaps you've noticed he isn't able to give or receive affection easily anymore?"

Emeline put her glass back on the table. This *docteur* seemed to want to help, so she shoved her shame aside. "He talks to President Coolidge, Doctor. And he has a dirty girl who makes him say things *vulgare*. He will not bathe himself." She wiped her eyes with her handkerchief. The one Truman gave to her himself for her birthday, soon after he earned his first paycheck from the quarry, the last handkerchief she had left that hadn't been twisted into shreds.

Henry took her hand. He knew how hard all of this was for her.

Dr. Stanley nodded vigorously, as if this was what he was expecting to hear. "Now, you should also know that we have determined from the police report, plus an interview with Truman, that he is not *criminally* insane, which determines which ward he is placed into. It also helps that no charges were pressed."

Mr. Thompson's decision not to prosecute was another reason to be grateful. Enough to have a lunatic in the family, much less a criminal. The inventory of the tobacco shop and haberdashery was covered by insurance, but not the building, which was in the middle of owner transfer. Henry agreed to hire a couple of quarry workers to rebuild the store and in return, no charges would be filed. Though barter arrangements were common around

Hopefield, Thompson was being generous to a fault, in Henry's mind, and he was beyond grateful. But hospitals don't barter and how he was going to cover Clemens' bills, plus the cost to rebuild the store, on top of the loss of yet another paycheck was beyond Henry.

"Doctor, I have to ask." Henry was surprised by the crack in his voice. Emeline visibly tensed. "What will the bill be for Truman's, uh, stay here?"

"I can assure you, Mr. and Mrs. Bates, that Truman is now in the state of Vermont's care. As such, the patients here are provided for through state funding and private endowments."

Henry could breathe again. God didn't give more than one could handle, that is what Pastor Anderson assured him. Having Truman here and cared for will be one less mouth to feed and that was a reason to be grateful.

"Now, times being what they are, our spending per patient has shrunk by sixty percent, yet our population grows, what with so many residual mental health issues as a result of our current climate. Plus... do you know what eugenics is?"

Henry and Emeline looked at each other. "No, can't say we do," replied Henry.

"Simply put, there is a movement to ensure the strongest Americans thrive and...provide a solid foundation for generations to come. So, there has been an increased interest in separating and caring for those that don't, how should I put it, fit in easily with mainstream society. It's a healthier choice for all, is the thinking, and I have to say I agree. There is government funding for that cause, though that said, donations of any amount are greatly appreciated and not a penny will be wasted."

The request for money was the only clear thing

Emeline understood about eugenics. She said, "Of course, we will give what we can. I will increase the baking and I am sure—" Henry squeezed her hand. Emeline stopped. "I'm sorry. It's just... we will do what we can."

"Thank you, Mrs. Bates. That is most generous. Now, back to your son. He will receive a lot of fresh air on our beautiful grounds, as well as multiple therapies. Please, can you tell me how long he's been showing symptoms of schizophrenia?"

For Henry, the room went blurry with sudden tears. He had been so *angry* at Truman. So betrayed. Now it suddenly felt different — like his boy had been stolen. The idea that all this wasn't Truman's fault, he needed some time to sit with that.

Henry pulled a handkerchief from his suit coat pocket and dabbed his eyes. "I'm sorry."

Dr. Stanley spoke softly, "There is no shame in it. This is overwhelming for anyone."

Henry sniffed and looked at Emeline. "What do you think, Emmy? Two years?"

Emeline seemed unable to speak, so only nodded.

Dr. Stanley sighed. "I wish you had brought him in sooner. You see, most psychotic breaks of this nature happen in early adulthood. Had he been brought in within a year of showing symptoms of this disease, the latest therapies would be most promising. On the other hand, being so young, he is, in no uncertain terms, an excellent candidate for recovery. And let me reassure you — this is the most ill, with the absolute worst symptoms, you will ever see in your son."

Emeline felt the tiniest glimmer of hope. Dr. Stanley went on. "To control agitation, we use hydrotherapy — the patient will be immersed in a tub of hot water, maximum ninety-four degrees, the temperature of which is strictly monitored, as are the patient's vitals. This can last for hours, sometimes days, with food and drink brought in. But the most promising therapy is brand new, from Vienna — insulin shock therapy."

Both Henry's and Emeline's eyes grew wide.

"No, no, not to worry — it is a simple injection. Given every day of the week over a number of weeks has shown remarkable results by restoring homeostasis in the cells through physiological shock, which prompts the nerve cells' defense mechanisms to engage, thus restoring balance in the autonomic nervous system." Dr. Stanley stood up and carried some papers with him around the desk. He handed each a copy. "Now, for insulin therapy, we do need family consent. If you could read it over and sign, we can begin treatment after some weeks of observation to ensure he is a viable candidate."

While neither of the Bates could fully digest the medical explanation, nor everything they read in the document, Emeline did come up with one conclusion, the only medical conclusion she needed confirmed. So, *docteur*, "*Est curable, oui?*"

Dr. Stanley leaned back and sighed. Giving a quick shake of his head, he continued, "As for curable, well, I like to think that it will be someday, but what we do know is that Truman has an excellent chance of getting back to a restored state where he can rejoin society."

Henry stroked his chin, freshly shaved for this meeting. "Is he considered a prisoner?"

Dr. Stanley replied quickly, "Absolutely not. That said, he is obviously not able to function in society, so he is what we call committed. This means that while he cannot leave without our say so, he's no criminal. What your son is, Mr. Bates, is ill."

Dr. Stanley buzzed his secretary. "The Bates are ready to visit now."

The secretary entered and following her lead, the Bates took their long wool coats from the coat rack and put them on. Henry picked up the suitcase of Truman's clothes they were told to bring and lugged it to the door that led to the quad. They were slapped by a bracing wind as the door was opened for them. The secretary, whose name neither of them would be able to recall later, explained to them that they were going to the Brooks Ward, where the majority of patients resided in large dormitories, seventy-five beds to a room. While they would not be permitted to see the sleeping facilities or any other part of the hospital, she went on, they were permitted to visit any day during visiting hours, as long as Truman was not receiving medical therapies. They stood outside a locked door. This building was more of what Emeline expected — thick granite foundation, charmless sandstone-brick, bars on the windows, painted white to match the sills.

After a brief explanation from the secretary, the Bates were handed over to an orderly, who welcomed them into a lobby, furnished with tall potted plants and the same chairs as in Dr. Stanley's office. There was a locked door on the far side with a window and bars. She appreciated the plants, the landscapes on the walls. Emeline started to overheat again in the room and started to remove her coat. She assumed they would wait here for Truman to appear, as they were told they would not be permitted onto the ward.

Instead, the orderly announced, "Now, you come with

me, and I'll take you to the visitor's room." Emeline pulled her coat back on with some embarrassment. The orderly picked up the suitcase and led them through the locked door, after which they faced a wall made of bars through which they could see a hallway lined with doors. There was activity at the far end, what looked like a lineup of patients being brought from one place to another. Some talking, a laugh, and a deep man's voice could be heard. None of the screaming Emeline had feared.

Untangling his keys with expert efficiency, the orderly unlocked the door to their right and brought them into a narrow, cheerless room with scuffed walls and three plain wooden chairs. There was a scratched wooden counter attached to the far wall.

"Excuse me." The orderly went back out to the vestibule, followed by a jangle of keys and the clank of another metal door sliding open and closed. He had taken the suitcase with him. They suffered through twenty minutes of worried silence, mixed with the anxiety of seeing Truman again. The tension was broken occasionally by Henry patting Emeline's hand and murmuring, "It's gonna be alright, Emmy'" and some comments on how the place didn't seem so bad.

They finally heard the now recognizable sound of the heavy metal door that led to the ward. The orderly then opened the door to their visiting room and ushered Truman in. The orderly politely exited as he left them with the assurance that he'd be right outside the door. In fact, they could see him through the window. Their twenty-year-old son's long, greasy hair had been cut short and his face freshly shaved. Emeline started to cry at the sight of how young and vulnerable Truman looked.

Henry watched as Truman stood and muttered under

his breath to whom Henry had, until now, considered "Truman's demons." The phrases seemed to repeat. *Mr. President. The flame. Burn it down. See it safe.*

Truman turned slightly to look at their chins with a slight smile on his face, but there was nothing to indicate that he even knew who they were. He let himself be hugged by his mother. When she let go, his smile was bigger and amidst the muttering, Henry and Emeline both heard the word, *Maman.* Emeline, now smiling herself, her first smile in two weeks, sat down and indicated they all do the same.

Emeline spoke first, "Truman, Dr. Stanley says that you are *un candidat* ..." she trailed off, not remembering the word in English.

"Candidate," said Henry. "A candidate for recovery. Because you're so young." He looked at Truman, not knowing what that information meant to him. Henry almost apologized for them not bringing him here earlier after hearing what the doctor had said about earlier was better but didn't. He still wasn't convinced that the Devil didn't have a hand in this mess.

Truman asked clearly, "Where's Clemens?" He went back to his cyclical mutterings.

Henry looked at the ceiling and asked himself how many times today his eyes are going to betray him. He grabbed his handkerchief and wiped his eyes while Emeline answered.

"Clemens has been badly burned, *mon ange*, but he will recover. He asks about you. He is so worried. I will tell him how well you look. Do you... do you remember what happened?"

Truman interrupted his murmurings to speak to them directly. "Clemens became the flame. He sees it safe."

Emeline, hoping she understood, replied, "Yes, Truman, Clemens was burned, but now he is safe." *And, she hoped, so are you.*

LATER THAT NIGHT, much later, after their other children were in bed, Emeline shared with Henry an unexpected feeling she felt upon leaving the hospital. It was the helplessness of leaving Truman behind, knowing they couldn't take him home whenever they wanted. Henry had to admit it was a disquieting feeling to relinquish his own flesh and blood like that. Henry Bates, who had always been a big man, in both stature and reputation, felt like everything he had worked for was slipping away, like slate chips skittering down a slag pile with nothing to catch them until they hit bottom.

11

———

1984: THE HUNTING TRIP

The week following Dante's witnessing of Pat's hallucination, no one heard from or saw Pat unless they entered his dark bedroom. Aside from his mental health, it was looking likely that not only would Pat miss the senior trip due to his high number of absences, but that he wouldn't graduate on time, either. Dr Garcia said that if he continued this behavior, he'd recommend Pat go to a private treatment center that specialized in depression in Brattleboro, three hours south. Candice pleaded with Pat to come out. The Brattleboro Retreat was not the state hospital, but it was too far away for her liking.

Dante was the one who got Pat out of his room, finally. He'd been asking Pat to get out on the snow machines all winter, but Pat had just told him to go alone, or ask the other guys, but Dante refused.

The heaviness Pat had been feeling was worse than ever — he felt pinned down, forcing himself to get out of bed for school, until the effort proved too much. And too pointless. Those few counseling sessions he had had at school were a joke — the counselor having him point at charts about feelings and create lists of positive things in his life. At least his father had stopped yelling at him to get his ass in gear. His family seemed to enter a quiet acceptance. But now his mom was losing it, crying and shit. What did it all matter? Who cared if he went to school? Pat didn't know what it was that changed that day when Dante finally convinced him; all he knew was on that day, the pale white light of snow reflected under the gray skies didn't feel so oppressive.

Plus, the buck was gone and had been for two days prior. It had improved Pat's mood considerably. Only Dante could have pulled it off, gotten Pat out of bed on that particular day and onto a sled. Candice was worried about him driving, but Bill was so thrilled to see Pat do something, anything, he gave it the green light.

Bill clapped Dante on the shoulder. "If for any reason you feel Pat can't handle it, you stop right there and get him on your sled and you come back. No jumps, nothing over twenty-five miles per hour, even on the straight-aways." Bill looked at Pat. "Dante's call, right, Pat? And I want you boys back here in an hour." Pat nodded in agreement.

The day was no different than any early spring day — low gray clouds, cold, snow everywhere. Pat suddenly craved to hear the sound of the engines, smell the fuel, see the exhaust billowing into the air. He wanted to feel the power and speed, the ups and downs, curves of the well-worn paths through his woods. He was fully awake for the first time in weeks.

Pat saw the excited look on Dante's face when he realized that it was actually going to happen, and he had to turn away. He felt bad because he hadn't been missing

Dante, or the boys, or any girls — he hadn't been feeling anything. He didn't know why Dante even came over anymore. Pat didn't ask him to be there. Most of the time he didn't really care if Dante was there or not. But today... today he loved his friend, the woods, the snow on the barn roof.

They crossed the driveway in their snow gear. Their snow pants made the distinctive whisking sound with each step. Pat pulled open the rumbling barn door and the sleds sat there as if waiting for this very moment. Pat checked the oil and the fuel — they hadn't been ridden yet this year — and everything looked okay. They fired them up and Pat rolled out first, leading the way to the miles of trails behind his house.

They cruised single file, taking it easy, Dante in the lead. He kept the agreed upon pace along the tight turns and sloping curves. They ducked under snow-heavy branches, engines buzzing. They stopped when they came to Route 2. Pat pulled up beside Dante and looked over at him.

Pat said, "Snotsicle, six o'clock."

Dante wiped his nose with his sleeve. Pat's sleeve, since he was wearing his old coat, and took a look at the smeared results. "Oh man, sorry."

Pat shook his head and laughed.

Dante looked at him, but Pat couldn't read his expression under all the gear. "That's the first time I've heard you laugh in weeks, Pat Bates."

Pat said, "Well, it's easy to laugh at a loser like you, Schnante." Dante could hear the smile under his face shield.

Dante grinned, too. "Dude, that better not be my new permanent nickname."

Pat said, "Hold up for a sec. I gotta armpit it." They both took off their gloves and unzipping their coats halfway, crossed their arms and tucked their bare hands up into their armpits.

Dante laughed. "As long as it's my own armpits. Don't forget the ravine. And next time let's remember those hot hand packets."

What Dante couldn't know was that this would be the last time Pat ever rode a snow machine.

~

As ALWAYS, armpitting it and mentioning the packets brought Pat's father to Dante's mind.

"Dude, whenever I do this, I think of your dad. Who, I am convinced, will always think I'm a bit of a douchebag."

Pat laughed. He remembered the first time Dante stepped into the Bates' living room when they were nine, he stopped dead and the color drained out of his face, prompting Pat to elbow him. Dante's eyes were glued to the large, antlered buck head mounted above the fireplace. His mouth open, all he could manage was a small sound.

Candice caught on right away. "Oh, don't worry about ol' Bucky, there. Bill bagged him years ago. Most points on a buck he's bagged yet! He can't hurt you."

"W-w-w-here's the rest of him?" asked Dante.

Bill had a restrained smirk on his face. "Go ahead, look on the other side." Dante walked through the doorway and walked into what was the master bedroom on the other side. Pat couldn't help it. He burst out laughing. Dante came back around looking bewildered. Pat held his stomach he was laughing so hard. Dante will never forget the look Mrs. Bates gave him, a mix of amusement and bewilderment. Her voice was soft when she asked, "Is this the first dead animal you've seen?"

Dante nodded his head and swallowed.

She put her hands up. "Well, if we're gonna eat 'em, we should know what they look like when they're dead." She walked into the kitchen before Dante could tell her he had never eaten an animal. It would be years until he was able to walk through the living room without his skin crawling. He never did get an honest answer to his question. It wasn't until they ate dinner after the hunting trip that he found out.

When Bill learned early on that Dante didn't eat meat — during that first sleepover in third grade when Dante wouldn't eat chicken casserole — he started bringing jokes home from the quarry. "*Sure, I'm on a vegetarian diet. I only eat vegetarians.*" The next sleepover, Bill snuck a carrot onto the table next to where Dante sat and said nothing about it. Just let it sit there. Pat thought it was funny. Kitty tittered, but kept her eyes down, perhaps embarrassed for Dante, or maybe about her father. That first time, Dante just looked confused, until Candice said, "Oh Bill. What are you doing? Give me that." She took the carrot back into the kitchen. Bill winked at Dante and said, "Thought you'd like it for dessert."

He did it the next time, but Dante wouldn't let Candice take the carrot and ate it before the meal. He winked at Bill and said, "Makes a better appetizer than dessert."

Bill laughed hard. "Good one, son." Pat never told Dante, but he felt a twinge of jealousy. He had never joked on an equal level like that with his father. Bill never laid out the carrot again.

Candice went on about how she admired the commitment people with special diets have — she could never stick to it, she said. From then on, she always made sure the family had pasta or pizza, plus salad, the nights he came over — meatballs on the side or an extra plain cheese pizza. She told Pat she liked Dante above all his other friends. Pat didn't know if his father knew Dante was Jewish or not, or what he would think of that. Pat's instinct told him to keep that under wraps, or who knows what the jokes would turn into. Besides, Pat didn't want to give his dad reason to pay more attention to Dante than he already did.

Pat had been so excited to finally go hunting with his father. His dad didn't feel he was ready enough in fourth grade for any of the gun seasons, but bow season was different. Plus, Pat was to just tag along and shoot a bow for practice. His father preferred bow season anyway — he liked the ancient tradition of the bow and arrow, the dignity of it. Plus, it was better for the balance of nature — after dressing a deer, whether in the field or back behind the barn, the carcass was left for the scavengers. Lead shot poisoned the blood and therefore poisoned the animals that picked the bones.

Pat figured that Dante thought his dad hated animals, which is why he hunted, but that wasn't it at all. Pat knew that his father revered the cycle of nature, which is why he thought not eating meat was not just stupid, but disrespectful. It upset the balance — God had created humans with the ability, and perhaps purpose, to digest meat; therefore, we were meant to eat it and participate in His plan.

~

IT TOOK until fifth grade to convince Dante to go hunting with them. Well, trick him into it was more like it. They had a sleepover on a Friday night, so Dante brought all of his sleepover stuff to school and then with him onto the bus, Pat helped him by carrying his sleeping bag. Bill told Pat he was looking forward to Dante coming along — to see how beautiful and natural hunting can be. And to toughen him up a little bit. Pat and his dad decided to keep it a secret since they hadn't been able to get Dante to willingly come along yet. Knowing how early they would need to get up, Pat pretended to fall asleep early so Dante would go to sleep early, too. Bill crept in quietly in the dark of 4:00 AM and woke Pat, who, in the dark, got dressed into his long johns and camo gear that he got for Christmas and his safety orange hat. There was one of those for Dante, too, who was woken up soon after. Bill stage-whispered, not wanting to wake the others, "Get ready for a big day, boys." He said no more.

In the darkness, Dante didn't see what Pat was wearing, only his orange hat that he had worn almost every day since Christmas. Dante yawned. "We're going outside?"

Pat replied, "Yeah, put your snow pants and jacket and stuff on." Dante groggily did as he was told. "What time is it?" No one answered.

They entered the kitchen, which had the only light on in the house and both Pat and Dante blinked against the brightness. The air smelled of eggs and bacon. Bill served them all a plate, bacon on his and Pat's plates only. Pat saw Dante register what everyone was wearing. "Wait, where are we going?"

Bill shoved some eggs toward him. "Just out back. It sure is a special time to be in the woods, at dawn."

Dante looked at the inky black beyond the frilly-curtained window above the sink. "Looks like the middle of the night."

"Eat up, boys. Gonna need your energy. We've gotta walk a bit." Pat did as instructed, but Dante only managed to eat half.

Bill saw it and said, "You're going to regret leaving that much when you get hungry in about an hour."

Dante shrugged. "My stomach won't wake up."

Bill smiled. "It's alright, just no whining about being hungry. Or cold."

Dante looked over at the door and saw two sets of archery equipment leaning up against the wall. He felt a drop in his stomach, which felt like he had swallowed a rock. They went out the kitchen door into the frigid morning air where Bill had a target set up behind the house. He named all of the pieces of equipment for Dante, who silently nodded at each one to show he understood. Bill showed Dante how to arm the bow, pull back his arm holding the string, fingers by his chin, and let go. Pat started firing arrows right away in the weak light, the first few either dropping or not flying far, but then he started hitting the target, or close to it. All of Dante's dropped or landed in the dirt. Pat told him not to feel bad, that only after a lot of practice had he started hitting the target.

They walked for about a mile into the woods behind the Bates' house, orange hats bobbing. Bill was talkative at first, puffing out steam as he told them about how he used to hunt these woods and how he had first met Candice. It was when he and his brother walked by the house tracking a deer. Candice had been outside getting wood from the stack on the porch and Bill asked if it was okay if they passed through. She offered them coffee, which they readily accepted and the three of them drank steaming mugs on the porch. He came back the next day and asked her out. They of course knew each other from school, even had the same last name, which Bill's friends joked about to no end. "Hey Bill, they're having a beauty contest in Barre. Why don't you *enter* your sister?" Bill was so lost in the story he forgot his audience. "Sorry boys. Inappropriate."

Pat and Dante looked at each other to see if the other one got it. They just shook their heads, not getting the joke. Bill went on, saying he had to grin and bear the teasing or be considered a whiner forever. They did the blood test, which a lot of people did back then, which proved there was no close relation, to their great relief. Candice said what a miracle it was she didn't have to go through all the hassle of changing her name all over town when they married.

Bill was obviously energized by having the boys there that frosty October morning. He had chosen today because it was the annual youth weekend. Any youth who had taken a hunting safety course can hunt this weekend, three weeks before the regular season, and can take a deer of either sex, no antler restriction. Bill went on explaining other hunting regulations and seasons, and Pat wondered how much Dante was listening. They followed the well-established trails, which made walking easier, but walking a long time in boots was wearing Dante out and he began to lag behind.

"I'm tired. When are we going to stop?"

Bill said without turning around, "We'll stop when we get there."

Pat spun around and put his hands up in an "oh well, that's the way it is" gesture.

"My hands are numb," said Dante. Pat's were, too, but he didn't want to say anything.

Bill stopped and dug in his bag. "Here you go and for you, too Pat. It was best to wait so they don't wear out when we're sitting." He handed them each a paper packet that started to heat up when rubbed. They put one in each glove and immediately felt the heat. "If you don't have these handy, go ahead and put your hands under your armpits. It's the warmest part of your body."

"Ahh," said Pat as he stuffed the hand-warming packet into his gloves. "That's the stuff."

Dante, humor returned a bit with the warmth, laughed and gave him a quick punch on the arm. Pat returned the punch, and they began to shove each other and giggle.

"Cut it out, now." They did as they were told but made faces at each other for the next five minutes as they continued walking.

A few minutes later, Bill said, "Okay, boys. Now Pat, you know the routine. We gotta be quiet from here on out." They walked in silence for ten minutes, breath visible in white puffs. Bill turned left into the woods at a bright orange ribbon tied around the tree and led them far off the path, where they followed about five more ribbons.

"There it is," Bill whispered. Bill dropped his gear and taking his bow and quiver of arrows, he climbed the wooden boards nailed into the tree in front of them. The boys looked up at the small platform, big enough for one.

"What's that?" whispered Dante.

"Deer stand," Pat whispered back.

"Pat," Bill said in as quiet a voice as possible, "Go and

see if the corn I put out two days ago is still there and if any of it is eaten."

Pat walked about twenty-five feet away from the deer stand, turned and came back. "It's been nibbled on," he loudly whispered up the tree.

"I'm hungry," said Dante.

"Quit that yapping," Bill whispered loudly, as he armed his bow with an arrow with a bright yellow tail. Pat glared at Dante and put a gloved finger up to his mouth in the "be quiet" gesture. Dante started to stamp his feet, which were quickly growing cold now that they stopped walking. Pat grabbed him by the arm and shook his head, indicating he needed to stop. Dante slumped down, his back against the tree, arms crossed, breath exploding in defiant puffs of white. Pat turned in the opposite direction that his father was looking and stood stoically, keeping his eyes peeled under his orange hat for any movement. He loved being out here with his dad, doing such a grownup thing, an important thing. His family would eat any deer they shot throughout the winter — venison steaks, sausages, and stews. He often thought Dante didn't know what he was missing. When he said that to him once, Dante agreed.

"You're right, I don't, so what's the big deal?"

After forty-five minutes of hunching and waiting, Bill stood up from his squatted position and stretched. He came down the tree and tapped on Pat's shoulder and pointed up. Pat went up with his gear and Bill took over his ground watch, turned away from both Pat and Dante while he searched for movement. Dante closed his eyes.

Pat saw movement by the opened sack of corn. He looked down at his dad to make sure he was watching, which he was. Pat leveled his arrow at the doe, aiming for her side up near her shoulder blade. He heard a terrible scream below him as he let the arrow fly. He looked down and Dante was gasping for air, his eyes unfocused and wild.

Pat turned back around and he saw that he had missed the doe, but hit a buck behind her, which he hadn't even seen — it probably stepped into view as the arrow flew. The doe sprung away. The buck, barely grazed by the arrow, and apparently not knowing from which direction it had come from, ran straight toward them. Pat loaded another arrow but was too scared to shoot it for fear of hitting his father. Bill already had an arrow cocked from his ground position and let it fly as the buck came straight for him. He got him right in the chest, but then was trampled flat by the terrified and injured animal, a hoof digging into his right shoulder.

He lay there groaning, unable to get up. Pat, dropping his gear, bolted down the ladder. "Dad. Dad! Are you okay? What should I do?" His voice screeched with panic.

Bill had the wind knocked out of him and couldn't speak. Dante stood behind Pat, his eyes wide with shock. He couldn't believe his nightmare had come true.

WHEN BILL finally caught his breath, he told the boys he was okay and to go back to the house and tell Candice what happened. Pat looked at Dante, "You go. Follow the ribbons back to the main path, turn right and it takes you straight home."

"I don't want to go alone."

"I can't leave him!"

"Take my hand, Pat." Pat put his hand out and Bill

grabbed it roughly, using Pat's counterbalance to sit up. He scooted himself backward to lean against the tree. He looked shaken and in a lot of pain. "You boys both go. I'll be fine. Probably can even walk before too long, but it's best if I take my time."

Pat left him his canteen and together the boys started running back along the narrow trail. Dante wore out by the time they reached the main trail and Pat kept going without checking if Dante was there or not. Pat raced into the house, breathing so hard he could hardly get the words out. Candice tripped on a chair on the way to the phone, but caught herself and called their neighbor and friend, Phil Robertson. He drove his pickup truck to the house and both Candice and Pat hopped into the cab. They drove on the trail until Pat saw the orange ribbons and told them to stop. They didn't pass Dante on the way, but that thought barely scratched Pat's panic.

The three of them made their way quickly, Pat first, then Mr. Robertson, dragging a toboggan that he kept around for his grandkids. Candice tried as best she could to keep up, but she winded quickly and silently cursed her love of baking that she inherited from her mother.

Pat stopped in disbelief. There was his dad, sitting and waving at them, and next to him was Dante, curled up in his good arm that was now waving, face dirty and tear-streaked, as if he was the one who was hurt. His disbelief turned to anger, mixed with relief that his dad was well enough to wave. Angry that Dante was curled up like a little girl, getting hugged by *his* dad when all this was *his* fault.

Dante untangled himself and came up next to Pat, watching Mr. Robertson get under Bill's good arm.

Candice caught up as Bill was explaining what

happened. "Trampled?" she cried. "I've never heard of such a thing."

Dante glanced at Pat, who refused to look at him. Dante saw the set look of his jaw. This was the same look he had when Russell Dupre stomped on his lunch last year. Pat hit him so hard he broke a tooth and got suspended for three days. Dante waited for the punch, but it didn't come. He wondered if, instead, it was their friendship that would get punched and broken.

Bill got to standing and together, the two neighbors lurched their way to the toboggan. Mr. Robertson squatted low and Bill followed suit, carefully, not without a few curses, reclining all the way back on the sled, facing the branches above. Mr. Robertson pulled while Pat and Dante pushed. Luckily there were a lot of leaves on the ground from the recent leaf fall and the toboggan slid along the path without much fuss. Candice scouted around for gear and draped on as much gear as possible, arranging the quivers so they lay in an X shape over her winter coat. When they got to the main path, Bill was again helped up and then reclined again onto the truck bed. Mr. Robertson had to maneuver his truck back and forth about six times to finally get turned around in the direction back to the Bates' so they could load Bill flat into the back seat of their Bronco and Candice could drive him to the hospital. She told Pat and Dante to stay home. Kitty was at a sleepover still, so Candice called her friend's house and told them briefly what happened and could they please drive Kitty home later that day.

When the boys were alone, for the first time ever, Pat didn't know how to talk to Dante. There were no words for what Dante had done. They shed their outdoor clothing in silence, leaving it in a pile on the kitchen floor. Pat went to his room and Dante followed, unsure from Pat's silence and tense jaw if he was welcome. He stood in the doorway. "I'm sorry. I know it was my fault."

Tears sprung to Pat's eyes. "Why did you scream like that, Strawberry? You made me totally miss and hit that buck. I didn't even know it was there!" He began to sob.

Dante walked over and sat gingerly on the edge of the bed. "I don't know what happened. I was tired and cold, so I closed my eyes to try to sleep. I guess it worked. I...had a dream. I had it before, too, that first night you slept at my house, remember? You were talking about hunting. I dreamed we were in the woods together and there was a doe and a buck. You raised your bow and the buck charged and leaped at me. It... it was *your* face on the buck's body as it jumped. Right as it was about to land on me, I woke up. But this time, this dream, it was different."

Pat waited, teeth grinding as he tried to stop crying. "Why were you the one crying when my dad was the one who was hurt? Why didn't you come with me to get help?"

"I couldn't keep up with you, so I decided to go back and see if I could help your dad. As soon as I got back there, I started bawling when I saw him sitting there, all broken looking. It was all my fault. Your dad put his arm out and said, "It's okay, Dante. Come keep me warm. So, I did. I told him my dream."

"Why was this one so different?"

"Because this time the buck leaped at *you*, Pat. It picked you up by its antlers and it..." Dante's nose quivered and his eyes welled with tears. His voice became a whisper. "It got you by the antlers, picked you up. And your body... sank down onto the points until they came up though the other side of you and there was blood, and you were just hanging there as it ran away with you."

Pat had stopped crying. He sniffed. "Jeezum, Straw. That's, well, I don't know what that is. Crazy. But it was just a dream."

Dante wiped his tears with the back of his hand. "I didn't want to go hunting anyway. And now it's all my fault."

Pat shook his head and shrugged. "We shouldn't have tricked you, that's for sure." Pat stood up. "Come on, let's get us some Swiss Miss."

BILL HAD A FRACTURED SHOULDER, bruises and sore muscles, but otherwise was fine. His arm in a sling, he told Dante a week later when Dante came over for a sleepover that he was glad for the paid time off. Dante looked at the floor — they hadn't seen each other since the incident. Pat had told him that his dad didn't blame him and agreed they shouldn't have taken Dante if he didn't want to go. But still, Dante felt responsible.

"I'm sorry, Mr. Bates. Really. I —"

"Dante, don't you worry. Things happen. And guess what, I don't know what you're going to think about this, but guess what's for dinner."

Dante looked at Pat, who was smirking. "I'm guessing it's not tofu scramble?"

Bill laughed. "Ow — stop being so damn funny. Nope. I guess you remember that buck — did you know I shot it right before it got me? But I got the last laugh. That neighbor, Phil Robertson, the one who came and got me, tracked that son-of-a-bitch down that same day, excuse my French. Finished it off, which was in its best interest at that point, dontcha know, dressed it and cut it into steaks for us. Didn't even tell us, brought a bunch of it over as a surprise."

Bill saw the look on Dante's face. "But don't worry, Candice made us some nice spaghetti for tonight."

Dante looked relieved, but Bill wasn't done. "Venison meatballs on the side." He roared with laughter and sputtered intermittent "ows" and various curses.

Dante told Pat later that night how weird it was to have an animal he saw alive, dead and cut up, passed around the table like dinner rolls. "After this, your dad he can't hate me any worse. I can't believe he still lets me in the house."

Pat just shook his head. "You are truly dumb. I don't know how you're gonna make it through school. Of course he likes you. All that joking around with you? You don't joke with someone you hate. Bugs me sometimes, you know. He doesn't joke around with me like that."

Dante chuffed. "Well, from what I know, making fun of someone means you think they're an idiot."

"Well, welcome to Vermont, where the dumber someone makes you feel, the more they like you. Why are we even friends, Strawberry?"

"Honestly, Pat Bates. I don't know."

BACK ON THE SLED, hands warm again, Pat and Dante zipped up, got back on the sleds and dashed across the road, racing across the field side-by-side until they got held up at a fence edging the woods on the other side. It hadn't been there last winter. "Well, that's not friendly," said Pat. They got off the sleds and started walking in different directions to look for an opening.

Pat started yelling. "There, there it is, I swear!"

Dante stamped over to him as fast as he could in the deep snow. "What, an opening?"

Pat took off his goggles. He had that look on his face that Dante had seen in his room. Fear. Dread. "That buck. The one my dad shot, the one that trampled him. He wants to get even."

Dante also took off his goggles and peered into the woods. He saw nothing. "I can't see anything." And he thought, 'Didn't you guys eat that damn buck?'

Pat clutched his stomach. "Ah, I gotta take a shit. Fuck." He tore his jacket off and brought down his layers of underwear, long johns, and snow pants. He squatted and shat.

Pat rubbed his behind with snow as best he could. He stood and saw the look on Dante's face.

"Fuck dude, sorry. No one should have to see that."

Dante said, "Did that buck literally scare the shit out of you?"

Pat pulled up his layers and grabbed his coat. "Dude, I can't believe you didn't see it. You would have shit yourself, too." He finished dressing. "We need to get out of here. Who knows where it is now."

Dante was alarmed by the urgency in Pat's voice. There was something about the way his eyes were focused, or unfocused, that made Dante worry. "You okay to drive back?"

"Yeah, I guess. But you go first again."

They went back across the field at a quicker pace, stopped at Route 2 and after two cars had passed, they crossed.

Once they got home, they drank their Swiss Miss, with

the marshmallows like always, and Dante stood. It was time for him to get home.

Dante put his hand on Pat's shoulder. "Dude, just get through whatever this is. Try those capsules my mom gave you. That shit helps."

Pat walked Dante out onto the porch and called out as Dante was getting into his rust-lined Tercel. "Why don't you stay the night?"

"Really?"

"Yeah. I'll let you beat me at Parcheesi."

Dante hesitated. That sounded like the old Pat. Fuck, he didn't know if he could take more… of whatever this was. He sighed as he shut the door and headed back toward the porch steps. "Should be easy. You can never get the rules right."

For the next couple of hours, it felt like old times, though instead of talking about comics, they talked about girls. Pat wanted details about Dante and Shannon. Dante hadn't been able to share much with Pat lately and it felt nice to have some attention on himself.

"Well, a gentleman doesn't kiss and tell."

Pat rolled his eyes. "Oh, come on. I've given you details. It's how you even know how to do anything."

"Shut up. I've seen Body Heat."

"Nuh-uh. When."

"Shannon's parents got a VCR a couple of months ago. They rented it and we watched it after they went to bed. And, well, let's just say we got inspired. My dad caught me coming in at 3:00 AM. He didn't tell my mom, though. See what you miss when you get all depressed and shit?"

"I bet your mom wouldn't even get that mad. They never seem to get mad at you."

"Yeah, but making them *disappointed* is its own hell."

"One detail."

Dante smiled. "Okay, you perv. Third base. A lot of times since that night." He lowered his voice. "We're talking about going all the way on the senior trip."

Pat frowned, which was not the reaction Dante was expecting. Dante said, "What, are you jealous?"

Pat hesitated, then shook his head. "No. I got other things on my mind."

PAT AND DANTE ate dinner with the family, the first time in a while Pat didn't get a tray in his room. Bill had railed against what he considered coddling, but Candice needed to know that at least Pat was eating. Kitty was quieter than usual at the table, unsure how to act around Pat anymore. She didn't want to say something that would set him off. Really all she could think of to say to him was that he needed a shower.

Candice tried to keep it light, like it was no big deal they were all eating together. All the usual inquiries about school and friends were directed at Dante.

Everyone was shocked when Pat started to talk. "It's bow season still. I want to go."

Dante halfway choked on his milk. Candice had heated him up two frozen vegetarian burritos; the rest of them had steak. "You can count me out." He laughed. "Obviously."

Bill and Candice looked at each other. Bill said, "Well, son. That's, uh, great to hear. Really."

Pat was nodding and taking bites of his tater tots. "Yeah, I haven't gone out at all this season. Dad, can we?"

Bill had been waiting for weeks for his son to want to

go outside, to do anything other than listen to that infernal Walkman and lay on his bed. But it was spring. Hunting season was in fall and winter, which helped control deer overpopulation and potential starvation from lack of resources. Which was something Pat should know.

Bill frowned but wanted to keep him interested. "Maybe you can help me check out the equipment. See what we'll need for next season." He glanced at Candice, who shrugged, meaning, "Sure, why not?"

"I want to track him, Dad."

Bill took a bite of steak. "Track who?"

"The buck. You know. The one that trampled you."

Bill swallowed. Was Pat serious? Hunt the buck that the neighbor had so generously tracked and butchered after the accident all those years ago? "Son, Phil Robertson took care of him for us, don't you remember?"

Kitty chuckled. "I still remember the look on Dante's face when you served the venison meatballs. He looked like the coyote on Bugs Bunny after he's been flattened by a rock."

Dante wanted to shoot a remark back to her, but he caught the looks on Candice and Bill's faces.

Pat stabbed a piece of broccoli. "Well, I can tell you he's still out there. And he's pissed."

Kitty waited for the rebuke about bad language at the table, but it didn't come. "Oh, so we can start cussing at the table now? Well, shit."

They all jumped when Bill's hand slammed on the table. "That's enough, young lady. You go to your room."

Tears sprung to her eyes. "Why is it Pat skips school and cusses at the table and I'm the one who gets in trouble?" She ran to her room without waiting for an answer.

Dante felt bad for her; try as they might, things just

weren't the same anymore. It was hard for her to get what was happening. He didn't understand it himself.

Bill wiped a hand down his face. "Pat, don't say bad words at the table. Dante, you probably should go home tonight."

Dante nodded. "Yes, sir." He slid back from the table. "Pat, I'll see you at school tomorrow, okay?"

Pat's gaze focused on a point behind Dante. "Yep. If he doesn't get me first."

12

1932–1933: THERAPIES

moke-eater and more flame. Grasping, don't desert me — you'll be president soon. Feel burning and swallow smoke. The flame is the only thing you need. Hear the crackle, pssshhh, the flame is done. Vienna sausage in the vein, medicine pssshhh the fire out. Until next time, you flat tire. I'll be waiting.

Silence.

It was time for recreation. Truman and fifty other men of all ages were led from the dormitory out into the chill spring air of the courtyard surrounded by brick buildings and dotted with maple trees. He had been here for eight months and now at age twenty-one, he was one of the youngest patients, of which there were few. His hand still wanted to stroke the black beard that had been shaved off and kept off. The oldest man near him appeared to be in his eighties, but there were more like him, as well. Truman was wearing one of three button-down shirts his mother had brought him. He normally avoided his scratchy wool trousers, but his other pants were at the laundry. There were three nurses and four orderlies. Nurse Mueller led the warm-up exercises.

"Up with the arms and down to the toes. Up with the arms and down to the toes." The other nurses demonstrated from their strategic placements along the edges of the rows with their starched smocks and white hats. The orderlies circulated, encouraging and helping those who were not complying. For some, it was due to agitation, for others, lack of comprehension. For the rest, it was a depression so deep they could not move their limbs through the fog that made colors dull, food tasteless, and raising one's arms exhausting.

"Arms up and sway like the trees." Truman was reminded of laundry drying on the line. Hanging laundry was his job, briefly. His inability to grip the clothing in tandem with squeezing clothespins was quickly made obvious by the number of shirts he left behind in the mud. In the few months he had been in the hospital, he was found incapable of doing any fine-finger tasks like weaving rugs or baskets, both of which generated income for the hospital, the profits of which were used for entertainment and recreation for the patients. One time when Coolidge was absent, Truman overheard Dr. Stanley during one of his weekly inspections of the facility. Truman heard him tell a nurse they were saving for indoor equipment to promote more stimulating physical exercise in the long winter months. He'd complained to her how it didn't used to be like that, but since the crash and resulting depression, everyone was suffering. Truman remembered something about a crash — it was around the same time President Coolidge began to speak to him. Maybe it was Coolidge's fault.

Truman was reassigned to custodial duties, which he

liked. He did them in the morning, after breakfast. He swept and mopped the dorm and took out the trash while other patients were doing their various activities. Wayne or another orderly or nurse would observe him and the others who were pulling off sheets for laundry, making the beds with new sheets, or washing the six windows, three on one side, three on the other, remarking on jobs well-done and demonstrating correct methods when needed.

"Alright, everyone knows this one – jumping jacks! One, two, three..." About thirty men out of the fifty men proceeded to jump in the expected style; Truman was not one of them. His arms went up, but his legs wouldn't comply. Wayne, his favorite orderly, told him he was doing great. Aimee told him otherwise. *Feel me? Lick me? What wouldn't you like from me? I will touch and lick and feel your prick in my ass.* Truman's hand went down his pants, grabbing and pulling. Wayne grabbed him gently by the shoulders and silently guided him back to the dorms as Truman pulled and jerked.

By the time he was back inside, Aimee was gone, and he was very thirsty. Wayne brought him to the bathroom and told him to wash his hands, counting down from thirty as he did so. Truman tried to pull his hands out from under the faucet, crying out — the snakes on his skin — but Wayne firmly held his wrists in place and didn't let go until count was done. Coolidge started up. *Water on the flames, the slither of the hiss, ssss, the voters will not relent.* Truman and Wayne walked together outside and then into another building to the day room, it was called, which was filled with another group of men of various ages playing cards, sitting, standing and looking out the window. Another smattering of nurses and orderlies were there, either silently waiting to be needed, or calmly talking with patients. Some patients were silent, others chatted together, and some were like Truman, talking to the people only they knew and only they could hear.

There were metal pitchers of water on a table by the large windows that looked out at the trees surrounding the thirty-six-acre complex. Wayne watched Truman get himself water, half of which joined the already soaked towels covering the table in anticipation of sloppy pours. Wayne told Truman he could wait here or go back to the dorm until dinner at noon. Truman took in Wayne's voice, separated it from Coolidge's and processed it. He recognized that he was expected to make a decision, but it was one that confounded him, so he remained silent. Wayne drifted away and Truman stood, getting hot in his sweater in the steam-heated room. He peeled it off and dropped it where he stood. A nurse came, picked it up, and put it on the wooden chair next to him and invited Truman to sit down. Truman did. He wished the chair would rock, like his favorite one at home. And a cigarette, the flame, didn't anyone care that was what kept Coolidge's mouth shut. If his Keeper of the Flame were here. His Clem.

"TREATMENT PATIENTS GIT TO THE DOOR!" Truman watched from his bunk while fifteen or so men shuffled sleepily to the door. He was surprised when the orderly, maybe his name was Jeffrey, tapped him on the shoulder. "You, too Truman. Today you're starting your new therapy, just like the doc said."

Truman arose, his thin frame chilled in the morning

air, Truman remembered no such conversation. Until now, his only therapy was when Coolidge berated him to the point that he couldn't sleep. President Coolidge learned to become alarmed when brought to the bathing room because cold water was splashed in his face, his power drained.

Truman thought water therapy was reserved for patients like George who threw grand tantrums every two weeks, pitching his lunch tray, or his shoes, or a chair. He'd be escorted by the largest of the orderlies and placed under jets of frigid water to stay his blood flow, to extinguish the fire that burned in his brain. When George returned as long as thirty minutes later, he was much subdued, exhausted in fact, his wrists colored with deeply purple welts from the straps attaching him to the white tile walls.

When he first learned of hydrotherapy, Truman hoped he would never have it, scared as he was of the snakes that would certainly coil around him like they did during his thrice weekly showers. The slithering was the worst between the time the shower done and toweling dry. That was when the snakes would crawl with abandon and until the last drop from his wet black hair was wiped away.

Then the cold-water therapy stopped and a new one was introduced. An orderly appeared at his bedside and with a "Hey, kid, let's get you to the water room," He took Truman by the arm and lifted him to sit. Truman twisted and pulled under the orderly's practiced hold on his arms until his legs went limp. He went boneless and almost slipped to the floor, the orderly cursing a blue streak. Why was he going to the cold showers? Coolidge wasn't even around at that time.

He was taken to a humid room of bathtubs instead

and brought to the edge of a tub filled and flowing. In it was a hammock floating weightless, fastened by canvas straps along the sides. The orderly that wrestled him through the halls to the water room helped him undress all the way, one firm grip on him at all times, his pants forced down. The nurse in attendance undid his buttons while the orderly held him from behind, grunting from the last vestige of Truman's resistance, his muscles like wires. The nurse talked him through the process of getting helped into the bathtub, one of five tubs attached to pipes pumping in water from an unseen source behind the tiled room. Two others were occupied that first time - one patient must have been soaking for some time – there was a dinner tray on the table next to him. Some, Truman found out later, could linger in here for as long as three days.

After he was secured into the hammock, head resting on rolled up towels, a canvas cover was drawn across him, keeping the steam in and the temperature stable. A nurse sat by his side the whole time, taking notes any time he moved or spoke, standing to check the temperature dials every fifteen minutes. She advised him to relax. This whole scene caused Coolidge to reappear and Truman continued to push against the restraints, told Coolidge what he really thought of him, to stop taking him vote, and that he needed to make the flame appear. Coolidge eventually settled down enough that a small pad was laid across Truman's eyes, keeping them closed.

Truman whispered into President Coolidge's ear that he didn't need his help, that the flame was not his to take and that the liquid heat would send him away, laughing at the President's pleading to fix the vote. At some point, he couldn't say when, the only noise he heard after he and

Coolidge ended their deliberations was the hiss of the radiator and trickle of the warm, running water that continuously flowed over his body without end. And he slept.

After six hours, he was brought up and out of the tub, and rubbed with soft towels by a different set of nurses and orderly, buffing him as if he were the body of a car. His skin glowed, the snakes stayed in their nests. He slept well every night for one week, then it began all over again.

IN THE YEAR since then that Truman had been in the hospital, he'd lined up for rec time, shower time, meal-time. His hydrotherapy was irregular, warranted only when Coolidge was at his worst. The other men from his dorm that lined up for daily therapy were others like him: talkative, uncoordinated, had special vision. There didn't seem to be many like them, or him. Truman watched these men transform from average size to large and soft-looking, like they had cottage cheese under their skin. Some had become quieter, others behaved no differently. They lined up every morning and Truman only saw them at lunch, at rec time, and at bed. Truman was moved to their group, his bed grouped together with theirs in a corner of the dorm, where a nurse sat with them all night under a small circle of lamplight. There was one his age, Polio Tommy, who turned, eyes looking at Truman's shoulder. "First Vienna sausage?"

Truman's focus was on Tommy's ear. "We gonna eat?" Aimee started up with her talk. *Your sausage is long and greasy. I will lick your sausage, will you lick mine?* Tommy laughed loudly when Truman said to no one he could see, "I will lick it. Touch it. Fuck it."

Wayne was on duty that morning, "Truman, you'll git breakfast after. This is therapy all the way from Vienna, ha-ha to Tommy here." Wayne clapped Tommy on the back. "You are a cut up."

Tommy grinned, eyes on Wayne's collar. "I know."

After a stop in the bathroom for morning toileting and brushing teeth, the men were walked down two separate corridors. Tommy, nicknamed Polio Tommy for his skinny legs and awkward gait as a result of his childhood illness, stepped as if his hips were on hinges and Truman was reminded of a puppet. Tommy used to be the skinniest man Truman had ever met, but now he was bigger than he was, especially thick around the middle. The men were led into a room Truman had never seen before. It had six beds, one for each of them. All the rooms Truman had ever been in at the hospital had large windows, but this room had none and it was quite warm. There were two doctors and four nurses waiting in the room, each with a sheen of sweat across their brow. The men were told to get onto the bed and lay back. Truman was glad he didn't have to get undressed. The rest of the room was taken up with equipment trays and thin metal stands with glass IV bottles hanging, rubber tubes attached.

The doctor talked him through it, it being his first time. Luckily Coolidge wasn't interested, and Aimee grew bored and went away. "This is the latest treatment, Truman. We have great expectations that this will make you well again." People had been telling Truman for a long while now that he was sick and that was why he was here.

Dr. Goddard was well-liked by the patients. He had a

kind smile, and he walked the ward often, observing, taking notes, talking to patients. Truman didn't see the other doctors doing that. He was glad it was this doctor speaking with him now. "You will come here every morning for what could be as long as two months. We will start slow, giving you small doses of medicine called insulin. This will increase and you will be sleeping for a short time as a part of the therapy, though to get to sleep may take several hours."

Truman had just woken up and hadn't eaten and now they wanted to put him to sleep. Coolidge protested. *This will never get the votes, the flame doesn't burn in bed. Get out and get the vote.* Truman began to get off the bed, but was put back by Wayne and held in place. There were straps on the side of the bed, which Nurse Hamlin secured. Wayne stood back and patted Truman on the shoulder. "There's a good boy. Don't worry, the doctors know best."

Nurse Hamlin talked to him about relaxing and letting her do all the work. Truman kept his eyes on the ceiling. He was poked in the arm and a clear liquid began to flow. Coolidge went on and on. Nothing seemed to happen, but then Coolidge became foggy, though he never completely went away. Truman was escorted back to the dorm to dress for breakfast, though some others remained in the room, attached to IVs. He was now a full-fledged member of the Vienna sausage group. His next sessions would become increasingly longer.

~

AFTER TWO WEEKS of increased dosage, longer fogs, shakes, and eventual blackouts, Truman noticed his pants were too tight. His shirts wouldn't fit right, could hardly button across his belly. He was given new clothes, he didn't know from where. Before he had only worn his own, from home, the ones his *Maman* had packed for him. He had been asking when he could see her again and was only told, "let's hope soon".

It now took up to three hours of clouded mind, dizziness, and intense salivation before the insulin being administered would knock Truman into oblivion. He had heard the nurses and doctors using the word "coma".

He had no idea how long the blackouts lasted. Now, each time he woke up, he felt a sensation in his nose — the insulin was administered through tubes up their noses, which were pulled out soon before they woke up, so it must be what caused it. Truman burped once upon waking and tasted sugar. He and the men on the beds were also grouped together at rec time with a nurse nearby at all times. Truman had nearly passed out several times during exercises and each time, a nurse immediately ran over to give him a cup of sugar water, after which he felt better.

Polio Tommy had not seemed plagued as of late by his special people clutching him around his waist, whom he usually spent a lot of time talking to and brushing away. He had also grown so large that Truman didn't recognize him from behind anymore. Tommy was still a cut up and was eventually placed into occupational therapy weaving baskets and rugs thanks to the improvements in his coordination. Another man in the group, Howard, didn't show up for rec time one day. His bed was stripped, and his things removed. They said he had left. Truman was given clothes just like Howard's soon after, one shirt he recognized because he had liked the with metal buttons embossed with a flower pattern. He wondered why Howard hadn't taken his shirt.

Truman hadn't seen anyone leave the hospital since he'd arrived, and it seemed more patients came every week. He'd heard there were over a thousand patients now. There was also a woman's ward now, on the other side of the complex. You could see them at rec time while they were doing their exercises.

After another month and a half of increasing disorientation, convulsions, and thirty-eight comas, Truman's Vienna sausage days were over. The original men who were with Truman at the start of his insulin therapy had been rotated back into the general population a few weeks before he was, and new patients were brought in to take their places and had become a part of the group. When Truman entered the hospital at age twenty, he weighed one hundred and twenty pounds. Now he was twenty-two and weighed two-hundred and four pounds. He only heard Coolidge's tirades once or twice a week these days, and Aimee not at all.

A week later, his mother, Clemens, and Ginny came to visit. It would be the first time Truman and Clemens would see each other in nearly two years, the first time since the fire.

13

1984: BEER, GIRLS, AND CARS

Kitty ran out from her room to answer the ringing phone that hung on the wall in the kitchen. She and Cheryl, her best friend, had agreed to call each other after they came home from school. They had some other friends to discuss. She picked up the receiver and flicked the light switch on the wall. It was starting to get dark. "Hello?"

"Hi Sweetie, it's Mom."

"Oh. Hi."

"Honey, is Pat home?"

"His car's here, but his door's closed. I'll go look." Kitty put the phone receiver on the counter and knocked on his door. She knew how it was with him now, so she opened the door a crack and peered in, ready to back out and slam the door shut if he was doing anything...gross. Empty. She glanced down the hall. The bathroom door was open, and it was empty, too.

She went back to the phone. "He's not here. Maybe he's with Dante, or the boys or something."

"Okay, thanks. I'll be home in a couple of hours."

"'K, bye."

PAT HEARD the echo of his dad's voice in his head, "*No such thing as bad weather! Only bad clothing.*" Hard to argue with a man who, between the quarry, hunting season, stacking wood, raking leaves, shoveling snow, snow machining, and fishing trips, lived almost his entire life outside. The first snow flew before Halloween and the last one, the first week in April. Summer was a contented sigh that came and went just as quickly. *Quit your bitchin'* was the now barely legible bumper sticker Bill got as a gag gift from one of his brothers. Bill stuck it on his truck that day and Candice laughed that she'd put it on his headstone, should he go first.

Being the middle of the day on a Tuesday, no one was home as he dressed in his hunting gear; camo pants, insulated brown jacket, safety orange cap, wool socks, heavy black boots, black gloves. He crunched across the thin sheen of corn snow, typical for April. He slid the barn door open.

He worked his way around the wagon that had resided along the west side of the barn his whole life. His mom said they had a mare named Daisy Chain when she was little, that she and the wagon were their transportation before the Model T, and again during the Depression. She would point out the pile of rocks they used for a headstone where they buried her at the edge of the woods.

When he and Kitty were little, like really little, the neighbor, Phil Robertson, would ride his horse a half mile over from his still-working farm and hitch her up to the wagon. Would let them alternate turns sitting in the back and then up front to hold the reins while they lumbered down the dirt paths Pat only saw now when hunting. The rest of the time, he used the paths in winter, only knowing they were there from their own snow machine tracks. Once they got too old for wagon rides, the wagon stayed put in the barn, no one having the heart to get rid of it.

Pat regained his focus and his light found what he was looking for, leaning up against the back corner behind the wagon. He slid the bow out of its covering and swung the light in search of his quiver. He saw the looks his mom gave his dad and him when he unwrapped this gift from last Christmas. It was a look of tenderness for his dad and one of pride for him. Almost a year ago. Seemed like a lot longer than that. Pat remembered being touched at the quality of the set — with proper care, it would last a lifetime.

CANDICE HAD USED up her ten-minute break using the bathroom and calling home, so she didn't have time to call the Zuckermans. She told herself to stop worrying.

When she got home at 7:30 after working the dinner shift at the college, the oven timer was going off. Bill had put in a frozen lasagna at 6:30 when he got home, as instructed that morning at breakfast. Candice removed her winter wear in the mudroom on the side of the house; the wood planks, hooks, and pegs were as familiar to her as her own face. The only thing that had changed over the years were the coats and boots. As she came into the kitchen, she heard Bill calling to the kids for dinner. Kitty came bounding out, ponytail swinging. "Jeezum *Crow*, I am hungry!" Pat's door remained closed.

There was no light under it, but that was normal these days.

Bill knocked. "Pat? You in there?" He opened the door. The room was dark. He peered in and didn't see the now familiar lumpy form on the bed. The bed was empty. He hadn't bothered to check when he got home. He figured Pat was in there, wanting to be left alone.

"Honey?"

Candice had just turned off the beeping timer. Kitty got the plates out and started setting the table. Candice walked through the swinging door into the living room. "Yes?"

"Where's Pat?"

Candice felt her heart start to pump faster. "I assumed he was with Dante, or the boys, or something." She frowned.

Bill's eyebrows knit together. "Isn't this strange for a school night? He didn't call?" He raised his voice a notch. "Kitty?"

Kitty came through the swinging door. "Kitty, did Pat call and leave a message?"

She shrugged. "I didn't hear the phone or anything."

Both Bill and Candice knew that Kitty had supersonic hearing when it came to the phone.

Candice said, "I'll call the Zuckermans."

PAT PICKED a tree behind the house, the small maple he could see from his room. He had seen the buck there several times, its antlered head always swiveled toward his window. Stomping one hoof on the ground, breath pushing out of his flared nostrils. It was behind this tree

Pat squatted, positioning the bow to shoot, arrow resting loosely in place. He waited.

CANDICE, Bill and Kitty each took their turn in the mudroom pulling on boots, coats, and hats. Bill went last, as he went to get the flashlights, which were used at least a couple of times a year during bad storms when the lights went out. They left the lasagna warming in the oven and filed out into the night.

Bill handed out the orders. "Kitty, go right back here behind the kitchen. Candice, you look on the other side of the house and I'll check out the barn."

Nobody spoke, tight with worry after calls to the Zuckermans, the Laguerres, and the Ibeys didn't reveal Pat's whereabouts. With his car in the driveway, this was the next best option. Even though it was dark and cold, Bill hoped he had taken a snow machine. It would be easy to track and, if Bill was being honest, it would show a spark of the old Pat.

Bill rolled open the large door and saw the sleds, parked and covered. He waved the flashlight beam around and noticed the small door on the other side of the barn was cracked open. He moved the beam around some more, passing over the tractor, the yard equipment, the hunting gear. His eye caught something and at first, he couldn't figure out what was amiss. As it dawned on him what it was, Kitty screamed for him and Candice. "Dad! Mom! Here's here! Come quick!"

They huddled around Kitty, flashlights trained on Pat, who was squatting in silence in all his hunting gear.

"Put the bow down, son." As soon as Bill saw Pat's bow

missing from the lineup in the barn, he was terrified at what he might find. And now he wasn't convinced that Pat wouldn't shoot one of them. God help him, he wouldn't know what to do then.

Pat had the arrow against the bow, loose but ready to aim in an instant. In the small circle of lights, Pat wouldn't look at them — either because the lights were too bright in his eyes, or because he was focused on something they couldn't see.

"I'm tracking it, Dad. That buck. Remember?"

Bill felt his stomach drop. "The buck? From that hunting trip with Dante?"

Pat quickly turned his head as if he heard something. "Totally. It's been outside my window almost every night for a week. I'm finally going to get that fucker."

Bill, Candice and Kitty all looked at each other. "Kitty, Candice, why don't you both go inside."

Bill could tell Candice didn't want to leave, but she put a protective arm around Kitty and guided her back to the house. Bill lowered the flashlight beam to the ground between them.

"Dad, I think my legs are asleep. You know how it gets, sitting for so long."

Bill did know. There was a lot of discomfort when crouched in a deer stand. He figured Pat hadn't been making small movements to stave off numbness. "How long you been out here?"

Pat looked around like he didn't quite know where he was. "Wow. When did it get dark? Um, I don't know. A few hours, I guess."

"Can you move your fingers and toes?"

Pat gave it a try, not changing his position. "Kind of. Huh. No, not really."

"Let me take over."

"I don't know if that's a good idea."

"It's okay. You can't shoot if you can't move."

"Shit, I guess not." Pat relaxed his position and the bow and arrow fell from his hands. Bill leaned over and picked them up. Slinging the bow over one shoulder and tossing the arrow aside, he offered his hands to his son.

"Take my hands, Pat. Let's get you inside and see how you are." Pat reached both hands up and Bill was reminded of when Pat was five and needed help getting out of a high pile of snow he had sunk into. Bill took one gloved hand in each of his bare hands and firmly pulled. Pat sank back down. His legs were completely numb, his feet frozen.

"Fuck, pins and needles."

Bill didn't bother about his language. "It's okay, let's wait a few until you can move again."

Bill sat down in the snow next to Pat, knowing his jeans would get soaked in a heartbeat. He wrapped his good arm around his son's shoulders. Actually, both arms were still good, it was the left shoulder that remained stiff after the hunting accident with Dante. With the dead buck Pat was now trying to kill.

Bill moved his bare hand, already red with cold, up and down Pat's arm trying to warm him up. It flashed through his mind that tonight was going to be real cold again and to leave the faucets running just a trickle to prevent the pipes from freezing, and perhaps bursting. This mundane thought calmed him.

"We got lasagna inside."

Pat nodded. "Awesome. I'm starving." After another few minutes, Pat struggled to stand.

"Dad, what about the buck?"

"It's not the buck that scares me, Pat."

After the family ate dinner in silence, Bill and Kitty loaded Pat into the car and took him to Central Vermont Hospital where they had what they called "emergency beds". It just about killed them both to leave him there, but it was time.

A few days later, Pat was still at CVH and visiting hours were almost over. Candice would be back soon with Kitty to deliver hot cocoa from the cafeteria. While they were gone, a nurse swooped in to change the bandages on his hands and feet.

A doctor waltzed in and stood at the foot of the bed, consulting Pat's chart. "You're lucky, you know."

Pat scoffed. Dante looked up from his comic.

"You get to keep your fingers and toes."

"So, any idea when I get out of this place?"

The doctor placed the chart back on its hook. "We'll wait for Dr. Garcia to give that answer."

Pat rolled his eyes. Dante looked back and forth between the doctor and Pat. Pat answered the question Dante wasn't sure how to ask. "They are working out which pills to give me because they think me wanting to shoot a deer is the same as shooting a person." Pat crossed his arms and looked down at himself on the bed. "Which it's not."

"Dr. Garcia will be here shortly." And with that, the unnamed doctor was gone.

Dante blinked. "Wait, you haven't, you know, thought about... fuck, dude. Have you? Like, to yourself?"

Pat looked out the window again. He squinted his eyes

like he saw something in the distance, then looked back at Dante. "No. But other things."

Dante waited.

"Okay, this past week, it's like, all I want is to be gray. Gray clothes, gray room, gray skin..." He looked over at Dante and read something in his face.

"Fuck off, I know how it sounds. But like, it's comforting. When I'm like this, bright color, like... mocks me. 'Look how bright and awesome I am. You could never be me.' Sorry, dude, really."

"For what?"

"For making you deal with this. You don't have to come, you know."

Dante shook his head. "You know that's not true. Look I don't know why, but you're the only one in the whole universe who gets me." Dante smirked. "And even so, continues to hang out with me."

Pat smiled back. It looked less strained than before. "That will never change, bro."

And for the moment, it was true.

AFTER TWO WEEKS at the emergency beds, Pat went home with medications that were going to affect his mood and hopefully, stop anymore delusional thinking. "Paranoid ideation" was what Dr Garcia called it. Given the family history, Dr Garcia was especially concerned at the direction Pat's mind was going. He had chastised Candice only once, saying that Pat should have been seen by a doctor long before now, especially given her family history.

Candice couldn't stop twisting her hands around each

other. "Does this have anything to do with the car accident last summer?" she asked.

Dr. Garcia shook his head. "Pat's condition may have matured a bit sooner due to his head injury. He is a few years younger than most people who develop this disorder." He shrugged. "It was going to happen eventually." He took off his glasses and cleaned them on his white coat. "Mrs. Bates, you need to be prepared. Pat has moved beyond depression and into delusion. He could recover very well, or not at all. Everyone reacts differently to medication and therapy."

Candice was so terrified that Pat was going to take his own life, she took only evening shifts and wouldn't leave until someone was home with him. Dante brought his homework to him almost every day, but didn't try to convince him to do it.

Lyle and Jeremy came by once or twice a week and on the weekends. If Pat was able to, he'd hang out like normal and they'd all talk about girls, cars, and parties. Well, Lyle, and Jeremy would, trying to convince Pat to go out again. They thought that if he just started up life again like before, he'd shake it off. Sometimes Pat thought so, too. Dante had his doubts. He stayed quiet and just kept coming over as often as he could. He also had Shannon to think about, though she was more understanding than he could have imagined.

If Pat was withdrawn, he lay on his bed curled up with his eyes closed. When that happened, the boys would take turns playing games on Pat's Nintendo. They left the lights off, like he wanted.

Bill complained about the video games and shook his head every time he walked by Pat's room, lit only by the screen, the boys sometimes quiet, sometimes loud in the dim light. Bill thought getting Pat out into the fresh air was the answer, but Candice explained that the medication prevented him from doing much at this point, even school. They needed to be patient.

Whenever Bill would get loud about what a waste of time the games were and questioned the doctors and medications, Candice knew he was hurting. She knew he missed his son. It was easier for Candice, who was able to feel useful by making meals, checking homework, cleaning. Bill, on the other hand, would come home from work and not know what to do with himself. He had tried to go sit with Pat in his room, but the unresponsive lump on the bed made Bill feel simultaneously numb and scared and he couldn't stay in there for very long.

Kitty would tiptoe into the room as if Pat were sleeping. She would whisper, "Can I play Nintendo?" and then turn it on without waiting for an answer. Sometimes Pat would force himself out of bed and play with her. She would come alive then and her bubbly banter about everything and nothing always made Pat feel a little better.

At first the boys felt bad because they didn't want Pat to know how much he was missing out on. Like the senior trip, which was coming up fast. Pat assured them that he was in no shape to go out partying, and until the meds started working, he said all he wanted to do was sleep. After about three weeks of staying in bed and feeling like a visitor in his own home, Pat began to feel a bit brighter. After a month, he was officially "stabilized."

It was Pat who started talking about their earlier adventures and laughing about how stupid they had been. The laughter from his room made everyone in the house, including the boys, feel as if they could finally exhale, could live and talk about their lives without guilt. It felt good to talk about the old days, to relive what had connected them in the first place, even the awkward times. The cabin came up a lot. Like the first time they drank beer, and the first time they brought girls there.

THAT SUMMER after their freshman year, the four boys started riding their bikes to the cabin so much that Pat and Lyle, who lived far from town, began to keep their bikes at Dante's. They had developed a weekend routine of Dante riding his bike about a mile up Route 2 to Jeremy's house to watch Saturday morning cartoons. Once the boring black and white Tarzan show started, they'd both ride to Dante's, raising their fists at the truckers that nearly blew then off the road. Pat and Lyle would each get dropped off after lunch. None of them liked lunch at the Zuckermans, which would often involve hummus sandwiches. Jeremy ate a ham and cheese sandwich at home before they left. After lunch, they'd all ride bikes to Ibey's General Store, the one owned by Jeremy's parents. They'd raid the snack aisle grabbing two bags of whatever they wanted, and the cooler to take one soda each, though Jeremy sometimes snuck out more, and stuff the spoils into their backpacks. There was a twirling magazine and comics rack — he had no interest in the Archie comics, but Dante was happy that there was a regular stock of Spiderman for him, and Super Friends for Pat. Pat never had enough money, so Dante would pay for the comics from his allowance. Pat had a lot of chores at home, but no allowance.

The group would finish with a trip to the freezer and

choose an ice cream to eat on the porch of the store, fighting over who'd get to sit in the two oversized rockers. Truman was usually there across the street on the wall, sitting, watching, and smoking. They'd all wave and he'd wave back. On the way out, they'd pass by and each say hello to him in their own way, "Hi, Uncle Tru."

"Hi, Tru."

"Hello, sir."

"'Sup, Pat Bates' uncle." That last one was Lyle, who had started listening to albums his sister Dana had bought, like "Rapper's Delight." Then they'd race down the railroad bed, either Pat or Lyle winning, and burst into the cabin ready to eat, drink soda, and talk about nothing. And everything.

The only piece of furniture was a rusty folding chair from Lyle's basement that they brought by taking turns holding onto it while on their bikes. Next was a milk crate from Ibey's General Store. They would each claim their spots — Jeremy on the milk crate in the far corner, Lyle on the wobbly folding chair next to him, Dante and Pat on the log they dragged in from outside. The crate was right under the hole in the roof where the woodstove chimney must have been. Sometimes Jeremy would stand under the beam and pretend aliens were abducting him while Lyle hummed the five-note *Close Encounters of the Third Kind* theme. Lyle brought his Walkman he got for his birthday and cranked up the volume, each ear straining to hear the music from the headphones placed in the middle of the room. They always ended up getting close to the Walkman by laying on the floor in a circle around it for the best songs. Lyle stole the cassettes from his sister Dana, too — Journey, Jethro Tull, The Runaways, Supertramp. The boys new favorite was Queen's album, *The*

Game. They would take turns listening individually when "Another One Bites the Dust" came on, stopping and rewinding for the next listener. They agreed that Jeremy, who had the next birthday at the end of summer, would ask for a boom box.

Sometimes when they entered the cabin, they noticed the milk crate would be moved, or the one chair folded up and resting against the wall. There would be a half-burned sage smudge on the floor, in a different corner every time. The boys would swear up and down that the smoke made them high.

The boys had been asking Jeremy to take beers from the store. He begged off, petrified of getting caught, but one day, Jeremy saw that two cans of Miller High Life had rolled under a shelf. When no one was looking, he stuffed them into his book bag and kept them in his room until the following Saturday. After telling the others what he had done, they kept giving each other knowing looks during school and making vague comments in front of other kids, like, "Hey Lincoln, you want to get high on life?"

"Pat Bates, didn't your family used to be... *millers*?"

When they were given puzzled looks, they'd just titter and say something like, "What's your problem?" Having this illicit plan that others didn't know about was as exciting as the prospect of actually drinking beer.

The day of the drinking, they did their usual Saturday routine, but this time, Jeremy had the beers in his back-pack. They got to the cabin, took them out and put them on the floor. It was a moment of reverence. Lyle said, "Jer-Bear, you should go first."

They discussed whether to open just one first and all share it or open both and split one beer between two of them. They decided on the latter and Jeremy pulled the tab on one and Pat on the other and each took the first sips. They both grimaced.

"Not bad."

"Yeah, it's good."

Jeremy passed his to Lyle and Pat to Dante, back and forth until there was no more warm beer to pass down their throats. Nobody would say that it was gross.

Convinced they were wasted, they mimicked what they saw in movies. They spun each other around until they fell down, saying things like, "I'm so wasted... Is it me, or is the world spinning? How many fingers am I holding up?"

Then they tried to ride their bikes in their "wasted" state. They went in circles around each other, pushing or kicking to try to knock each other down. Pat was the winner. He always won their contests — who can touch the wall first, who can jump their bike the highest, who can get to the top of the tree first. Lyle would come in second, Jeremy third, then Dante. Pat was the one who usually started the contests and cared the most about being first. Dante didn't care too much either way; not that he liked being called a pussy. He felt that this was where he was different from them; even if he wanted to, he couldn't follow sports too well without a TV. He just didn't like competing. But, he had to admit, it would have been nice to win once in a while. Or just not have any contests at all.

ONE SWEATY SUMMER DAY, they rode some girls out to the cabin. One of the girls was Pat's cousin, Tippy, who lived in Barre. The rest were her friends whom none of the boys had ever met. They had asked their parents to get dropped off in Hopefield one Saturday, saying it was just for something to do. This plan had been brewing for two weeks, ever since Tippy came over for Candice's birthday.

Tippy was showing everyone at the party her school pictures, which Candice had asked her mother, Bill's sister Desiree, to bring, and one included her whole class photo. Pat asked about one cute girl and Tippy told him that was her best friend, Carla. Pat asked Tippy to set them up, plus two more, and the first cabin make-out plan was hatched.

The girls got dropped off at Ibey's store, where the boys were waiting and had been pacing, for an hour, their bikes piled up on the ground at the bottom of the stairs. Pat chucked the comic that Dante had bought for him behind the trash can and rushed over to introduce his friends to his cousin. Surprised and oddly hurt, Dante quietly went and picked the comic up during the introductions and put it in his backpack before he joined the group.

They all stood there looking at each other, a girl occasionally giggling. Pat broke the awkward tension when he smiled at Carla and said, "We want to show you our hangout." He picked up his bike and told Carla to hop on.

Carla asked, "Who's that creepy guy on the wall?"

Pat glanced at Dante and said, "My uncle."

"Oh, I'm sorry." Carla looked at the ground.

"I'm not," said Pat. Dante was still pissed about the comic, but glad that Pat wasn't a total asshole about Truman anymore.

～

THOUGH DANTE HADN'T EVEN TALKED to any of the girls yet, he was blushing furiously by the time he got matched up with the last girl, Amelia, who had long brown hair, glasses, and seemed as unsure about all of this as he was. He and Shannon had gotten to the point of sitting together at lunch sometimes, so Dante hoped she wouldn't come to town that day and mess that all up. He was just here because everybody else was.

Dante held the bike for her while she got on the seat. He stepped in front of her and she put her hands around his waist, which was unsettling. He prayed he wouldn't fart and started pedaling. The bike wobbled and they almost fell, but he caught it in time and smoothed it out when he got some speed. After they passed Truman, Dante realized he had been so nervous about the girl on his bike, he forgot to say hello. He didn't hear anyone else say it either.

"Cool cabin! How'd you find this place? Where do we sit?" was the chorus of questions when they arrived. To Dante, it was unsettling to have it so noisy and crowded. Pat shared the log with Carla and Jeremy shared the crate with his girl, Wendy. Lyle had been paired with Tippy and his folding chair was too small to share, so he offered it to Tippy. She sat down for a second on the chair, then changed her mind and sat next to Lyle on the floor. Dante and Amelia stood next to the door until Pat told Dante to come and sit down already.

Jeremy had gotten his birthday boom box, which he had tucked away in the cold storage space in the wall, just in case. Once in a while, it was obvious somebody else other than Truman had been there, evidenced by a granola bar wrapper or a juice bottle, probably a hiker.

Jeremy took it out of its hiding place and began

digging through his bag. "Let's see... Journey, Air Supply, Van Halen —"

"Oh, Air Supply," said Wendy. "They're my favorite."

Tippy rolled her eyes. "It's all she ever listens to. Van Halen next, please!"

Jeremy complied and popped in the Air Supply tape, which started in the middle of *All Out of Love*. Wendy squealed and made him rewind it to the beginning, which took a couple of tries. Finally accomplished, he said, "I got a ton of snacks from the store. My family runs the general store where we met." He started throwing bags of chips and cookies onto the ground and taking out sodas more gently, though not by much. The girls squealed and each grabbed a bag and a soda. From their positions around the room, the girls all started talking to each other about some fight that happened at their school in Barre and the boys sat watching them. When they abruptly stopped chattering, Pat lunged toward Carla as if waiting for just that moment. They started kissing and they all could hear it over the music. Lyle took that as his cue and started making out with Tippy.

Dante hadn't felt this out of place since the horrible hunting trip he finally had taken with Pat. He wondered if he would ever stop being the odd one out. Dante, blushing beet red, looked at Jeremy, who looked as uncomfortable as Dante felt, minus the red cheeks. "You guys want to go outside? There's a cool tree nearby — split open by lightning." The two girls looked greatly relieved and the four of them left quickly. The girls appropriately oohed and aahed over the lightning tree, its inner trunk charred and exposed to the sky. None of them seemed particularly interested in making out, so they walked around the woods, talking about favorite movies, favorite songs, favorite food.

When they got back to the cabin, Dante and Jeremy hadn't seen it, but their girls had given each other a signal. Before Dante opened the door, Amelia touched his arm and he turned. Wendy did the same with Jeremy and they all, not so quietly, stood next to each other and made out for one minute. Dante kept his eyes open at first, but when he saw hers closed, he closed his, too. She tasted like Doritos. He couldn't believe the amount of spit that got made and wasn't sure if he should wipe his mouth once she pulled away. When they stepped inside, the others had finished their make-out sessions and were digging through the cassettes trying to find the next one to play. Pat looked at Dante with his wet mouth and red face. He smiled at him with raised eyebrows and Dante smiled back.

TOWARDS THE END of sophomore year, after getting his license, Lyle bought his uncle's used 1978 Subaru Brat with the money he had saved up from the previous year, ever since his father let him start helping out at their body shop. This meant that Lyle became the hub of the group, from which their world expanded exponentially. Jeremy had his license, but no car. Pat was next, then Dante. Until then, Lyle was constantly getting asked to drive them all to Barre to hit Exile, the record shop, on Main Street. Cassettes for the boombox, vinyl for personal favorites. Always a stop at Price Chopper Grocery on the Barre-Montpelier Road: comics from their large racks for Dante and Pat, Entenmann's donuts for Jeremy, Hostess Snoballs for Lyle. The boys would take turns being in the front of the Brat and buckling into the open seats in the back that were welded up against the cab.

The Brat was key in setting up the cabin to make it more make-out friendly, a goal for Lyle and Pat in particular. Wherever the miles-long railroad bed intersected with a main road, there was a metal gate to prevent cars from driving on it, although it was undrivable for most of the year due to the long winters and ensuing spring mud season. The gate was built from yellow metal tubes welded into the shape of a triangle that could swing open in the event of a fire to give firetrucks access. Jeremy got a bolt cutter from the storage shed behind the general store and cut the lock that joined the two ends of the chain wrapped around both the post and opening side of the gate that was next to the Rose Garden Apartments' parking lot, their access point. They simply replaced it with the same kind of lock from the hardware store and made it look closed, but didn't click it locked. To any passerby, the gate looked locked, not that anyone ever looked, nor had there been any fire in those woods since time out of mind. If there was a fire, the lock was open, so no harm done.

Donna Hicks said yes, finally, to going steady with Lyle right after he got his car. Pat seemed to kiss a different girl every month. Jeremy hadn't had any luck with girls, yet, but didn't seem too bothered. "More time for video games," he said. Dante, who was struggling to be bolder with Shannon, but she still seemed to gravitate towards Pat.

~

ONE DAY while Pat was at CVH, Shannon and Dante hung out by the waterfall and she told him how over the years, she never knew that Dante liked her. He had always seemed to shut down around her and so she figured he was not interested at all. She kissed him hard after she said that and told him what a great friend he was to Pat and how lucky she was to be his girlfriend now. How she understood that Dante needed to focus on Pat for a while and that they would get their moment on the senior trip.

After a month of medication, Pat started to get out of bed on his own every day and complained about being bored and how he wanted to start driving again. He hadn't had any hallucinations or ideations in a week. Candice checked in with Dr Garcia. He said these were all very good signs and meant the meds were working and that Pat was ready to go back to school and that he should start therapy. The doctor warned that he would have to be watched very, very carefully. She didn't need to be told; at this point, Candice wouldn't let Pat try a new toothpaste unless it was approved by the doctor.

Pat started doing his hair again like Shaun Cassidy, wearing his trademark cutoff sweatshirts and tight acid-wash jeans. Candice, after asking Bill to go with him a few times at first, allowed Pat to start driving himself and Kitty to and from school. Kitty was under strict orders to report anything "off."

"Aren't you going to blast your Twisted Sister or what-ever?" asked Kitty, peering into the rearview mirror while she applied strawberry-flavored Bonnie Bell lip gloss.

Pat shrugged. "I don't know. Not now."

Kitty sat back against the passenger door and looked at her brother frankly. He was different now, but better now that he wasn't a dark lump on his bed. She couldn't put her finger on what she was feeling.

"What are you thinking about?" she asked.

What Pat didn't say was that the reason he wasn't playing music was so he could listen for hoof stomps. For foggy breath. For the scritch-scratch of antlers against the windows. It didn't matter that the car was moving. This is what people didn't understand. The medications had calmed his fear, made him feel better about everything in general, but the worry was always there.

"How good it feels to get out of the house. Even if it is to go to school."

"Shit, you did have it bad."

They laughed together at that. Kitty thought some more. How was he different? He was...cautious. Distracted. Subdued.

The spark that had made him an asshole also made him her brother and she missed it. She didn't know how to be with him anymore. She knew she would always love her brother, but feared she wouldn't be able to find a way to like him anymore.

14

1984: THE BRIDGE

Candice's youth, while mostly sweet once Truman was gone, had some darker parts that she finally shared with Pat, who had been asking a lot about his uncle since his return from the CVH. Along with Truman being whipped behind the barn, and the fire, of course, there was her brother Samuel getting knocked around after missing a day at the quarry, and her sister Felicity eloping too young to get out of the house and moving to Boston where she became a teacher — she was a presence that Candice had sorely missed. By the time she turned ten years old, things had improved — people were working again, thanks to government programs and a faraway war that took her older brother Samuel away from the sheds that had already been making him cough and returned him a hero. Papa had beamed with pride and his dark moods lessened as the Rock of Ages began to thrive again with people fixing up their homes, buying nicer headstones, and the building of Greyson College stone by stone.

Candice's earliest memories of her eldest brother were

of his recovering at home after being disfigured by the fire that Truman had set. She was so proud to be given the responsibility of bringing Clemens lunch in his room and he would ask her to read to him, which she now attributed to her love of books, especially romance novels. She recalls holding her breath whenever she entered the room, bracing herself for Clemens' face, but that passed in time when she saw how lovingly his high school sweetheart, Ginny, tended to him and kissed his scars. Candice was told by her mother not to blame Truman for the fire or for Clemens' burns, as he was plagued by spirits, though once she was an adult, she learned it was a hereditary condition in his nervous system. She remembered her father saying, "God help us all if any more of you children get afflicted."

The thought of this terrified her throughout her childhood and made her dread the dark, which was, she imagined, the perfect time for the hereditary spirits to come, and she would end up like Truman. She was the only one of her siblings that spent time with Truman now, all of them having moved away or died, though she would see birthday cards on Truman's kitchen table every April from Felicity and Annabelle. Samuel wanted nothing to do with him, or any of them it seemed; apparently, he ended up retiring in Guam. Henry Bates had died years before, when Candice was in high school, from stonecutter's TB.

The last time any of them saw Samuel was at *Maman's* funeral when Pat was little and Kitty was just a baby bump. Candice told Pat how she had brought Truman to the funeral, and he was more agitated than she had ever seen him, arguing loudly with that Coolidge voice. So loudly, in fact, she had asked Bill to escort Truman away from the service until he calmed down. Truman, through no fault of his own, had broken their mother's heart and perhaps the fact, if he could comprehend it, had broken his.

Pat learned from her that Truman took a variety of medications, some of which were developed relatively recently, and others that were originally for seizures, but somehow were useful and helped with the voices and his coordination. He also learned that Truman was in the system under Section 8, which, from what Pat understood, was for people with mental illness. He learned the name of Truman's condition: schizophrenia. That he had a case worker named Alex, who handled his Section 8 paper-work and loosely monitored his activities, given that Truman was stable, had reliable housing, and regular family contact. Alex had told Candice how blessed Truman was, that most of his clients were lucky to have even one of those elements in place.

CANDICE ASKED Pat to pick up Truman for Kitty's fifteenth birthday dinner in mid-March. She had him call Truman before to make sure Truman didn't get it in his head to drive out himself, which worried his mother to no end. Candice couldn't even bring herself to ask Truman anymore if he had a license, much less insurance. She decided she didn't want to know because there would be nothing she could do about it. He was an adult after all, he had a right to make choices, poor as they may be. Anyway, it was raining, as it had been on and off for days, and the dirt roads were a mess.

Pat idled outside of the Rose Garden, keeping the truck running and the wipers beating fast against the rain.

He honked the horn and Truman came out in his beige cardigan and wool winter coat that Candice said he'd had since time out of mind. It was nice, in a weird way, to be alone with him. Pat could always be himself with Truman, like he couldn't be with anyone else. Truman would never dream of judging, scolding, or even praising him. He asked questions, but never asked him what was wrong. Even Dante could drive him nuts with his questions.

Truman hoisted himself into the passenger seat, muttering quietly to his voices. That he could keep a conversation going at the same time never ceased to amaze Pat. During the ride, he asked Pat about school ("sucks"), girls ("taking a break"), if he'd been working ("not exactly"), or hunting (Pat hesitated. "No, but I aim to, soon"). He asked about Dante, which made Pat smile, him thinking of Dante like family.

"He's got a girl now."

"That so?"

"Yep. Name's Shannon. You'd like her, she's nice."

"Shannon-a-Bannon. A rose. Good for the garden." The windshield wipers beat back and forth. Pat turned the dial on the handle to slow them down as the rain began to ease up.

Pat knew now that "rose" meant Truman was talking about a girl. It made him think back to junior year, when he and Lyle went crazy together over girls. Lyle had been dating Donna again and they talked about going all the way. Pat helped Lyle plan it out. The night it happened, Pat drove them all to the cabin in his truck since Lyle's Brat was in the shop. Pat had come out of one of those early depressions he had that year and was dating Lori Fletcher for a couple of weeks and she came with them. Lyle and Donna went into the cabin, and they stayed in the truck. Pat felt her up under her bra and she pushed his hand down into her open jeans. She gave him his first blowjob that night, both of them awkwardly positioned on the bench seat, her body bent over the stick shift, warm mouth sliding up and down his erection. He'd never come so hard until he lost his virginity three weeks later. Like Lyle, it happened on the futon they'd dragged into the cabin. It was with Sheila Retton, who graduated two years before and knew a thing or two about liquor, pot, and sex.

Pat shook his head at the memory of that year, and what he did in the cabin that night of the class of 1983 graduation party. He must have been beyond girl-crazy to pull a stunt like that. Or just an asshole. This year's party, *their* graduation party, will be different. Not only because he's not graduating until he takes a ton of summer school, but he can't drink either. Not with the medication. Should keep him from doing anything too stupid.

Dante had told him when he got back from the senior trip to Montreal that he and Shannon went all the way. Pat had missed out on the trip entirely — no one thought it was a good idea for him to go, not even Pat. Lyle and Jeremy were eighteen by then, so they were more than happy to clear out of the shared room for a couple of hours after curfew and go to bars for the very first time. They gave Dante shit for not joining them, but not too much given the circumstance.

Dante told him it wasn't as scary as he thought it would be, not knowing exactly what to do. It was with Shannon, after all. She said she wasn't as scared, either, because she was with him.

Pat couldn't even jerk off anymore; girls were far from his mind. Which he hoped wasn't becoming a regular thing. He looked over at his uncle. He took a deep breath and released it.

"Uncle Tru, who is Coolidge? I mean, I know he was a president. And he was from Vermont. But, like why do you talk to him?"

"He keeps the votes."

Pat sighed. "Tell me more about Brunella." He turned off Route 2 onto the dirt road that led to the two other dirt roads that took him home. The trees were sprouting early green leaves. Given that year's big snow melt and recent rains, the road was thick with mud. Pat slid around, but was in control.

"Brunella-Newtella. Only one to make it rise. Feel it grow. Clemens, Bringer of the Flame, a man for her."

Pat finally understood what he meant. "Did he love her?"

"Don't tell Ginny, but Clemens and Brunella loved it together. He won't with Ginny, not since the burn, but Brunella is the rose who can. The cabin is the where."

Pat thought he understood. He remembered from his mom's stories that Ginny was Clemens' wife and they never had kids. "So, why the sage?"

"Brunella, the lover of the brother. I love the brother. I love the Brunella that loved the brother. Clemens is gone. Brunella is the bridge."

Pat nodded. So, the cabin was the last connection Truman had to his brother. Burning the sage was purification, or for Truman, maybe a way to honor that connection. A ritual, at any rate. He probably would never have figured it out if he hadn't spent so much time with the Zuckermans.

Pat's eye caught something to the left. He slowed down. The buck. He heard the hooves. The defiant snort.

The buck's majestic rack was turned toward them. Pat slammed on the brakes. Truman braced himself against the dash.

"Uncle Tru. Look out my window. Tell me that you see that buck." Pat's blood had turned to ice and his bowels loosened. He fought to maintain control of his body. He whispered, "Do you feel how angry it is?"

Truman craned forward to look out Pat's driver side window. "Buck-a-truck. Not my view."

Pat pounded the wheel in fear and frustration. "Look! He's right *there*."

Truman pulled a cigarette out of his cardigan pocket and struck a match. "The flame. The flame keeps it calm." He shook out the match. "They gave me the clock of pills. They are what give Coolidge the votes."

Pat closed his eyes. Truman sat silently, smoking, indifferent to whether they were driving or not. When Pat opened his eyes, he didn't dare look to the side of the road. He drove on and Truman returned to his mutterings until they pulled up to the house. The house where Truman grew up and where Pat was almost done growing up. Pat parked in front of the porch, trying to get as close as possible so Truman could avoid the muddy driveway. Pat predicted correctly that Truman would head right for the porch rocker. Pat went inside, announced that they were home and brought out a blanket for his uncle. They sat for a minute, Truman rocking and Pat up on the porch railing, cold and wet through his jeans thanks to the misting rain. Pat stayed through Truman's first cigarette of many that he'd smoke that visit, coming in only to eat. Together they listened to the rain pattering softly on the new, green leaves of the dooryard maple.

Pat looked beyond the barn, only to become overcome

with the now familiar feeling of dread. There he was again, rack as big as life.

"Truman! Look he's right there! Right fucking there!"

No reply. The rocker was empty and swinging on its own. Pat heard his mother calling everyone in for dinner.

15

1984: THE LAST FIGHT, THE LAST PARTY, AND THE LAST HUNT

Graduation for the class of 1984 was a week away and they were all going to Tommy Fallen's graduation party. There were no hard feelings with Tommy after what happened at Dougie Frasier's graduation party for the class of 1983 last year. After all, everyone was so wasted.

Last year, Dougie Frasier was the Trojan High School quarterback, and the party was at his family's farm. The crowd had included nearly forty graduates, including the football team, the cheerleaders, and smattering of underclassmen, including the boys. This wasn't their party, the boys didn't graduate until the following year, but Dougie and Jeremy's parents were old friends and so the families had spent a good amount of time together. Jeremy thought it was really cool of Dougie to invite him to the party, which Pat, Dante, and Lyle took to mean that all of them were invited. At this point, Pat had been doing great — he hadn't had a round of depression for weeks and wouldn't again until after the car accident.

Around nine o'clock, any adult presence slowly

dissolved until there were only Trojan students left around the bonfire in the large clearing behind the barn. Word got around about the four cases of Miller Lite stashed at the tree line at the far end of the Frasier's backfield. A stampede scrambled across the field, eager to chug at least one lukewarm graduation beer. The handful of kids who weren't interested remained around the fire, talking quietly. Others disbanded from the main pack and formed intimate groups that melted away into the warm night and settled randomly around the backfield. Pat, Dante, Lyle, and Shannon made up one such group, nestled in among the high grass.

Jeremy was among those scrambling. He had promised his cluster of friends that he wouldn't return until he had accomplished his mission of a beer in every hand. Across the fire-lit night, all could hear his cry, "Beer for all and all for beer!"

"No one hustles as hard as Jer-Bear when it comes to beer," remarked Lyle.

Pat laid back and looked at the starry sky. "You can say that twice and mean it. Hope he gets here quick."

Lyle followed suit and reclined in the tall grass, hands behind his head. "Well, no worries. We have plenty back at the cabin, thanks to Dana who will take any excuse to use her ID to buy alcohol." Dana was Lyle's oldest sister who recently turned twenty-one. "Shame we already went through the ones we brought."

Shannon scooched closer to Pat, which did not go unnoticed by Dante. She settled back against a cool clump of grass. Her hands went up to readjust the feather clip in her hair.

Dante suddenly took off his baseball hat, the one that he'd worn for years with the band name, Rush, embossed on it. He wouldn't listen to Pat that he should get rid of it. Now he was wondering if Pat was right; ratty caps were probably not a chick magnet. Maybe the hat was why Shannon didn't seem to like him back. That and his nickname Strawberry. It made him sound like a wuss.

Pat suddenly sat upright. "Wait. Shhh." The full moon coming over Spruce Mountain highlighted the edges of his feathered blond hair. "Did you hear that?"

No one moved except to tilt an ear upwards to catch the sound. Nothing.

"Shit. Thought I heard a deer or something."

"Probably just two lucky lovers having a lay in the hay," commented Lyle.

Shannon adjusted her tasseled, red-suede jacket to cover up against the oncoming night chill that arrived when the moon crested the mountain. As she did, she moved another inch closer to Pat. Dante noticed that, but Pat acted like he didn't. The truce was still on. Dante had really wanted to ask her to come to the party with him, but he was so worried about blushing he couldn't do it.

"Jer-Bear is taking way too long." Dante reached into an inner pocket in his jean jacket and pulled out a big baggie of pot.

In the clear light of the moon, Dante saw Pat's mouth drop open. "Holy shit, Straw. Where have you been all my life?"

Dante had been hesitant to steal weed from his parents, not wanting to risk the disappointment talk, so he had only ever taken the smallest amounts. But tonight he took the risk and took enough for a few bowls.

"Nothing but the best for someone else's graduation!" laughed Dante. Maybe this would impress Shannon. He reached back into his inner pocket. "Oh, shit." He could immediately feel his flushed face.

Pat immediately caught on. "Okaaaay... who's got a pipe?" asked Pat.

Jeremy burst through the tall grass, arms crammed with cans of beer. "Pipe? Who said pipe? I got mine, just in case. Dante's got the weed?" Jeremy dropped a tepid beer can into everyone's lap, and then plunked down next to Dante, breathing heavily under his Bass Pro baseball cap. He took out the metal pipe he got when his cousin took him to a head shop in Boston earlier that year. Dante passed the baggie over to Jeremy, who started packing the bowl tight.

Jeremy, taking the first hit, burst out in a chortling cough. "Oh my Gawd." he choked out. "This shit is *rad*."

"Rad?" asked Pat. "Ever since that *Valley Girl* movie came out. It's got everyone talking like a moron around here."

Lyle grinned, taking the pipe from Jeremy. Dragging in a hit, he held his breath, then raising his voice to a falsetto, said, "You're, like sooo bitchin', Pat." He let go his hit.

Pat ignored Lyle in favor of the pipe, which Lyle passed to him. Shannon took the pipe from Pat. "Who's got the lighter?" Pat flicked the lighter and lifted the flame to the pipe in her hand. Their faces lit up as she inhaled. Dante watched her look up at Pat while she took her hit, but Pat fixed his eyes on the flame.

Pat took his thumb off the lighter and it went out. Shannon took a toke. She loved *Valley Girl* but couldn't admit it now.

It was Dante next. He toked and held it in. Dante held his hit as long as he could, chortling noises coming from his nose, then released it in a fragrant stream. Jeremy accepted the pipe back from him and tried another toke. "I think it's cashed."

Before anyone could speak, someone yelled out from about fifty feet away, "Okay, I smell weed. Who's holding out?"

Lyle put his finger to his lips, "Shhh, everyone," he whispered. "That's George McKinney." He dropped his voice even lower and said with exaggerated lip movement, "Asshole."

The five of them sat perfectly still while they listened to George search through the grass for them, but it was all they could do to stifle bursts of stoned laughter until they finally cracked up for real.

"GO!" shouted Lyle and the group shot up and ran into the woods. They outpaced George, who yelled, "Why are you being so lame? It's graduation!"

They disappeared into the trees. When it was all clear, they walked along the edge of the field back to where their cars were parked. No one asked Shannon to come along, but no one said no, either, so she grabbed Pat's passenger door to his pockmarked Ford truck and climbed up onto the bench seat. Dante took a big breath and climbed in after her. Jeremy got into Lyle's Brat. Lyle's headlights shining into the woods, revealing Tommy Fallen and Debby Miller locking lips, pressed up against an evergreen tree. Lyle stuck his head out the window and yelled at them to stop dry-humping and come with them. They laughed and hopped into the open back of the Brat and strapped themselves into the seats behind the cab. Pat and Lyle turned their rigs around one-by-one and started down the Frasier's quarter-acre long driveway, Pat in the lead.

THEY DROVE on the rough back roads so as to avoid any cops on the way to the cabin. Pat parked on the street when they got to the Rose Garden. Everyone in Pat's truck got out and jumped into the back of the Brat. They drove up to the bushes that covered the entrance and Jeremy hopped out, walking over to take off the lock that was never locked.

While he did that, Tommy knocked on the window and yelled, "What the fuck? Where are we going?"

Lyle knocked back. "Shut up, Tommy. You're gonna wake everyone!"

They all turned around and stared at the Rose Garden windows. No lights came on. Jeremy closed the gate behind them, put back the lock, and got back into Lyle's Brat.

At the cabin, someone flicked on the battery-run boom box tuned to WORK, the Top-40 station. The DJ was taking call after call from friends and family congratulating their loved ones on graduation night. Def Leppard's new hit "Photograph" came on.

Jeremy Ibey held the can of Budweiser on its side and punched a sloppy hole in it toward the bottom with a screwdriver. All eyes on him, he carefully tipped the hole up to his mouth. The spectators started to chant; "Jer-Bear, Jer-Bear, Jer-Bear, Jer-Bear!" All eyes were on him in the cabin, which was lit by the single kerosene lamp hanging from the ceiling.

Jeremy lifted his free hand to pull the tab, but the U-curved rim of his battered baseball hat blocked his hand, so he turned his cap backward. The chant got louder, near to deafening on the Bear syllable. Jeremy tucked his finger under the tab and tugged it upwards with a sharp crack and hiss. The small crowd let loose, hooting and hollering. He finished shotgunning his beer in three successive swallows. After the final gulp, Jeremy smacked his lips at the crispness of the beer, made freezer cold by the now nearly liquid five bags of ice in a large metal tub in the corner of the room that they had stopped off to buy at the gas station. He lifted the can, crushed it in his fist, and then released the deepest and airiest of belches. Leaning back, he hollered, "So long class of '83. Class of '84 RULES!"

As the night deepened, Pat sat back from the crowd, wasted, one arm up on the back of the futon, while his other hand loosely dangled a half-finished Bud. Dante and Pat locked eyes and they both grinned. Dante raised his chin and rolled his eyes to indicate "check out those two," meaning Tommy and Debby, who were making out on the other end of the futon, hands in all directions. In the next moment, Shannon sat down next to Pat and before Dante could blink, she started making out with him. Pat didn't miss a beat and in the next moment, his hand was up her shirt. The truce was over.

Shannon and Pat finally came up for air, lips red and wet. Lyle and Jeremy saw what was happening, glanced at Dante and turned away in unison. In low voices, they started confirming if they had seen what they thought they had seen. Dante staggered to the newly hung hammock and tried to sit in it without spilling over. God, they were all so wasted. But still.

Pat didn't seem to notice that Dante had retreated. He waved the hand that was still gripping a beer in a circle, as if casting a spell on his group of friends. There was still a trace of wetness shining around his mouth. His words slurring together, he turned to Shannon and said, "These guys — you see 'em — these guys are the best guys in the whole fucking world. Our junior year was the best in the history of... history. And next year *this* senior class will be even better." Pat weaved himself up to his feet. He addressed the crowd, "You hear me, assholes?"

Lyle and Jeremy had turned back around at his voice and Lyle let out a "Hell, yeah!"

Pat balled his free hand into a fist and punched the air. "Senior class of '84!" Pat wobbled as he stared at the floor, which was beginning to turn in circles. "Let's give a Fighting Trojan cheer!" He swayed and took an unintentional step backward.

Jeremy jumped up next to him and shouted, "When I say 'Trojans', you say 'Fight'! Trojans!"

The crowd responded, except for Dante, raising and spilling beers, "Fight!"

"Trojans!"

"Fight!"

Pat belched. "Where's Strawberry, my favorite asshole?" He was slurring.

"Right in front of you, Pat Bates, you wastoid." Dante untangled himself from the hammock and stepped into the light. His voice was barely clearer than Pat's.

"Look Straw. I know it and you know it, and everyone here knows it. I'm gonna say it and you can't stop me."

Dante froze. Was Pat about to announce that Shannon was his girl now, so Dante could just fuck off and deal with it?

Pat chugged the rest of his beer and wiped his chin. "You are my best fucking friend, the best fucking friend in the whole world. And here it comes. Are you ready? I love you, Strawberry."

Everyone cried, "Eeeeewwww!" and chucked as many empty and near empty beer cans at Pat as they could find.

Dante had trouble remaining standing. "Will you, then, you fucking redneck, stop calling me that fucking nickname once and for all?"

The room fell silent. "Jeezum, who put the stick up your ass?"

Dante, for the second time in their friendship, leaped at Pat and knocked him to the ground. The two rolled around on the floor. Someone knocked the kerosene lantern while backing away from the fighting bodies on the floor and it swung wildly.

Jeremy and Lyle had picked up the tub of ice and beers and dumped it on Pat and Dante. Suddenly, ice, water, and beers rolled across the futon, tables, chairs and floor, soaking everyone from the waist down. Their aim had not been very good.

Shannon, who had been behind Pat on the futon, stood up shakily, holding her head. "Ow!" She sat down hard on the floor.

Dante thought he saw a light outside the window, but figured it was because he was drunk.

Pat sat up first, soaked top to bottom, his feathered hair flat and dripping. "What the fuck, assholes, there were still full cans in there!"

A hush came over the room. Tommy and Debby went over to Shannon and checked on the goose egg that was already forming on her forehead.

Dante struggled to sit, his hair stringy and wet. He stared hard at Pat, who put his hands up in exasperation. "Strawberry, what the incredible fuck was that?"

Dante was still drunk, but no longer slurring. "Stop calling me fucking Strawberry. I'm fucking sick of it."

The door to the cabin opened and in stepped Ephraim Zuckerman.

Dante scrabbled to his feet. "Dad!"

"Mrs. Bates called. Truman called her. Said he saw you boys driving down here and he had a bad feeling. I saw the lock wasn't closed on the gate and figured out how. How long have you been doing this?"

Dante didn't know how to answer. "Sorry, Dad. Things got out of hand."

"Why the hell is everybody wet?" Ephraim saw Shannon clutching her head. "What happened? Are you okay?" Shannon replied by bursting into tears.

"Okay, party's over. The Brat stays here — Lyle, give me your keys. I'll give the girls a ride home. Everyone else, you walk back to our house."

Dante said, "But —"

"You better just stop right there, Dante."

Tommy shuffled his feet. "Mr. Zuckerman, I gotta work in the morning. Could you drop me at Debby's? I live near her."

"Fine. Lyle — keys."

Lyle handed them over, mumbling, "Sorry Mr. Z." The girls and Tommy got in the Subaru wagon and Ephraim K-turned the car around and drove back down the path, headlights creating a tunnel of light that shrank as he got farther away.

Since Lyle and Jeremy did the dousing, they were drier and much more wasted than Pat and Dante, who walked ahead of them. Even if they didn't make it all the way to the Zuckermans, it was a warm night if they ended up passing out on a pile of overgrowth. At first all the boys were silent until Jeremy and Lyle started horsing around again, shoving each other to see who was drunker.

Pat and Dante walked at a distance from each other. They didn't talk for a long while.

"You know how wasted we all are, right?"

Dante shook his head. "Doesn't make it right."

Pat threw his hands up. "When, Strawberry? When? After all this time? I mean, you got one year left to get together with her. What's your problem?"

What did he have to do, beg? Voice raised, he said, "I don't want to be called Strawberry anymore. It's a stupid nickname and I hate it and I hate you for giving it to me." Dante turned back to the drunk duo behind him. "You hear me assholes? No more of this Strawberry shit."

They heard an "oof," which sounded like Jeremy. He might have tripped, but it was too dark to tell. They heard a "Whatever, dude," which was followed up by the sound of retching.

Pat stopped and Dante did, too, crossing his arms. Pat said, "Fuckin' A, Dante, it's just a nickname. And it fits, don't you think? You blush at everything. Kind of a ridiculous habit, don't you think? I mean, you still read comics and shit. When are you going to grow a pair?"

"Fuck you. You have it so easy, with your pretty hair and showing off your abs twenty-four-seven. How can Shannon, or any girl, possibly like anyone with a nickname like Strawberry? It sounds like I'm some kind of fucking idiot." Dante started walking again. "And it shouldn't matter. You know I like her and then you feel her up, right in front of me."

"We were *wasted*, dude. And I'm sorry, but *she* jumped *me*. It felt good. You should try it some time."

"Up yours. Sorry I'm not a big fucking Casanova." Dante wanted to pounce on him again, but suddenly felt more tired and dizzy than he had before. He hunched over and puked.

"If you think I'm holding your hair back like a girl, you can forget it."

Dante sat down hard next to his vomit. "I hate being me. You're right. I am the biggest fucking loser." Dante lay down and curled onto his side next to his puke.

Pat sat down next to him. He looked back but didn't see the other two. "I'm sorry, Straw... Dante. You're right. You may be a loser, but I am king of the assholes."

Dante sat back up and Pat put his arm around him. Dante said, "Well, you said it first. But you forgot redneck. You are king of the redneck assholes."

Pat pushed him over. "Vegetarian pussy."

Dante came back up. "Oh man, you pushed me into my puke."

Pat tried to hold back a laugh and failed. Soon they were both cracking up. Pat said, "I am going to call Shannon tomorrow and tell her that was not cool of me. I mean, dude, do *I* have to be the one to tell her how you feel?"

Dante shrugged. "I should just call her, too. Ask her out. Okay, you call first, then I'll wait a day and call."

"God, you're such a girl. Okay, fine."

Jeremy and Lyle staggered up, debating whether or not they could make it all the way back to the Zucker-mans, which was at least a mile and a half.

Dante said, "Well, I don't have a choice. I think my ass is actually going to be handed to me this time."

Jeremy and Lyle looked at each other. Lyle said, "We're going back to the cabin. Too fucking wasted."

Pat looked at Dante. "I'll come with you."

Jeremy said, "Straw- sorry... Dante. Fuck, that's hard. Anyway, hope you don't get too reamed out."

"Thanks, Jer-Bear. And if you want to stop being called Jer-Bear..." Dante pointed to Lyle, "or Lincoln, just say the word."

Lyle's large teeth shone in the dark. "Four score and seven assholes ago, Dante Zuckerman got a stick up his butt. Hold on." He weaved in place for a moment, hand to his mouth. "Nope, I'm good. Later losers."

Lyle called back after a minute, voice faded from the distance. "Bring me my keys tomorrow!"

EPHRAIM WAS WAITING for them at the kitchen table. They didn't have to be told, they just sat down across from him. "Where are the other two?"

Dante said, "They were too, uh...sleepy to make it back."

Ephraim rolled his eyes. "Look, I want you boys to know that Truman did the right thing."

Neither of them said it, but both boys were thinking it. *Fucking loud Tommy.*

The boys stared at the table.

"But the worst thing, the truly stupid thing, was drinking and driving around like that. If you want to party, I get it. I was your age once in case you forgot. But you can't be driving around. You know what's worse than killing yourself?"

The boys knew the answer but remained silent.

"Killing somebody else, like your best friend." Ephraim ran a hand down his face. "Damn, I don't know how to do this. Dante, you should really have gotten caught more so I could have practiced for this. For the record, this is *bad*."

"My folks make me do all the laundry in the house when I f-, sorry, screw up. Last time was for one month."

Dante's eyes widened and his mouth dropped open as he kicked Pat under the table.

"Okay, our laundry for one month. And you work at the store for free until further notice. Oh, and uh... you're grounded for one month, too."

Dante looked at the table. He calculated a month from then. He looked at Pat, then his father with wide eyes. "What about the Foreigner concert? That's in three weeks!"

"Well, let's see if you make any more horrible decisions between now and then. So, before we conclude this pow-wow, do you two have anything to say for yourselves?"

Dante sighed. "I'm sorry, Dad. Really. You're right, it was dumb. It won't happen again."

"Totally, Mr. Z. It won't happen again."

Darlene came bustling in wearing an oversized tie-dye with a peace sign on it. "Okay, boys. Eat a banana to help with dehydration and take these vitamin B supplements. Oh, good God. Is that puke on your sleeve?"

Dante turned his arm and looked. "Uh, maybe?"

"I don't even want to know." Darlene handed out bananas, capsules, cups, and water.

"Thanks, Mom."

"Thanks Mrs. Z."

Darlene turned to Dante. "Get the sleeping bags out of the hall closet. Wait." She peered at Dante, searched his face.

"What?"

"Huh, well, you're a little pink, but not beet red as I expected. Huh."

Dante rolled his eyes as he started to go fetch the sleeping bags, but gave a small smile as soon as he was turned the other way.

Pat was left to sit in the kitchen with Darlene and Ephraim. Darlene sat down and reached across the table. Putting her hand on his arm, she said, "Pat, I know you've had a rough time, on and off, lately."

"Yeah. Dante helped a lot."

"Well, I'm glad for that. You two are lucky to have each other."

"Thanks, Mrs. Z."

"You'll see, next year, your senior year, will be so much better."

That's what everyone had hoped. That's what everyone always hopes.

THE END of the school year for 1984 had arrived. The boys couldn't believe it. It was finally their turn. With graduation less than a week away, Alice Cooper's song *School's Out* could be heard blaring from the school parking lot at any time during those final days.

Tommy Fallen's party was on the Saturday night five days before the ceremony. Dante was picking up Shannon and Pat and Lyle drove Jeremy. Jeremy had finally gotten a car when his father upgraded his Bronco, giving Jeremy his old one. But there was a problem with the starter, so it was in the shop. Tommy lived on the other side of Number Ten Pond, so it was a lot of curvy back road driving. Mud season may have been over, but there was plenty of wash-board to make for a bumpy drive under the canopy of lush, green leaves whose colors washed out in the headlights.

Dante gave two short bleeps of his horn. Pat came out almost immediately. He looked like normal Pat, tight jeans and feathered hair. This was the first time Pat will have spent time with anyone other than the boys since his time at the emergency beds at CVH.

Pat got in the back seat and gave an extra pull on the creaking door to shut it completely. "Well, if the door falls off, at least it's summer coming up."

"So funny I forgot to laugh." But then Dante laughed anyway, mostly with relief. Dante hadn't realized he had been so tense, waiting to see which Pat was going to show up.

Shannon turned in her seat to look at Pat. "You look great. Heather's been asking about you, you know."

Pat took a deep breath in and gave a short huff. "Let's do this."

Dante started down the dirt driveway. "Don't be nervous, dude. If anything gets too weird, or whatever, we'll just bail."

"You know, I'm not supposed to drink or anything. This might be too fucking hard."

"Well, remember what happened last year after Dougie Fraiser's party?" Shannon punched him in the arm. "What's wrong with you, bringing that up?" Dante grinned at her. "I'm an asshole, that's what's wrong." He turned towards

Pat in the backseat. "Maybe not getting wasted isn't so bad."

Pat focused his gaze out the window, like he was

searching the darkness. "Whatever, dude. I am prepared for the worst."

PAT WAS SEATED on the couch by the picture window that looked out over the pond. He had what looked like soda in his red solo cup. Heather sat next to him and leaned in. Her breath smelled sweet and sticky. Rum.

"Did you get some rum from Tommy's room to put in your Coke? I took a shot, too. It totally burned!"

Pat forced a smile while he lied. "Yup, sure did." He thought of the endless drinking lectures from his parents before the party. His mom couldn't stop rubbing her hands around each other as they waited for Dante to pick him up. His dad wouldn't shut up about how they were counting on him to be smart, do the right thing, and hadn't he already put the family through enough?

Heather flopped back, sloshing her icy drink, but not spilling it. "Can you believe it? We're done! Totally done with this shit. With high school!" She held her cup up for a toast. Pat lightly tapped his cup against hers. Pat was surprised. He figured everyone knew he wasn't graduating with them. He stayed silent.

Frankie Goes to Hollywood's *Relax* began playing. "Oh my God, I love this song! Come dance!" Heather jumped up, this time spilling her drink onto the floor. She bent in half and gave an open-mouthed laugh. "Good thing my drink matches the carpet!" Either forgetting that she asked, or remembering that most guys didn't dance except for ones like Nate Hubbard, she flounced to the other side of the table where other girls, and Nate, were dancing.

Pat scanned the room. Dante and Shannon were

nowhere to be found, so they could be anywhere doing anything. He looked out the window and saw Lyle's lanky silhouette making out with Donna's equally lanky form at the edge of the moonlit pond. There were a few couples out there. Jeremy looked like he was with someone, too. Pat peered more closely to see who it was.

Right when he did, there was a ripple in the lake and his body tensed with icy dread. His mouth dropped open as twelve-point antlers rose dripping with water. As the buck rose to its full, impossible height, Pat's view was blocked by the buck's angry puffs of vapor that inexplicably began fogging up the glass in the window.

He should never have come. He had to lead the buck away from here. What if someone got hurt?

He hurried unnoticed out the side door. He knew that Dante always left his keys in the ignition of his Tercel because there was no one in the world who would be desperate enough steal it.

"HELLO?" The voice was groggy, as expected. It was just after midnight.

"Mrs. Bates?"

"Yes, Dante. What is it? Are you okay?"

"Yes, but it's Pat. We, uh, don't know where he is."

Candice sat bolt upright in bed. "What?"

"He, uh, kind of... borrowed my car."

"He's *driving*? Oh, God, tell me you boys haven't been drinking."

Silence on the other end. "Not Pat, I swear. I saw him. He had the chance, but he turned it down."

There was a flash of light outside.

"Hold on, Dante."

Bill was already out of bed and looking out the window. "Is that Dante's car?"

Candice put the receiver to her chest. "No, well, yes, it's Pat. He...borrowed Dante's car." She began to talk into the phone again. "Dante, it looks like he's here. Are you able to come get your car?"

Bill put his hands on either side of his face as he pressed up against the window. "He's running toward the house."

They heard his footsteps up the porch steps and the door crash open. "Dad! Dad?"

"Mrs. Bates, what's going on. I hear—"

Candice wasn't sure why, but she needed Dante to come. "Dante, can you come now?"

"Yes, I'll take Lincoln's car. They can all get a ride home. Be there soon."

BOTH BILL and Candice stopped as soon as they entered the living room. Candice clicked on a lamp.

Pat was pacing, frantic. "Dad. It came to the party. This is really serious. I had to leave. I *had* to." He stopped and looked at a point on the wall beyond his parents, who were frozen in place. Bill looked behind him, at the buck head on the wall.

"Patty, what are you talking about? That buck? Again?"

Candice came forward and grabbed him by the shoulders. She knew that look on his face, his eyes looking past her with small darting motions. Truman had that look, when he was what the doctors called "agitated".

"No, no, no, no, no...not my darling boy." Her ability to stand left her and she sat hard on the floor.

Candice couldn't catch her breath. She wanted to call out, but all that came out was a wheeze, "Bill." She was panicking. "Bill."

Bill rushed over. "Pat, help me with your mother."

Pat's body weaved slightly in place as he stood over his mother and father. Pat stared at the buck head mounted on the wall, looking both vacant and terrified. Bill looked at Candice, then Pat, then back at Candice. "Honey, are you alright?"

"Dad! Dad! I'll go look for him."

Before Bill could react, Pat ran out the door to the porch and they heard him clomp down the stairs.

"Candie, what is this? What?"

She shook her head and caught her breath. "It's happening again. Our boy..." She broke down then and sobbed, Bill holding her tight.

Kitty came out, sleepy and scratching her eyes. "What's going on?" She looked at her parents on the floor, her mother ghost white and her dad flushed red, trying to help her up. "Oh." It was the only thing she could think of to say. She began helping her mother onto the couch.

Bill heard the barn door slide open. "Oh, Good God."

Bill, barefoot and in pajamas, raced out the door. His heart was beating so hard he was worried he'd collapse before he got to his son. Pat was in and out of the barn in a flash. Bill watched Pat's form disappear into the night, he could make out a bow slung on his shoulder and a quiver in his hand.

"Shit." Bill ran back inside to get dressed. He had a feeling he knew where Pat was headed and needed Dante's help.

LYLE'S BRAT pulled into the driveway as Bill was coming back out, flashlight in hand. Dante started to get out of the car.

"Son, stay in there. We're heading into the woods."

"The buck. Is it the buck?"

Bill nodded, his face sadder than any Dante had seen before.

"Hold on." Dante dashed out of the car and ran into the house to get something. Candice, on the phone with the police, looked at him strangely, but was busy giving the details of Pat's manic departure and said nothing. He threw the buck head, the one that had scared him so badly as a kid, with a clunk into the back of the truck and they took off down the snow machine trail after Pat. Dante figured he knew where they were going.

DANTE SAW the orange ribbon tied to a branch and stopped the truck. The trail to the deer stand was too small for a vehicle.

Dante lifted the buck head out of the truck and Bill grabbed on to the antlers. With the head between them, they made their way quickly down the trail. The heavy burden between them made their movement through the dark difficult as they rushed under moon-illuminated tree limbs, through shadows, slipping in splotches of wet leaves leftover from mud season.

Pat was right where they figured he'd be. They looked up and Bill trained the flashlight on Pat's face. "Dad! Dad!

It's here. I can hear it. I can't see him through the branches, I can't get a clear shot."

Dante saw the tears streaking down Pat's face and nearly cried out at the look of terror that went with them.

Bill spoke to him in a low tone. "You keep your back to him as you flank the perimeter, keeping it in front of you. You don't want him to see it until we're ready."

Taking the head from Bill, Dante nodded and began his sideways walk around the trees that surrounded the deer stand, his back to Pat. Bill immediately began talking to Pat, trying to get him to look at him, only him. He didn't want Pat to think Dante was the buck. Not yet. He took slow steps as he started toward him.

"Patty, we know about the buck. I...am sorry... that it's, um, here. But I think, well... Shit." Dante froze when Bill stopped talking.

He heard Bill take a big breath. "Patty, we need to get better gear if we're gonna track this thing. I need my gear, you need your camo, your—"

Pat shook his head wildly, like a toddler not getting his way. "He's here, Dad, can't you hear him? Oh God." Pat folded in half and began to weep. "He wants me so bad."

Bill took this opportunity to climb up the stand. Dante knew now was the time. He lifted up the buck head he had taken from the Bates' wall and began to work it into the branches of the tree directly across from the deer stand. He tipped the antlers so he could swing the face toward Pat. The idea was to position it and then get out of the way so Pat could shoot at the head and after his quiver was empty, get him to come back home with them.

Pat had settled into quiet sobbing as he watched his father climb to the top of the stand. They all heard it, in the otherwise still and silent night, the snap of a branch as

Dante made the last push to position the head. Pat inhaled sharply and turned his dirty, tear-streaked face toward the sound, arrow cocked. He aimed and shot. Dante didn't have time to move behind the tree and fell back as the arrow pierced him, the absolutely best shot Pat could have made from the deer stand.

Pat's face lit up with joy and relief. "I got him, Dad!" He laughed and in a deep voice no one had ever heard before said, "I got that bastard. I got 'im good."

16

1935–1966: A HOMECOMING

It had been six months since Emeline's last visit, and she announced it was time to return to Waterbury. She and Henry had gone again after that first visit, but the New Deal program had finally reached central Vermont and construction picked up again, along with headstone orders. Henry didn't want to risk taking time off and jeopardize his coveted supervisory position, so they hadn't returned. When she asked about weekends, he said he needed his rest. It was hard enough to get to church. If it wasn't that, then he blamed bad weather and risky driving conditions.

Emeline had tried to phone Truman, but that first call was a frustrating mix of silence and irrational mutterings. Plus, Mrs. Osbourne was probably listening on the party line, and who knew who else. Emeline didn't want Truman to be anymore the village spectacle then he already was. She had talked with a Dr. Goddard, who seemed to know a lot about Truman. She was thanked for signing the papers that allowed Truman to receive the new therapy, straight from Europe and that they had been administering the therapy and were seeing improvements. He told her that the incident, the fire, that prompted his being taken to the state hospital was, perhaps, a blessing in disguise, as it got Truman here to the hospital and he was making remarkable progress.

Emeline knew she would not be telling that to Henry, who had been forced to take out a loan to keep his promise of payment for reconstruction of Mr. Thompson's shop, which had thankfully been completed. Henry was still paying it off, however, with interest. Plus, who could ever be grateful for Clemens' disfiguration and the tarnished Bates' reputation? Henry was convinced that it was only due to his generational tie to the quarry, his father having been stonecutter there before him, that he kept his employment. This tenuous position, along with Clemens' permanent disability, was not something Emeline could picture Henry forgiving, illness or not.

Clemens had been convalescing at home since he left the Central Vermont Hospital burn ward. Ginny had been by his side every minute she could since she saw his charred body brought in that day. She was a certified nurse now and had gotten her driver's license. This allowed her to be at the Bates' most days, either before or after her shift, and from morning until night on her days off. She helped Emeline change bandages, prepare poultices, kept an eye on Annabelle and Candice, often picking them up from school. Ginny began to think how silly it was she had to go home every day. Wouldn't it be more practical to get married?

She began to drop hints about this around her parents, but Ginny's father had more than a few reservations about his daughter marrying a cripple. He had stopped trying to put other men in her path, handsome men, employed men, educated men, when it was clear she would not be turned. The thought of his best and brightest child burdened by a disfigured husband made his stomach clench.

It turned out Clemens felt the same. He encouraged Ginny to go out and have fun like their friends, who in sunny weather went on picnics on Bald Hill, swam at Number Ten, went joyriding to Burlington to enjoy Lake Champlain, or drank rye at the regular gathering in Jerry Frasier's back field. In winter, it was cross-country skiing through the woods, or even downhill at the Sarducci's where a hand-pull tow rope had been fashioned around a large pine atop the steep slope behind their barn. There was the movie palace and soda shop in Barre. But where Ginny ended up going the most when she was not at the Bates' was the library in Montpelier, so she could bring books for Clemens to help him while away the hours recovering in bed and eventually, able to sit in a chair.

It killed Clemens not to be able to chop wood, drive to town, fix the roof, shovel the snow, rake the leaves. His mother reminded him that it was not forever, just while he was healing. His father, whose mood had improved some since he was getting regular work again, he never quite regained the raucous laugh that had been a regular part of family supper. Clemens told Ginny that he would not marry her — he loved her too much to saddle her to a lame horse. She ignored his protests and continued to come, day after day.

The protests were finally declared as useless as Clemens' left arm. When Clemens' skin had healed enough for him to stand without undue strain on his delicate, deeply scarred skin, the date was set.

Ginny and Clemens married in a June ceremony in

the Bates' living room filled with posies and ribbons. Ginny wore her favorite Sunday dress, the white one with high bodice and intricate lace trim. Felicity was in charge of the decorations, and she had spent four hours the morning of the wedding sewing together the bridal bouquet and the flower garlands that lined the fireplace and windows. Annabelle and Candice were the flower girls, Ginny's younger brother the ring-bearer, her older sister the bride's maid. Samuel was the best man and while everyone knew that it should have been Truman standing up there, Clemens respected the good face Samuel put on, both knowing he was there only by default. But when Samuel first heard the news about the marriage, he approached Clemens with his hand out with congratulations and shook it firm, patting him gently on his bad shoulder. This was the first glimpse Clemens had of Samuel and the well-respected gentleman he would become. It was ill-advised for Clemens to travel yet, so instead of a proper honeymoon, Ginny simply took over Truman's old bed starting that night and her things were brought over the next day. Emeline was thrilled to have another woman around, not just for chores, but for company. It was Ginny who offered to drive her and Clemens to visit Truman so that they could deliver the news, a visit that was way past due.

GINNY INSISTED ON DRIVING. Clemens said he felt the fool riding shotgun to his wife, but he had barely started helping around the house again, must less driving. There was hope his left arm would return to partial use in time, but that was a wait-and-see. Emeline packed Truman a bag — when she called to tell the hospital of their visit, it was requested that she bring large-sized clothes as Truman had put on weight. She couldn't imagine her wiry son any larger than when she last saw him, but she did as she was told. She dug through Henry's half of the closet and took out two shirts and two trousers that she knew were not his favorites. She carefully folded them into the suitcase, along with two pairs of socks, underwear, and a belt.

Clemens was anxious to see Truman. He had confessed to his family, when he could speak again with his now permanently slurred speech, about the plan that day of the fire to steal tobacco from the shop. He told them what a low point he had reached about his job, Ginny, Truman, everything. That while he didn't lose his brother, he lost his best friend and it was he who, in his anger and grief, tried to use Truman instead of trying to help. Clemens had convinced himself at the time that the robbing of the tobacco-haberdashery was also to Truman's benefit — tobacco was the only thing other than Emeline's French lullabies that had calmed him, or at least ceased his mutterings.

Clemens said that he'd had a long time to think, and he came to the conclusion that while that may have been part of it, another part had been more deeply rooted. He had wanted another caper with Truman. Wanted the two of them to do something risky and secret, like when they were kids. He told them he felt as responsible as anyone for the fire and for his own disfiguration. Henry shook his head and sighed, wondering what the hell he had done to turn his eldest into a thief, on top of spawning a lunatic son. He didn't think his despair and humiliation could go any deeper, but upon hearing Clemens' story, he couldn't speak for two days.

EMELINE'S DESCRIPTION had not prepared Clemens for the sheer size of the state hospital. There were six buildings in full view and hints of others behind those. Ginny parked and Emeline directed them to the central building, the original Victorian structure that housed the administrative offices. Emeline told Clemens and Ginny that they had been asked to visit Dr. Stanley first, to discuss Truman's treatment, which was lauded as groundbreaking.

Clemens carried the suitcase with his good arm into the waiting room filled with large potted plants intermittently placed among wood gilded sofas and floral-patterned chairs, Ginny and Emeline sat together on a divan. Clemens stood and gazed out the window that faced the large green surrounded by functional-looking sandstone-brick buildings.

After a short period, Dr. Stanley's secretary, who clasped Emeline's hands and greeted her warmly, ushered them into Dr. Stanley's office. Dr. Stanley couldn't hide the shock of seeing the left side of Clemens melted features, but composed himself professionally, asking them to sit.

"I can't tell you how wonderful the timing is for your visit. Truman has completed his treatment and as I told your mother on her first visit, it's the most modern medical therapy in existence. It was administered over the course of two and a half months and in Truman's case, has yielded excellent results."

He paused, smiling and waiting for a reaction.

Clemens was feeling diminished by the books on the walls, Dr. Stanley's opulent desk, and by the doctor himself. He hadn't spoken with many people other than family and he was self-conscious of his slurred speech. He remained quiet. Ginny took his hand and looked at him. "That's wonderful. Isn't that wonderful, Clemens?"

Emeline had a look of hope on her face. "He is better?"

Dr. Stanley nodded. "Yes, definitively better. As for fully cured, I cannot say that will ever be the case. But his auditory hallucinations have diminished significantly, and his agitation greatly lessened as a result. His physical coordination has improved to the point of his being able to participate in occupational therapy."

Clemens shook his head and spoke, trying to enunciate as clearly as possible. "Auditory hallucinations — are those the voices?"

"Yes, that's right."

It was clear the doctor could understand his words and Clemens felt encouraged to ask more.

"No more talking to President Coolidge or that nasty girl?"

"Well... it is lessened. He has long periods of silence now, which, as I am sure you remember, was not the case upon his arrival here."

"Are there many like him here?"

Dr. Stanley shook his head. "Our population is mainly made up of patients with melancholia, especially since The Crash, as I am sure you can imagine, plus we've had a large influx of patients with developmental disabilities, such as retardation, in an effort to keep society functioning more efficiently. We have a fair number of patients with mania, energetic mood swings if you will, as well as senility. Our numbers, including the addition of a women's ward, have swelled to well over a thousand."

If Clemens could have formed his mouth to whistle, he would have. "Truman is special, then?"

"Very. Schizophrenia, as it is more commonly referred to now, is a disease of the central nervous system, which is, of course, regulated by the brain. We have been able to stabilize his system to the point of improved overall function and cognition."

Dr. Stanley shuffled some papers. Clemens saw this as a signal that the meeting was over and began to rise.

The shuffling, however, was only a transition to the bad news. "It is fair to warn you that Truman, while having mostly positive changes, has also experienced side effects."

Clemens settled back into his chair.

"He has gained a considerable amount of weight. His therapy involved injections of insulin, followed by doses of sugar to awaken him from his therapeutic comas. Sometimes more was needed to balance out the sometimes-overwhelming effects of the large amounts of insulin. This is why you were requested to bring Truman larger clothing, which I see you have. His weight should return to normal, or near normal over the next year."

Emeline sat up a bit straighter. "He is ready to come home soon, *non*?"

Dr. Stanley considered the question. "Please remember that this therapy is new and that we need to observe the long-term effects. It is in his best interests, especially if there is a relapse."

The look on Emeline's face showed she was struggling with this new information that was tarnishing her previous hope.

"Well, why don't you have your visit then? And you can call anytime to ask about his progress or to come again."

As BEFORE, they were escorted to another building, where an orderly took the suitcase and they were brought into a private room with a window in the door. There were the same wooden chairs as Emeline had seen on each of her previous visits. They waited for fifteen minutes until there was the unmistakable sound of multiple keys on a ring being rearranged, and the door was opened.

Clemens thought they had brought the wrong man into the room. This man was not large, he was obese, buttons straining over his bloated belly. "Excuse—"

Truman smiled, then spoke as if bumping into a familiar face on the street. "Bringer of the flame!"

Tears sprang to Clemens' eyes. That was the nickname Truman, or President Coolidge, had given him after the disease — not spirits, as he was now beginning to understand it — had come upon him. Had come upon *them*. He sprang across the small room, tripping on the corner of Ginny's chair. She reached out a hand to steady him and the brothers embraced.

Clemens could not believe how difficult it was to get his arms around Truman, but as he pulled away, he saw it was the same black hair (though short now), the same eyes and tenor of voice. "Truman. It is so good to see you." Truman kept smiling as he stood still for the hug, though he did not return it.

Truman's smile faded as he heard Clemens' slurred voice. "Can I touch it?"

Clemens thought he was talking to the dirty girl again, but Truman reached up to feel the wilted skin that slid down Clemens' left side of his face, starting from just below the eye and ending out of sight at the collar bone.

Truman's eyes roamed around Clemens, never meeting his eyes. He looked like a blind man trying to read a street sign as his fingers pressed into the flesh. Though healed, the skin was sensitive, and Clemens reflexively flinched. Truman drew back his hand. "The burn is flesh, votes are in."

Clemens, face smarting and hope of connection faded, withdrew back to his chair. Emeline took his place by Truman's side, squeezing and patting his rotund front. "What is this — another man in there?"

Truman flashed a smile, though his eyes remained flat. The smile disappeared as quickly as it came. Clemens looked at the floor.

Ginny said from her chair, "Truman, guess what. I'm your sister now! Clemens and I just got married! I wish you could have been there. It was a beautiful ceremony, especially with all the garlands Felicity made." She sighed and clasped her hands.

Truman reached out and touched her shoulder in a way that was more like a poke. "Sister-mister." Ginny laughed. "That's right. I'm the sister to your mister." Emeline smiled at the senseless word play, but Clemens apparently would have none of it.

Emeline said, "I was told on the phone we can walk on the quad during visiting hours. Let's do it, *oui*?" She knocked on the door and the orderly who helped them earlier opened it. Emeline made her request to go outside and the orderly led them down the hallway of visiting rooms, where they glimpsed the tops of heads, hats, a few

faces, and heard muffled conversations though the rein-
forced glass windows in the doors.

They emerged onto the green with instructions to
return to that same door when they were ready to leave.
There were other families, some walking in small groups,
some sitting quietly on benches. There were couples, too,
and at times it was not easy to tell who was the patient
and who was the visitor.

Ginny chatted on about the family like she would with
anyone who had been away. How Samuel was going to
join the Army, how there was a war in Europe and while
there was no talk of our country joining in, Samuel said
he wanted to see the world and so he hoped we would.
Clemens lagged behind, taking it all in. Before he had
come, he imagined Truman and the doctor sitting in an
office much like Dr. Stanley's, Truman on the couch and
the doctor taking notes on his ruminations. All he knew
about all this was what he saw in the movies. But his body
is inflated like a zeppelin, and for what? Sure, Truman
was no longer muttering as much, but his words still
made no sense, his eyes would not lock. Clemens cursed
himself for expecting the old version of his brother to
return.

Truman suddenly dropped in step with him while
Emeline and Ginny walked ahead, pointing to the trees,
the benches, the other groupings of families. Truman was
on what was now referred to as Clemens' "good side."

"Clemens."

Clemens was so startled to hear his name he stopped.
Truman took his hand. It felt bloated and soft, any
callouses from quarry labor long dissolved. "Clem. My
married Clem."

Clemens stared into Truman's eyes, which held his for

a few seconds. Clemens never thought his heart could swell with so much love and hope.

"My Keeper of the Flame." Truman dropped Clemens' hand and his eyes began to rove again.

It was enough and Clemens smiled as best he could with his transformed face. He put his arm around Truman's shoulders as they continued their walk.

SEVEN YEARS LATER, the day had come for Truman's release. Medication had been developed in pill form that patients could take from home. The wards were emptying as therapies and programs were being developed outside the institutional model. With so many young men away at war now that the United States had engaged, people with handicaps were being introduced into the workforce, especially at factories.

Henry and Emeline drove to what was now called the Vermont State Hospital together, leaving Clemens at home against his protests so that they would have room for Truman's luggage. Emeline had brought Truman four more suitcases of belongings over the years, the last set of clothes only one size larger than his original set as his weight gain gradually tapered off, much slower than predicted.

In the time Truman had been away, Ginny and Clemens had a home of their own in Barre, so Ginny could commute easily to her nursing job at Central Vermont Hospital. She worked mainly in the burn ward, by request. Clemens had gotten a job at the clothespin factory where he was able to utilize a vise instead of using his left hand to hold the pins during assembly. No children had blessed their home, but no one dared to complain, or pry. With Clemens being so disabled, perhaps in ways that were not to be discussed, it seemed best to accept what could not be changed. Their dedication to each other was never in question.

Annabelle and Candice were the only children left at the Bates' residence. Felicity had realized her dream to become a schoolteacher and married a man from Boston, where she resided. Samuel was in Europe fighting with the US Army. Annabelle was a senior and Candice a freshman at Hopefield High. They had helped Emeline prepare for Truman's welcome home party, with Clemens and Ginny expected as the only guests. Not wanting to traumatize the children, the youngest were never brought to the hospital on a visit. Other than Clemens, none of Truman's siblings had seen him since he had been committed at age twenty. He was now close to thirty.

Once all packed up in the car, Truman was practically buried under all of the suitcases. There was not much talk on the car ride home. Emeline twisted her body sideways as much as she could from the front seat and talked over the engine of their new Plymouth about what Truman's brothers and sisters were doing these days, which included Annabelle's being courted by the son of the mayor of Montpelier after they met at a dance, but of course no marriage until after high school. Candice was struggling with her schoolwork, but was a very good cook and loved to bake, in fact providing the lion's share of the baked goods drive for the Ladies' Auxiliary fundraiser to provide care packages for local boys fighting overseas, like Samuel. Felicity was expecting her first baby, making Truman and his siblings aunts and uncles, wasn't that wonderful? She joked that with the gray hair she and Henry had now, it was only proper they become grandparents. While she talked, Henry quietly focused on the road ahead, while Truman tried to relax and listen to his favorite of all voices in the world, that of his mother's. Truman was not able to take in all of what she said. He had trouble picturing his siblings as the adults, or almost adults, they were now. It felt fine to be in a car again.

Upon arrival, all Henry could think about was the last party where Truman was in attendance, Truman's own birthday party, and the humiliating behavior that ensued. Truman's mutterings appeared to have decreased, thankfully, but the doctor had said there was no permanent cure. God almighty, what would it be like to have Truman at home again. And for how long? Forever? Christ have mercy.

Clemens and Ginny were waiting on the porch in the crisp autumn air. The colorful fall leaves had already turned brown and fallen, crunching under Clemens' feet as he sprung down the steps to help Truman with the luggage. Truman got out of the car and stood there, waiting to be told what to do. Clemens put a suitcase in his hand and told him to carry it to their old room. Truman followed Clemens inside and greeted the girls, dressed up for the party.

Truman looked over their heads. "Hello Bell Hop. Hello Candy Cane." The sisters looked at each other and giggled as Truman addressed them by nicknames from their childhood, which no one had called them in years. They squirmed as they stood there, not knowing if it was okay, or even safe, to hug their haggard, black-haired brother, who looked much older than they could have imagined. Truman flashed a quick-fading smile and continued to follow Clemens, much to the girls' relief that they wouldn't have to make conversation, or touch him.

Truman walked right to his bed and put his suitcase on it, while Clemens put the other on the floor. Henry came in with the last two and placed them next to the door. Truman turned at the appearance of his father in the doorway.

Henry said, "Welcome home, son."

Truman gazed at the door frame. "Thank you."

Henry sniffed and wiped his eyes. "When you're ready, come on out and we'll commence the festivities."

Henry departed and Clemens laughed. "By festivities, he means, 'Let's eat, I'm starving'." Clemens watched Truman as he opened the suitcase on the bed and began unpacking bottle after bottle. Clemens picked one up. "Reserpine." He wasn't sure if he pronounced it correctly. He continued to read, "Antipsychotic. Take twice a day." Clemens could not get used to associating words like psychotic with Truman and wasn't sure he ever would.

Truman handed him a paper. "This is for *Maman*." Clemens looked it over. It was a list of side effects. "Loss of appetite, weight gain." Clemens stopped. "Well, that don't make sense. What else, let's see, depression, nasal congestion, decreased sex drive. Well, Truman, gonna be hard for you to make babies."

Truman continued to unpack. "Can't. Knife to the cut to the balls."

Clemens stared at him. "What? I mean, you said yes to that? What if you get all the way better? You're still young. Plus, you've seemed to have gotten rid of the dirty girlfriend."

"They just did it. Did it to most everyone." This must have triggered something in Truman because he began muttering. "Wasn't always the votes. It was the flames and fixing. Coolidge said so."

Clemens replied, "I don't know what to say about that. I mean, doctors know best, right?" He sighed and shook his head. "But still, it's only right to ask a fella first. What if you get better?" Clemens sat on the bed by the door. "Well, I ain't had no luck in that department neither, so be it." He reached into his pocket. "Smoke?"

Truman's eyes remained fixed on the packet Clemens pulled out and licked his lips. "The flame."

Clemens put one in his mouth and shook out another for Truman. "Come on, follow your Keeper of the Flame to the porch. Your chair's waiting for you."

The brothers smoked on the porch together while the last of the food was being prepared. Clemens didn't know how, but the tobacco soothed his brother's spirits or illness, as he had to keep reminding himself. From then on, he made sure Truman was never without them.

The party started when they reentered the house, bringing in a rush of crisp air with them. Emeline shouted at them to close the door. She was beaming. Clemens knew what it meant to her to have this much of the family together again.

Henry, on the other hand, sat silently at the head of the table, tense as a bowstring. The table was bursting with food. The table fell silent for grace and all hands automatically went up to take the person's on either side. Truman's hand remained on his lap until Ginny scooped up his right hand and Emeline, who was at the opposite end of the table from Henry, his left. Truman began to mutter. It occurred to Clemens that Truman probably hadn't been touched by anybody but a doctor for the years he was away. Clemens knew that Truman and his father would have to find a way to be in the same house and during grace, he prayed for Truman to readjust quickly to home life and for his father to have patience.

Ten minutes into the meal, Truman had finished his plate, stood up and left the table, plate in his hand. Henry opened his mouth to protest, but Clemens put his hand on his father's and asked him to wait. Truman didn't know where to go and he remained standing, muttering under his breath. Emeline stood up. "Truman, dear, sit down, *non*? We worry about the dishes later."

Truman sat down again and put his plate on the table. "I made baskets. Sometimes worked the loom."

Clemens blinked. "You did?" Henry looked at Truman with surprise.

"I never worked the kitchen. Dishes were not mine to clean. I mopped the floors."

"Baskets?" asked Emeline. How wonderful! Where are they now?"

"They sold 'em. Got us some barber shop quartets that way. A singing cowboy, once."

Truman got up twice more during the meal, did a lap around the table each time and sat down again. Compared to the last party Truman attended, Clemens thought this odd behavior was mild. He could only hope his father thought so, too. If his father laid another hand on Truman, Clemens wasn't sure what he would do, but he'd make sure it never happened again.

Heartened by hearing about Truman's work at the hospital, Clemens arranged an interview for Truman at the US Clothespin Factory where he worked. Mr. Haverford, the owner, had a sister in the state hospital at that time and was very interested in Truman's story. He told Clemens it gave him hope for his sister, whom he would hire in an instant if she could show an aptitude at all for working again.

When Clemens, who could drive very well now, pulled up, Truman got out of the car and stared at the larger-than-life clothespin that adorned the roof. Clemens said, "Remember when we'd come here to Montpelier near-to-once-a month until winter after we got the Model T? We'd run off after our picnic on the state house lawn and roam all over. The first time you saw this, you stared at it just like you are now. You said something like, 'Hope I never get fat enough to need a clothespin like that'."

Truman nodded. Clemens wasn't sure if that meant he understood or if he shared the same memory, but it was a fond memory for Clemens, and he was glad to tell the story.

Truman's mutterings were starting up, so Clemens delayed going inside and brought Truman around the side for a peek at the water wheel that generated the electricity needed for the machines. The workday had already started, and the building rumbled with the rumblings of the assembling machines. Clemens figured that noise was no worse than the granite sheds and so maybe it would be alright.

The interview was brief and Truman's voices only acted up once. Mr. Haverford was mainly concerned that Truman could put in a day's labor and withstand the racket of the machines, which shook the wooden building from clock-in to clock-out. He had hired others upon release from the hospital, he said, given the shortage of young men enlisted in the war. There were a lot of women working there, too.

Truman started a week later, Henry dropping him off at Clemens' house on his way to the quarry. At the factory,

Truman had trouble sitting for any length of time, but after more than generous patience from Mr. Haverford, he eventually found his niche carrying full boxes of pins off the line to the loading dock. When the noise didn't appear to bother him at all, Clemens remembered how Truman used to like the radio cranked up to the highest volume to help stay the voices.

ONCE IT WAS clear that Truman would be keeping his job at the factory, Truman went to live with Clemens and Ginny. It was only practical as it would be easier for Truman to get to work and to keep his twice annual doctor visits at the medical offices down the street. Clemens saw the sadness in his mother's eyes when Truman left again, but he knew that Henry and the girls were not adjusting to Truman's strange habits and avoided him until forced to share a meal together. Clemens explained to his mother that she couldn't expect the girls to suddenly love a brother as strange and old as Truman, of whom they only had few, and unpleasant, memories.

The couple lived in downtown Barre, which meant most places could be walked to, like the hardware store, the grocery store, the bakery. Ginny would smile whenever the brothers donned their hats and walked out the door to eat at The Pine Run Diner down the street on their days off together. Or to Gino's Deli to buy cigarettes. The two of them cut quite a couple of fine figures, she mused, what with Clemens' burn scars and Truman's regrown long, black beard and unpredictable behavior.

While Ginny may have found it endearing, it bothered Clemens until he realized they were not the problem, it was everybody else. Women would startle and men would stare. Young children would either silently clutch their mother's skirts or burst into tears. Truman didn't seem to notice one way or another, but with the help of Ginny's encouragement and love, Clemens turned his shame into dignity. Then he took it one step further, which made him feel like himself again, the first time in years.

There wasn't much to be done about startles, gasps, or tears, except tip one's hat and keep moving. Older children, however, had little fear and a lot of curiosity. They'd always start with Clemens.

"What happened to your face, mister?"

Clemens began to dream up a new answer every time. "Well, I was out checking my maples lines one day when, wham! I got struck by lightning."

"Nuh-uh."

"Uh-uh, did so. And my brother here, he was with me, and got zapped by the electricity and it crossed all his circuits. Now his brains are as scrambled as eggs. Isn't that right, Tru?"

All eyes would shift to Truman. How Truman would play along depended on if Coolidge was with them, too, which meant Truman was in a somewhat agitated state. If he was, Truman would smile his quick smile, like he did when people directed their attention to him, say something like, "Stop stealing the vote, Mr. President. The flames will eat your victory."

That would shock the boys into silence and Clemens and Truman would continue on down the street.

Or it might go something like, "Why does your face look like that?"

Clemens would reply, "Don't ever kill no one, boys.

They could send you to the electric chair and you know what's worse than getting fried until dead?"

They'd gasp, mouth agape.

"Well, I'll tell ya. It's getting fried and *living*. And my brother here, *he's* the one that threw the switch on me! He felt so bad, he was just doing his job, you know, as executioner. But he felt so bad, he leaped onto the electrified chair to pull me out. That's how he got to be like he is now."

All eyes to Truman. If Truman was clear in his mind, he might start digging around in his pockets. "I got that switch around here somewhere. Never know when you might need it." Then he'd look one of them right in the eye and say, "Whatcha been up to anyway, son?"

That would get the boys beating feet down the sidewalk as quick as they could.

Clemens would more likely than not clap his arm around Truman's shoulder. "We still got it, Truman. The adventures of the Bates boys are far from over."

After a few months of Truman and Clemens taking their regular jaunts around downtown Barre, things quieted down for them on the sidewalks as people got used to seeing them. Some even began to say hello. Clemens had no doubt that word had gotten around about how they were to blame for the fire all those years ago and Truman's hospitalization, but it didn't bother him. Not anymore. He had a beautiful, loving wife, a family that had loved and supported him all these years, and even if they couldn't quite give as much to Truman, that was okay, too, for he and Ginny wouldn't flinch from their commitment to him. Nothing he could do about their father, but the girls were young, perhaps they'd come around.

As for Truman, Clemens still missed him, missed *them*, Clem and Tru, as they used to be.

But he also realized their relationship would have changed over time anyway, as all relationships do. At least now, he spent time with his brother every day and how much luckier could he be than that.

AFTER TEN YEARS of working and living in this way, the unthinkable happened and Clemens was diagnosed with colon cancer, rare in someone so young, but there it was. Ginny took a leave from work to care for him, but the cancer was too aggressive. During Clemens' illness, Truman was so agitated, he had to quit his job at the factory.

One day before he got too sick, Clemens asked Truman to come sit with him as he had something to get off his chest. He told Truman about Brunella, the woman, the whore, to whom he had given his virginity and had continued to see after he had healed from the fire. Things took a hard turn when Brunella caught tuberculosis and was thrown out of the brothel. At that point, rumors had started that the CCC funds were drying up and the railroad project was to be aborted. The rumor did come true in time, but before then, the workers were being moved so far down the line that they wouldn't be coming to Hopefield anymore for supplies or whores, so the brothel was going relocate. Having nowhere to go, Brunella told Clemens that she was going to the cabin, now abandoned, to die.

Brunella didn't have the strength, she said, to start over again somewhere else. The railroad tracks were never laid, so Clemens was able to drive along the railroad bed to bring her supplies for a few weeks, until she succumbed. He buried her in the woods behind the cabin. Clemens still went there sometimes. Clemens said he was telling Truman so that she would be remembered. But to not tell Ginny, it would only hurt her. But if he could go to the cabin, for him, once in a while, just to sit with her spirit, it would mean the world to Clemens.

After Clemens passed, Ginny tried to remain in the house with Truman, but she surrendered to her grief by overdosing on medication she had stolen from the hospital. When she fell into a deep sleep, so deep it scared Truman, he called Emeline, who called an ambulance. Ginny thanked Truman for saving her because as soon as she swallowed the pills, she realized that as a Catholic, if she died by suicide, she'd never meet Clemens in heaven. She apologized for not being able to take care of him anymore, but the pain was too great. Ginny never returned to the hospital and moved in with her parents, who were ailing and needed care.

Truman did not want to be at the factory without Clemens, but could not afford to rent the Barre house without an income of his own. He didn't want to move back home and live so far from town. The owner of the clothespin factory, Mr. Haverford, always sympathetic to Truman's condition, helped him apply for disability and housing vouchers under Section 8. Truman moved to the Rose Garden Apartments in Hopefield, which had been converted to cheap apartments when the brothel was shuttered. Truman honored his dying brother's wishes. When he learned from the Zuckermans one day when he was visiting the Indian that burning sage was a common form of purification, Truman brought some along with him every trip. To purify the air for Brunella's lungs, to clean her spirit.

Truman made sure to take Clemens' driver's license with him when he moved to the Rose Garden and though Ginny took their car, as was only right, Truman saved a bit every month until he could afford a used coupe. When he wasn't sharpening his driving skills on the dirt roads around Hopefield, Truman settled into a routine of solitude, broken up by Annabelle and Candice's marriages, Henry and Emeline's funerals, and a couple of short visits from Samuel. When he discovered that the church wall was a fine place to pass the day, that was where he could be found most of the time.

Then something remarkable happened. Truman didn't know if it was the new medication, chlorpromazine, or if it was divine providence, but he suddenly saw the world with a clarity that he hadn't had in years. It wasn't that Coolidge was ready to pack his bags and leave, no, he would always be witness. It was when Truman was driving around one day that he first noticed it. Or *them*, rather.

Fossils. Everywhere. He was driving over them, they were in his dirt driveway, along the railroad bed on his way to clean the cabin. He couldn't believe he hadn't noticed it, especially during his quarry days. It all made sense. That was why they were calling out to him, screaming when the machines dug into the earth. They were once living creatures and when disturbed to such a degree, their souls were roused to protest.

And so, he began to collect them. Brown ones, red ones, mottled ones, striped ones, first filling his bedroom in cardboard boxes, separated by patterns that marked what kind of fossils they were. The collection spilled out to the porch until his doorway was nearly blocked by boxes of his fossils. If Truman was home when the kids that lived there got bored and began throwing them around, he came out in a rage that was new to him and his neighbors. The cops were called after Coolidge got into the act and started ranting about flames and votes. The easiest solution was to move the fossils out of the children's reach.

Officer Gary Hollister, who responded to the call, had grown up with the Bates boys and had accompanied them a few times on picnics to Number Ten pond and drinking parties on Bald Hill during high school. He remembered when Truman stopped coming along and that Clemens had always made excuses for him. For a time, after the fire, Gary thanked God every day for his good fortune in comparison. He had an idea. The church not only owned the graveyard up the hill leading out of town, but also the patch of land across from it. Officer Hollister asked Pastor Douglas if he wouldn't mind Truman using a part of the land for his collections. When Pastor Douglas gave his blessing, Officer Hollister came on his day off and he and Truman loaded up the crates into the back of his pickup, where there were also some of his own barrels and crates that had fallen into disrepair. When Truman discovered the fossilized chicken foot, he knew this was where he was meant to house his collection. He thanked Gary, whom he remembered vaguely from somewhere in his past, and told him to come see the collection anytime. Gary did, bringing his younger children to hear the stories about the fossils.

Sitting on the church wall and collecting fossils occupied Truman for nearly a decade. Then along came Patrick. Truman didn't know that he had the capacity for love anymore until his youngest sister's son pestered his way into his life.

Until then, Truman didn't feel he was capable of much, but Patrick apparently thought otherwise. Whatever form Truman's abilities took, Patrick, a bold and eager little boy, never seemed to take note.

17

______

1984: LITTLE BUCK

*S*cratcha-dacha. *Revenge is sweet. The brother is here. Can you hear him? He's in the wall, I can hear him. Scratcha-dacha. Ten-point rack, rack me up. I'm a goner.*

"FRED, can you hear him? I shot him, the buck. He's pissed. He's trying to come in."

The orderly, Fred Johnston, whose brother was on the same ward as Pat, nodded. Fred's brother Devon had been in and out of the hospital and the CVH emergency beds what seemed all his life. It's why he became an orderly at the Vermont State Hospital. So he could always be there for him.

Fred put a small tray on the bedside table. Pat sat up on his bed as he took the paper cup of water and drank down the pills that he shook out from the other paper cup. He crushed a cup in each hand and gave them back to Fred, who was relieved this new patient was so cooperative. Devon always tried to pocket them, but Fred knew all the tricks. Fred believed in the medication, though it was a rough transition, deeply sedating at first. Always a gamble until enough combinations were tried, until the doc got it right. Sometimes they never could, like with Devon. Maybe again with this Pat. Schizophrenia was a bitch.

"Fred, how strong are the walls?"

Fred put the crushed cups into his pocket. He reached out and knocked on the wall next to Pat. "Hear that?"

Pat nodded.

"When you hear that, can you hear the *scratcha-dacha*?"

Pat shook his head. "You mean I can knock on the walls, and he'll go away?"

Fred shrugged. "Couldn't hurt, just a little knock, though. Don't want to startle him. Try it."

Pat tapped lightly on the wall. His face lit up. "Thank you, Fred. Thank you."

Fred smiled and turned to leave. "Just a light tap, now. It's all it takes."

Pat gave him a thumbs up, then yawned and lay back in his bed. Fred closed the door and knew this young man was in for a long, hard ride. It was best he slept more now as his body adjusted to the medication that may or may not get him to back to a level of independence. For now, Pat would need to rely on others for everything. He would need both assistance and medication his whole life, but this didn't necessarily mean he wouldn't be able to eventually hold a job or have his own place.

If there's one thing Fred knew, this shit was on a case-by-case basis.

~

DANTE SAT at Truman's greasy kitchen table, trying not to breathe too deeply for all the smoke in the air. His bandaged shoulder throbbed. The ashtray was buried under cigarette butts and Truman was lighting another. Dante had felt compelled to come see Truman, to feel out what it would be like for Pat in the hospital.

Truman was muttering. "The flame comes again. Clean and go. Protect the buck. Light it and go. Scrub it clean and go."

Dante nodded. "So, Mrs. Bates told you, huh? About the buck that Pat sees? Or thinks he sees?"

Truman didn't respond, kept talking about cleaning and scrubbing.

"What's the hospital like? I mean, you haven't been there for a long time, right? But like, is it all straitjackets and stuff?"

Truman slammed his hand on the table. The cigarette it was holding went flying and landed in Dante's lap. He stood, knocking over his chair. "Jeezum, Truman!"

Dante bent down and picked it up. "Here." He threw the smoking butt on top of the pile in the ashtray.

Truman stood up. "Take me to the cabin. Gonna clean it. Scrub it out. Feed the spirit and scrub it forever clean."

Dante didn't know what to say. "The cabin? Now? I mean, why don't we go see Pat or something? His mom said he can have visitors." Dante was scared to go to the hospital alone.

Truman opened a drawer in his kitchen and rattled things around until he found what he wanted and stuffed some items in his sweater pocket. He walked past him and opened the door and walked past Dante's Tercel to his own car. He took the keys out of his pocket and got in.

As much as he didn't want to get his own car stuck in the winter slush, Dante wasn't sure he wanted to drive with Truman, either. It would be the first time.

"There's too much snow. We'll get stuck." Dante wasn't sure if that was true. They had a significant thaw the previous few days and the snow wasn't even high enough to make a good snowman. At any rate, his arm was still in a sling from the arrow and he wouldn't be any help digging them out.

Truman pointed at the small metal letters on his car, the ones that said 4WD. "Read it and beat it."

Dante sighed and joined Truman at the car. They got in and drove the short distance to the entrance. Dante got out the shovel from the back and handed it to Truman, who began clearing the snowbank created by plows that cleared the Rose Garden parking lot. Elderly or not, Truman was strong. When he was done, Dante removed the fake-locked lock that his dad threatened to report, but never did, and swung the gate open.

Truman had to dig them out twice on the railroad bed, but they made it to the cabin. Truman got out, but when Dante started to follow him, Truman's eyes focused on something behind Dante and he said, "Feeding and scrubbing is my business." He entered the cabin. Dante figured if Truman wanted him inside with him, he'd say so, which he didn't, so he might as well try to turn the car around. He climbed in the driver's side and began the many one-armed turns needed to do so.

Between the windows being rolled up and the crunching of the tires under the snow, he didn't hear the crash of the kerosene lamp or notice when smoke began to billow out of the glassless window, through the many cracks between the planks of the walls, and the hole in the roof where the woodstove must have been.

Truman stepped out of the cabin and watched Dante finish his final turn. When Dante looked out his window, his jaw dropped and got out of the car. "Truman, what did you do? What is this?"

"Burn the sage, feed the spirit. Clean it with forever flame. Brunella-Newtella free and clean."

Dante threw his hands in the air. "We have to put it out! Oh my God, what are we going to do?"

Truman walked over to him and put his hand on his shoulder. It was the first time Dante had ever had physical contact with Truman. His breath smell like a thousand ashtrays. "Go to the garden. Call the Keystones."

Dante blinked. "Keystones?"

Truman turned around to look at the flames licking out of the glassless window. "Coppers of the Keys, Stones of the Cops, baton and hats."

Dante finally got it. "You want me to call the cops on you?"

"Go now, Dante. Bringer of the Keeper. Go on."

Dante shook his head and turned back to the car. It didn't take him long to realize that was the only option now. He stopped, took off his jacket, and gave it to Truman, who was only in his sweater. "Put this on, at least."

Before Dante left, Truman put his finger to his lips. "This stays with the flame. No one to tell about you."

Truman pulled on the jacket and turned around. Against a strong feeling of dread, Dante did as he was told. He saw Truman through the rearview mirror, muttering and watching the flames transform the cabin into a pile of coal and ash.

THE FOLLOWING DAY, Darlene and Ephraim sat Dante down at the kitchen table. Dante hadn't told them that he had gone to the cabin with Truman, as Truman instructed. At least, that was what he thought Truman said. To keep quiet about his part in it.

Ephraim started. "How's your shoulder?"

Dante was in a lot of pain from driving the day before at the cabin. He shrugged, which he shouldn't have done. "Ow."

"Dante, I can't possibly know what you are going through. This has been the most incredible and devastating thing I can imagine, and now Truman."

Darlene said, "Honey, there's no way you could have known. All you did, all you have ever done, was try to help. I'm so proud of you, Dante."

Dante put his head in his free hand. "The buck. I knew about it. He would see it outside the window." He picked up his head, tears on his cheeks. "It's just, I thought I was just missing it, you know. Couldn't see it, or something. But the look on his face whenever he mentioned it. It was... it was... terror. And then... he'd just be normal again." He made a scoffing sound. "Normal depressed, I mean. I should have said something sooner."

Ephraim put his hand on Dante's. "You can't take responsibility. This was going to happen, no matter what."

"I should've told his folks. I mean, they knew about his depression, but this was different."

Darlene was crying now as well. "And what would they have done? Who wouldn't believe Pat saw a buck out his window? *You* did."

Ephraim said, "Look, about Truman. I don't know if

this is the right time to bring it up, but Candice told us the police said that there were tire tracks in the snow that matched Truman's, that's not a surprise. There were two sets of footprints, which is the surprise." Ephraim leaned forward, "I noticed you borrowed my jacket this morning to take the trash out. Where's yours?"

Dante didn't see the point in lying. If he got in trouble, so be it. "I didn't know he was going to do it. I swear. But even if I did, I would've helped. I think I know why he did it."

Ephraim and Darlene looked at him expectantly. Dante continued, "He did it to be with Pat. I know it. I asked him what the hospital was like and that's when he insisted I take him to the cabin. He *wanted* to get committed. He's not crazy. Shit, wrong word, but you know what I mean."

His parents were stunned into silence. Ephraim broke it by saying, "Well, I hope you know the hospital is nothing like when Truman was there. A lot has changed in fifty years, thank God."

"I have to go see Pat. Am I grounded, or can I go?"

Darlene said, "Of course, you can. I'll call and set up a visit." Bracelets jangling, she laid her hand on his arm and smiled. "Not every choice we make, even when it's to help someone, is perfect. But choosing to help, that *is* perfect."

THE PREDICTION that Pat would get worse before he got better came true. In the hospital, he spent most of his days in his new room terrified the buck was going to gore him, just like in Dante's dream all those years ago. When he hadn't eaten for two days, saying that he had to keep knocking on the wall, Fred stood outside his door and called his name until he opened it. Fred knocked on the wall for Pat while he ate the meal Fred had brought. It became routine for a few weeks, until Pat was able to stop for periods of time.

Sometimes there was a lot of screaming and crying in other rooms and in the hall. While overall nice guys, the orderlies at times had to get a little rough to keep a patient from hurting himself or someone else. Unlike Truman's time, the state hospital was now only for patients that were a true danger to themselves or others and had shrunk considerably. Patients became clients of Washington County Mental Health once they left and were monitored by their case workers wherever they lived in the community, be it their own apartment or a group home.

Until Pat was stable enough to leave the hospital, he was on a rotation of appointments with doctors, counselors, and occupational therapists. He spent the rest of his time alone in his room, or in the rec room next to the smoking area, where he soon picked up the habit. Cigarettes were given out at the discretion of the staff and only the orderlies had lighters, which they held onto while lighting the patients' smokes.

Truman came to visit Pat in his room every day and tell him stories of how it used to be and how different the hospital was now. About the water therapy, the Vienna sausage room. Truman said he missed the water therapy, which had apparently been traded up for pills. How fat he had gotten on the insulin. Pat would listen and sometimes he understood what Truman was saying through his word salad. Other times his brain was so foggy, he could only catch a word or two. Truman was released before Pat after someone finally had the right ear to understand Truman's answers to the questions. Truman had never been a liar and told why he had set the fire. He asked to stay but was denied. The federal government owned the cabin, but no one pressed charges, though he was told if he pulled a stunt like that again, he'd go to jail, not back to the hospital. VSH could not help someone who knew that what he was doing was wrong.

DANTE COULDN'T BELIEVE the size of the Waterbury hospital, even though he was told how much bigger it used to be. After reporting himself to the receptionist in a wood-paneled office, Dante was told to have a seat in the sterile waiting room with vinyl chairs. His name was called and a large, metal door buzzed open with a stout orderly who waited for him. Dante was shown to a small room that had a couple of wooden chairs and a scratched-up counter attached to the wall. The door closed automatically and through it, Dante could see the back of an orderly's head outside through the thick glass window that was crisscrossed with thin black lines. He heard speaking, then the door opened and Pat walked in. His hair was limp and stringy. He looked skinny. His blue eyes were dull. He smelled like cigarettes.

"So, uh, hey," said Dante. He had never felt so useless.

Pat remained standing. He ran his hands down his pale face. He didn't, or couldn't, look directly at Dante for more than a second. He walked to one wall and knocked a few times. He went to another and a did the same, and again, and again.

Dante leaned forward in his chair. "I'm here, dude. We all are, anytime. Jeremy, Lyle, just say the word. They want to come, but I told them I wanted to see you first. Are you okay in here? What's it like?"

Pat's feet made a shuffling sound as he walked over to the window. He knocked on it. "He didn't follow you, did he?"

Dante tensed. "Who, Pat?"

Pat turned back to him. "You know, you saw him. You saw me shoot him." Pat began to pace back and forth. "Did I get him? You saw me. You were there. Did I get him?"

Dante suddenly felt the pressure of saying the right answer. If he said yes, would that end the delusion? Would that make the buck go away?

"Yeah, man. You got him." Dante realized Pat was probably never told that he had shot his best friend. He wondered if Pat even noticed his sling. He decided to change the subject. "You see Truman much?"

Pat looked at him, then knocked furiously on the wall. In a terrified whisper, he said "It's here, dude. We gotta go."

Dante knew the visit was over. Tears spring to Dante's eyes and a sob he didn't know was coming escaped. "Okay, Pat. Let's go. Whatever you need."

Dante opened the door and waved to the orderly who had let him in, now seated at a small desk down the wall. Pat was escorted and after a jangle of keys, was sent to walk alone through the door that opened to his wing. Dante saw Pat reach out to the wall as if to knock on it as the door swung shut behind him. The orderly stayed behind with Dante and showed him the way out.

Dante managed to hold it together until he got to his car. Once he got in and closed the door, he began weeping so hard it hurt his ribs, his stomach, his healing shoulder. Sobbing like he wouldn't ever see Pat again. Sobbing like someone he loved had died.

EPILOGUE
ICE CREAM AND ASHES

Pat was released from the Vermont State Hospital two months after his medication had taken hold and he was deemed stable. He was placed into a small group home in Montpelier, created by the agency when the community-based mental health model started to gain traction. He was now a client of Washington County Mental Health. His caseworker's name was Brenda and she helped him schedule doctors' visits and enrolled him in a work program. The group home was staffed by a counselor at all times, who handed out the strictly controlled medications. Each resident made their own breakfast and lunch and were expected to cook one night a week. They planned, prepared and shopped for the meal with as much or as little assistance as needed. Ostensibly, the group home was a transitional space from the hospital to society, though some clients had been there for more than five years. Residents were free to come and go as they pleased, catching rides on agency transportation or with their case worker to appointments, or walking into town. Clients typically lived on SSI (Supplemental Security Income) and whatever money their families could spare, so typically a walk was just that. A walk.

Pat had his own room and shared a floor with two other residents. One was Greg, who was a few years older and also had schizophrenia. Greg used his fingers to draw in the air in front of him and often brushed off what he called "yartels" from his clothing. The other floormate was a middle-aged woman with severe bipolar disorder named Deidre who wore heavy makeup that was often smeared. She took a liking to Pat and would get upset if she wasn't able to sit next to him at meals.

Pat's work program was a type of occupational therapy. Gone were the sheltered workshop days of basket-weaving and picture-frame assembly. The WCMH work program connected clients with local businesses in the community that hired the agency to pick up recycling and piles of confidential documents to be shredded. Neighbors hired them for cleaning, moving furniture, mowing lawns, and stacking wood. The crew was driven in a van by a counselor who oversaw their work, and the clients were paid a few dollars an hour. Young, energetic clients like Pat were glad to get out of the house and he participated in the program almost every day. His extra income mostly went to cigarettes and soda.

Candice was horrified at Pat's new smoking habit that he picked up at VSH. The doctor told her that schizophrenics commonly smoked, that there might be some correlation between nicotine and dopamine that somehow affected their mood. In fact, he had never worked with a person with schizophrenia who didn't smoke.

Dante and the boys would pick him up and they'd

joyride to Number Ten Pond or Bald Hill. As soon as they got into the car, Lyle liked to announce, "Gentleman and Assholes, we are now leaving Washington County Mental Health and entering... Washington County *Metal* Health," and push play on Metallica.

Maybe it was his illness, or maybe his medication, but the boys had to drive slow as Pat couldn't stand the car going over thirty-five miles an hour. His eyes would grow large and he'd say, "What is this, Thunder Road?" They wouldn't let Pat smoke any weed, afraid of what might happen, which Pat didn't seem to mind as long as he had cigarettes. Pat kept his eye out for the buck, though he didn't get all worked up about it anymore. He had taken to repeating things that seemed to be an endless loop in his mind — "I'm gonna get my truck on the road, I'll get my GED next year." Sometimes the boys got fed up with the loop, but there was no way to get him to stop. When one day he said, "I am the father of KISS," they stared at him for a minute, then busted up laughing. He laughed, too. Dante loved to see him smile, which wasn't so much anymore. "It's true," he laughed. "I wrote all their songs." That joined the loop.

Bill and Kitty would take him out for fast food and fishing. Candice would show up a few times a week and stuff his room with snacks, accompanied by lectures on smoking.

Dante knew when fall came, things were going to change. That first summer before college, he would come alone a few days a week and just sit with Pat on the porch. Pat would chain smoke and tap on the walls while Dante did most of the talking. How dating Shannon was going well, but with Shannon going to school in Arizona, neither of them was sure about their future together. How his parents wanted him to go to Greyson, but Dante was seriously considering a major in psychology, so was relieved when he got into UVM. How Lyle started full-time at his family's body shop after graduation and Jeremy enrolled in business classes at Vermont Community College to see if he had a knack for it. Maybe one day he'd take over the general store or start something of his own. After Dante told Pat things like that, Pat would say, "That's good stuff," then pick up a chain from his loop-speak.

His freshman year, Dante came back once a month to visit his parents and Pat. The staff at the group home said they never had a resident that got as many visitors as Pat. After a few months, Candice, whom Dante often saw at the group home, told him how Pat was showing remarkable improvement. The getting better part had started. The doctor said that his treatment had started early enough after the onset of symptoms that he had an excellent chance for recovery. While there was no cure for schizophrenia, they were told, it could be well-managed enough that he would be able to participate in life again, though never to the degree he had before. Schizophrenia made visual processing a challenge and made reading impossible, so he would never be able to finish high school. Expectations should be managed.

Through the WCMH work program, Pat got a job at the local Ben and Jerry's shop cleaning tables. He talked less about the buck, though it would never completely leave him. But he was well-liked at the ice cream shop, so much so that the manager recommended that he transfer to the factory in Waterbury. Pat made a joke about how he was never going back to Waterbury, even for ice cream. The truth was, he was pleased. He moved out of the group home and into an apartment in Barre, where he got picked up for his swing shift by a friend he had made on the factory floor, who was happy to split the gas.

Uncle Truman would stop by his apartment once a week to collect his favorite ice cream, Maple Walnut, that Pat got for him special, straight from the factory line. They would sit and smoke and eat ice cream together. Or when Dante was visiting, they would visit Truman together at the Rose Garden. Dante and Pat sometimes walked up to the ComeSee, just because. If Truman was up to it, he'd drive the short distance in his powder blue VW Rabbit to meet them there and tell them all about the fossils. They were too big to ride the chicken foot, but they listened to Truman as if they were hearing it all for the first time.

When Truman died in the early spring two years later, Candice had him cremated, as everyone suspected that was what he would have wanted. Pat and Dante spread his ashes at the ComeSee. They also planted a rose garden in his honor at the Bates' house, six bushes planted along the front porch. Everyone assumed it was because Truman had lived at the Rose Garden Apartments for so long, but Pat and Dante knew that wasn't the whole story. Pat had his dad help him build a miniature cabin to adorn the garden. Once in a while, when Dante was visiting, Candice would make a big dinner for Pat and all the boys, complete with vegetarian options and jokes from Bill. Dante would tease back saying that now that he had a bad shoulder, they finally had something in common.

Dante made sure to burn a piece of sage in the tiny cabin whenever he came to the house. He would sit in the rocking chair on the porch with his feet on the railing and watch the smoke come out of the hole where the wood-stove pipe must have been.

RESOURCES

Mental health challenges and the systems designed to help you navigate them can be overwhelming and scary. Please know that if you have a mental illness, or love someone who does, you are not alone. Here are some resources:

National Institute of Mental Health

MentalHealth.gov

International Society of Psychiatric-Mental Health Nurses

Substance Abuse and Mental Health Services Administration: Living Well with Schizophrenia

National Alliance on Mental Illness: Find your local chapter

Vermont Care Partners: Supporting Vermonters to lead healthy and satisfying lives community by community

ACKNOWLEDGMENTS

My heartfelt gratitude goes first and foremost to the clients of Washington County Mental Health with whom I had the pleasure of working when I was a counselor at Green Mountain Workforce and at the group home in downtown Montpelier. Many years have passed between now and then, but you are all in my heart and I thank you for all you have given me.

The same gratitude goes to the staff who influenced me at that time, at my first real job. Thank you Jane Devereux, for taking me under your wing and becoming my close friend and confidant; thank you Paul Miller, for mentoring me and being a great ally; thank you Sue Swindell, for hiring me because I ate the Smarties at the interview; and thank you Brian Wightman, who gave me my first shot. You each took a chance on me, and I hope I did you proud.

There are many locations mentioned throughout the book. Some are real places: Washington County Mental Health, Vermont State Hospital, Central Vermont Hospital, Number Ten Pond, Rock of Ages, the clothespin factory, Route 2, Spruce Mountain, Bald Hill, the railroad bed, the waterfall, the church wall, and the Winooski River. The geography of Hopefield is loosely based on the village of Plainfield in central Vermont. The Rose Garden Apartments is inspired by both the Plainfield apartment building referred to as the Heartbreak Hotel and the former brothel in Adamant. Thank you to the village of Plainfield and its residents, many of whom I call friends.

The ComeSee is a real place, and maybe still is — I haven't been back in twenty years. I added the word "museum", though the hand-painted sign on the side of the road on Maple Hill simply said, "Come See". The fossilized chicken foot is real, according to the curator whom I happened across one day, but, unfortunately, I am not able to confirm his name. There are first and/or last names of people I know or used to know sprinkled throughout the book as they came to me without much rhyme or reason, which was fun for me and is hopefully okay with everyone (I'm looking at you, my dear friend Phil Robertson!). For anyone whose name is not used, please know that you are woven throughout every word of this novel. The nickname Strawberry was given to an old classmate of mine for the same reason as Dante, and I bet he hated it as much as Dante did. The nickname 'Pat Bates', if indeed it was a nickname, was inspired by an old friend who was always called by his first and last name, same initials. Not sure if it was cool to use your name here, but you know who you are.

Thank you to my husband Philip for encouraging me to make the time and space to write. Thank you to my OG read and critique group: Ely Rareshide, Linda Salem, and Kim Schultz, for helping me mold the foundation for this novel. Thank you to Leslie O'Brien of Goldenwest Editing for smoothing out my format, grammar, inconsistencies, and other rough edges.

Finally, the biggest shout out ever to Tim Gmeiner and his dad Mark Gmeiner for being the first two people to read this novel. It was your support and feedback that inspired me to aim higher and dig deeper. I cannot thank you enough.

A NOTE ON TRUMAN'S THERAPIES

I researched treatments for schizophrenia in the 1930's while writing about Truman's stay at VSH. I was impressed with the efforts taken in this pre-medication phase of psychiatry and psychology, which by today's standards seem harsh and uninformed. However, doctors had to start somewhere. I truly believe that in most cases, therapies were invented with the intention of helping. That said, there were consequences; insulin shock treatment, while at times achieving desired results (not a cure – there was and still is no cure for schizophrenia), caused obesity. At times, patients died.

In addition, eugenics was a popular trend at this time and was practiced at VSH. While not a major part of this story, knowledge of this practice lends itself to understanding the mindset of people in this era towards people who were differently abled.

Links to information about Vermont's history with eugenics:

From University of Vermont: <u>Vermont Eugenics: A Documentary History</u>

Interview with Dartmouth College researcher on Vermont Public Radio in 2017 (includes a photo of staff and patients at the Vermont State Hospital): <u>Coming to Terms with Vermont's Dark History of Eugenics</u>

ABOUT THE AUTHOR

JJ Holbert has a BA in Sociology from Hunter College and an MA in Teaching English as a Second Language from St. Michael's College. She informed her father a long time ago that she would take the career path less traveled. Case in point: in addition to working in mental health in Montpelier, VT, her choices have led her to dishwashing and cleaning hotel rooms in her hometown of New Hope, PA; slinging falafel in Boulder, CO; being a bike messenger, interior design showroom sample assistant, and a movie theatre usher in NYC; an assistant professor in Kanazawa, Japan; a zoo tour guide, a teacher, and a writer in San Diego, CA. JJ feels confident that she did what she said she would do. She currently lives in southern California with her family, where she and her husband run a sailing tour company. It has nothing to do with writing, but they love it.

She is currently working on a novel based in San Diego County. *Big Flame and Little Buck* is her first publication.

Go to https://jjholbert.com/ to read her blog.